The Maidstone Conspiracy

James Osborne

James Osborne

Acclaim for

The Maidstone Conspiracy

For anyone who enjoys a page-turning plot filled with shocking betrayal and criminal intrigue … THE MAIDSTONE CONSPIRACY was created just for you.

-- Tim Young, bestselling author

A fast read with one twist and turn after another. You think you've got it figured out; but wait! The surprise ending is a bonus. I predict you'll lose sleep over this one. I did.

-- Edna Bell-Pearson

Perfect for a trip to the cottage or beach, or as a companion on a road trip, I give THE MAIDSTONE CONSPIRACY five stars.

-- A. B. Funkhauser

James Osborne is a skilled writer who really knows how to keep one's interest by leading his readers on a suspense-filled journey.

-- Gayle Moore-Morrans

Absolutely loved reading THE MAIDSTONE CONSPIRACY. Extremely captivating and very well written. WOW Jim!! You have really aced this one – your best yet!!!

-- Eliza

I was drawn into the plot on the very first page. Much that follows is … unexpected twists and turns that propel the reader forward until the very last page.

-- Lois W. Stern

The Maidstone Conspiracy

Cover design by: Art Paynter

Second Printing 2021

Published by Fairfax Books
an imprint of Fairfax Publishing Unlimited

Prologue

Colorado Springs, Colorado
April 12, 2010

Paul Winston walked from his modest office, down three flights of stairs to street level in downtown Colorado Springs. He eagerly inhaled the fragrant spring mountain air while heading for his pickup at the curb nearby.

A few steps from the truck the wealthy entrepreneur and philanthropist felt himself thrust forward forcefully from behind onto a parking meter. He grabbed the meter to keep from falling. Unable to hold on he landed on his back. Paul looked up. A disheveled young man stood over him, an old-style revolver clutched in his right hand. Smoke drifted from the rust-etched barrel.

Good god! he thought. *That son-of-a-bitch shot me!*

"What the hell?" Paul tried to challenge his assailant. The words were a garbled wheeze. He recognized the unshaven face but couldn't quite place it.

Paul watched helplessly as the shabbily dressed man raised the antique weapon. His mind was demanding he flee, but his body wouldn't respond. The gun jumped, then jumped a second time. Paul heard loud bangs as two bullets slammed into his chest with enormous force. He couldn't breathe.

"Right! That'll fix you, ya greedy bugger," he heard the man say. "Bloody well serves you right!"

'Why?' Paul tried to ask, noting the British accent. Only his mind was able to form the words.

Chapter One

Durham, NC,
20 Years Earlier

Paul Winston was studying hard for the last of his MBA final exams at Duke University's business school when his cell phone rang.

"Hello?" he said.

He sensed a presence at the other end, but no sound.

"Hello?" he repeated. "Who's there? What's going on?"

There was a muted cry of anguish.

"Oh, Paul!" He heard Emily's voice cry out, convulsed with grief.

"What is it?" he said, suddenly alert. "What's going on? Are you all right? Do you need help?"

"It's Mom!" his sister cried. "It's Mom and Dad!" she corrected herself. "They're gone," she sobbed. "They're both gone! A crash! Dad's plane! They were killed, Paul. They're dead. Oh my God, Paul!"

"What?" Paul said. He struggled to grasp what he'd just heard. "What … what's happened? How?"

"The plane, Paul. Dad's plane," Emily said. "It crashed and exploded. Dad was landing at the ranch … on the airstrip. Mom was with him. George said the plane blew up while landing. He says Mom and Dad must have died instantly. Oh my God, Paul! Can you come right away, please? This is terrible, and there's something not right about this. I need you, now!"

Paul tried to console his sister while she struggled to share with him the few details available about the tragedy. They sat in silence on the phone for a few moments, then exchanged a few words of comfort, knowing that nothing they could possibly say would bring them solace. Finally, Paul said, "I'm on my way, Emily. I'll see how soon I can get a charter and let you know. Are the police there?"

"Yes, they're here," she said. "But something's wrong. I'll explain when you get here. Hurry, Paul!"

"I'm on my way, Emily," he repeated, too shocked to think of anything else.

Paul called Garrett Aviation at Raleigh-Durham International Airport. He was told a Learjet would be landing soon from a one-way trip. They could get it ready in less than two hours for his flight west across the country. Garrett knew the wealthy Winston family. They were eager to oblige. His next call was to a friend at the Colorado State Patrol. Major Joshua Schroeder confirmed what Emily had told him.

"I'm so very sorry, Paul," Schroeder said. Paul and Joshua had been buddies through high school. "For what it's worth, Paul, I will personally see that we do everything we can to find out what happened. Right now, all we have are a lot of questions and not many answers. We both know your dad was an excellent pilot. This doesn't make any sense at all; it's very troublesome."

Paul was at the top of his MBA graduating class at Duke University's Fuqua School of Business in Durham, NC. He'd enrolled at the request of his father, Ted Winston, a successful Colorado entrepreneur and rancher, after being asked to take over the family's rapidly growing business interests. At 28, he was the eldest of three children. Both of his sisters were married and pursuing their own successful careers.

During the 17-mile taxi ride to Raleigh-Durham airport, Paul tried to shake off the fog of grief clouding his mind. He needed to think clearly. He knew that as the eldest, his two sisters would look to him for leadership through this calamity that had befallen their family.

Chapter Two

Colorado Springs Airport

"This is terrible, horrendous, Paul. I'm so very sorry," George Underhill said as they met on the apron of the airport in Colorado Springs. The ranch foreman's eyes were red. He grasped Paul's hand and then put a muscular arm around his shoulder. They walked together into the executive flight terminal building.

"What in the world happened, George?" Paul asked, struggling to hold his composure. "How could this happen? Dad had thousands of hours on that plane. He's landed hundreds of times at the ranch. This makes no sense, George! What went wrong?"

"We don't know yet," George said. "People from the NTSB (National Transportation Safety Board) have just arrived. Maybe they can give us some answers. The Sheriff's Department has the site cordoned off."

"Where are Mom and Dad?" Paul said. "Where did they take them… their bodies?"

"Colorado Springs," George said. "The coroner took them, and the sheriff has ordered autopsies. It's normal in accident cases."

"Paul!"

He turned quickly when he heard Emily's voice calling out. His diminutive sister was running across the small reception area. She collapsed in his arms, and her cries of grief drew everyone's attention.

"Oh, Paul," she said after a few moments, tears streaming down her face. "I'm so glad you're here! Let's go home!"

"Where's Roberta?" Paul said.

"She's out at the ranch," she said. "She drove out with Stephen and the kids."

He wasn't looking forward to seeing Roberta. There'd been a strain between him and their youngest sister since they'd been teenagers. Paul didn't understand why, and Roberta steadfastly refused to discuss it. He'd finally decided to just let it go. That wouldn't be quite so easy now, he thought.

Emily grabbed Paul's arm and began pulling him toward the entrance.

Paul glanced back at George. The big ranch foreman raised his right eyebrow and tilted his head sideways sympathetically.

Chapter Three

Earnscliffe Manor,
Maidstone, England

While Paul's chartered jet was landing in Colorado Springs, Lord Percival Winston, the 11th Earl of Prescott, was dying. His frail body lay in a huge four-poster bed dominating the master suite at Earnscliffe, a 500-year-old manor house nestled in the picturesque hills of Kent, southeast of London.

"Willard," he whispered to his second cousin, "It's time."

Lord Percival's breathing had become shallow, but he still managed to whisper a few words from time to time, despite the cancer ravaging his internal organs. He'd ordered all life support disconnected.

"Don't talk like that, Percy," Willard said, mostly for the benefit of the few family and staff gathered at his bedside. "You'll be up and about again before you know it. This is just a setback. It'll pass."

Percival managed a weak smile. At 83, he was the eldest of five children. His only surviving sibling, Ted, was the youngest. Their other brother and two sisters had been small children when they were killed in an air raid during the Second World War. Percy regretted that he and his late wife Mary had been unable to have children. He missed her terribly, the love of his life. She'd died 17 years earlier.

I wonder if Willard has any idea what comes next? Percival thought.

He was aware Willard expected a large inheritance. That wasn't going to happen. Percy would see to that. He'd told his second cousin many times that for 25 years he'd been living from the inheritance he

9

might have hoped to receive. Percy had grown tired of giving Willard handouts. So, in the absence of a direct heir, Percival had bequeathed the bulk of his considerable wealth and his title to his only sibling, his brother Ted Winston, in America.

Willard had always refused to believe he was not the natural heir, even though being a second cousin put him some distance from the usual lines of succession. He wasn't about to let matters rest. Secretly, he'd made plans to challenge the will after Percival's death. Willard could see that he wouldn't have long to wait.

Percy had anticipated Willard's nefarious plans. He'd put in place appropriate countermeasures to neutralize Willard's greedy intentions. He regretted that he would not be around to see the measures applied. Just the same, it made him smile inwardly

Chapter Four

Two-Dot Ranch, Colorado
Three months later

"Looks like an avgas leak may have caused the explosion," the man said. "We're positive that sparks coming from the starboard brake while landing ignited a gas leak from a fuel line. It caused the explosion that killed your parents."

Ray Alvarez was not one to mince words. He was in charge of the NTSB team investigating the deaths of Ted and Catherine Winston after they'd died in a fiery plane crash on their ranch west of Colorado Springs.

"We've not ruled out foul play," Ray said.

"Why is that?" Paul said.

"We found evidence the fuel line going into the starboard engine may have been tampered with," Alvarez said. "The same with the brakes. In fact, CSP is treating this as a probable homicide. The Colorado Bureau of Investigation is also looking at the evidence. We'll hear back in a few weeks."

"Are you serious?" Emily said, her eyes wide. "Who would want to harm Mom and Dad? They were just ordinary people … really nice people who went out of their way to help others. This makes no sense."

"These things rarely do," Alvarez said as he rose to leave. "I'll make certain you're kept informed."

11

"Thank you, Mr. Alvarez," Emily said as she led him to the door. "We really appreciate you coming all the way out here to give us your report. That was very kind of you."

Alvarez nodded. As the NTSB investigator walked across the wide veranda of the big two-story stone ranch house, Emily noticed a brown van coming toward them on the long gravel road that led from the highway to the ranch.

"Looks like someone's sent us a package," she said over her shoulder to those gathered to meet with Alvarez: Paul, Roberta and her husband Stephen, Emily's husband Jeremy, ranch foreman George Underhill and his wife Elizabeth.

They had also attended the release in Colorado Springs earlier in the day of the coroner's report on their parents' deaths. Listening to the report had been difficult. It had stopped short of identifying a cause, which is normal procedure for coroner's reports, but they were disappointed just the same.

Emily watched as the UPS van pulled up. The deliveryman jogged from the van across the wide paved driveway, up the six steps and across the 20-foot covered veranda.

"Sign here," he said. The strange-looking package was addressed to her brother. It had an unusual, almost regal appearance to it, and bore a return address in the United Kingdom.

Paul opened the package while the others were busy discussing what Alvarez had shared with them.

"I'll be damned!" he blurted out, commanding everyone's attention.

Paul chuckled, sitting back in what had been his dad's favorite armchair.

"Well now, if that don't beat all," he added using a country colloquialism. "Will you look at this?"

Paul held up a document even more regal-looking than the package. He handed it to Emily, who scanned the cover letter and then, barely containing her excitement, said, "Paul, is this for real? It says you're now an English nobleman, an earl. Is it true… that you're the most direct descendant of Dad's brother, of Uncle Percy?"

Paul grinned and shrugged his shoulders.

"You know," Emily added, "I never gave it much thought when Dad used to tell us stories about his older brother, that he was an English nobleman, like Grandpa Winston used to be. It says here that Uncle Percy's official name was Lord Percival Winston, the 11th Earl of Prescott.

"The letter says he passed away two months ago," Emily said to the rapt attention of those gathered. "It's from his solicitor, that's 'attorney' to us Americans. I wonder why nobody from the family over there called us. Anyway, Uncle Percy had no children … no direct descendants, anyway, so apparently this means that you, Paul … you're the next in line to inherit his title and his estate.

"All I can say is 'Wow!' and congratulations, big brother!" she said, a smile lighting up her face.

Paul stood to his full six-foot, two-inch height and stretched, stunned by the news. Everyone was grateful to hear some good news for a change. Everyone understood that the title would have gone to his father, Ted, had he and Catherine not died in the plane crash.

The group congratulated Paul, then gathered around Emily, wanting to read the letter from the English solicitor that she was passing around. All except Roberta, who stood apart, looking askance at her brother.

"What does this all mean?" she demanded, repeating her sister's question with an entirely different tone. There was a hard edge in her voice. She sounded like the trial lawyer she'd become. Her crisp words belied a mixture of annoyance, impatience, and envy. "Are you the only one to get an inheritance from Uncle Percy's estate? Will you be moving to England? Does this mean George will be taking over running the ranch on his own? Who'll be running Mom and Dad's other businesses?"

"Hold on, Roberta," Paul said. He struggled to be patient. "I'm not sure about any of this right now. It's all rather sudden. I don't know what to make of it yet. First, we'll have to find out if this thing is authentic … not someone's idea of a cruel joke. I'll call that English solicitor in the morning. It's after business hours there now."

The next morning, Paul phoned his late uncle's solicitor, Malcolm Witherspoon in London, and then called his sisters together in their parents' den, "Mr. Witherspoon confirmed what we know: that Dad would have inherited Uncle Percy's title and the bulk of his estate, had he still been alive. Evidently, how this works is the eldest of each succeeding generation of Winstons inherits the title and all that goes with it.

"Mr. Witherspoon told me that Uncle Percy's will expressly continue a centuries-old tradition that requires each subsequent Earl to swear under oath to, above all, use any inherited financial resources to preserve Earnscliffe Estate and the honor of the title. Failure to do so means forfeiture to the next nearest relative. Beyond that, the sitting Earl or, in the case of a woman the countess is free to use inherited monies as he or she considers appropriate."

"That's not the least bit fair," Roberta protested. "We're heirs too!"

"I really don't care," Emily piped up. "And we are not heirs. Regardless, we have the money and the shares of Mom and Dad's ranch and businesses they left us in their wills. Thanks to them, Jeremy and I have more than we could ask for. To be blunt, Roberta, I'd rather have Mom and Dad and Uncle Percy still alive rather than be discussing their money. Besides, all of us have successful careers. So, who cares? And good on our big brother, the soon-to-be Earl of Prescott! How exciting is that?"

"Well, I don't think it's right!" Roberta shot back.

"Frankly," Paul said. "I have no idea whether the financial resources involved are all that substantial or not. We'll just have to wait to find out. Mr. Witherspoon wouldn't go into detail on the phone. He promised to courier me more information. The first thing I need to do is check out what all of this means, in detail, and then go from there. I'll keep both of you in the loop. That's the best we can do for now."

Until going to Duke University, Paul, and his dad, along with foreman George Underhill, had operated the thriving 5,400-acre spread called Two-Dot Ranch, one of the largest beef cattle operations in southwestern Colorado. Paul was unmarried and immensely popular among single women for miles around. Each dreamed of marrying this budding businessman/rancher with movie-star good looks. His charm, laid-back manner and ear-to-ear grin had left a trail of sparkling eyes and fluttering hearts among scores of eligible young women, and tears when he'd left for Duke. The school had granted Paul his MBA based on the high honors marks he'd maintained throughout the two-year program.

*

During the weeks following the emotional trauma of their parents' funeral and the probate of their wills, Paul had to grapple with another decision – whether to leave the life he was being groomed to pursue, especially with the cause of his parents' deaths still unresolved.

"What do you think, Emily?" Paul said over the phone. "Should I go?" It was his fifth or sixth call to Emily – he'd lost count – since receiving the letter from England. His sister and her husband, Jeremy, had returned to their home and careers in Somerville, Massachusetts, near Boston.

"Paul," Emily said, chuckling warmly to the brother she loved dearly. "My answer is the same as the last five times you called and asked me the same question. Yes! Absolutely! Go to England. Become an earl. What the heck? What have you got to lose? Not a thing!"

"Have I called you that much?" he said, embarrassed. "Sorry. It's a hard decision, Emily. George thinks I should go … assures me he can

15

handle the ranch. I know he can. Besides, he has an added incentive now, with Dad and Mom leaving him a 10 percent interest."

"Go, big brother!" Emily said. "Go, for heaven's sake!"

"One other thing, Emily," Paul said. "My friend Josh called this morning about the crash to brief me on the investigation. Josh says the fuel line on Dad's plane was definitely sabotaged. The forensic unit at the Colorado Bureau of Investigation is convinced Mom and Dad were murdered. CSP has started a full homicide investigation."

After a long silence, Emily said, "Have you told Roberta?"

"I called her," he replied. "She just said, 'That's what I expected.' A bit odd; she sounded distracted. Maybe she's into a big trial or something right now."

Josh had told him leads were generating no results and the investigation appeared close to being stalled. He encouraged Paul to get on with his life, and if that meant a move to England, then he should go. Josh promised to keep him posted and to stay in touch, as friends do.

Paul knew it would not be easy to leave behind his hometown, growing business interests and thriving ranch. He and George had debated the pros and cons during those weeks. George argued that even if Paul changed his mind, the experience would be well worth it. Besides, he was still young and had the option of returning home anytime.

Although his late uncle's will mostly involved his late father, Paul decided that he must honor the request that the new Earl relocate, at least for a while, and pursue the responsibilities of an English nobleman. He admired his uncle's foresight, having included the phrase *at least for a while* among his wishes and had not made permanent relocation a condition. Paul decided that's what his father would have done and would have wanted him to do now.

Before moving to England, Paul gathered the businesses his parents were building under a holding company separate from the ranch. He called it Prescott Enterprises in honor of his uncle. Paul also asked

George to become general manager of the ranch, instead of foreman. After all, he now was a partner and would be in charge. George had worked hard over the years. His new status represented quite an achievement. George was the son of a hard-drinking cowboy and a promiscuous bar room 'entertainer' who never married. He'd been forced to support himself before reaching his teens.

Paul admitted he was curious about living in England, given his heritage, especially what life would be like as a nobleman. Paul and his sisters held dual citizenship, all three having been born in England like their father. They hadn't been back since they were small children. He was intrigued by the prospect of living in an ancient manor filled with a host of support staff.

From conversations on the phone with Percy's solicitor, his uncle's will had left him numerous valuable properties and an abundance of financial resources.

Chapter Five

Earnscliffe Manor,
Maidstone

The news had spread like wildfire. Excitement rippled through the social elite of picturesque Maidstone and area. The newest Earl of Prescott was about to take up residence in one of the city's most imposing landmarks, nearby Earnscliffe Manor. The historic estate was nestled in the lush rolling hills of Kent County, aptly nicknamed The Garden of England.

Earnscliffe had been home to the earls of Prescott for centuries. His uncle's many friends and admirers, his neighbors and the Manor staff joined together to plan a gala evening reception and ball welcoming the 12th Earl. It would be the social event of the season. The guest list included nobility, ambassadors, prominent politicians, and local dignitaries. Planners arranged for a grand entrance in the great hall of the meticulously restored manor, where Paul would be formally presented to the 247 invited guests.

Willard Winston, Paul's distant cousin who occupied a luxurious gatehouse on the estate, volunteered to advise Paul about preparing for the welcoming party. Paul was grateful for his cousin's help. He was unfamiliar with English customs, particularly concerning formal events like this. Willard, 23 years older than Paul, strongly encouraged the charming young bachelor to make his appearance with a date and offered to find a suitable young woman to join him.

"Are you quite certain about this, Willard?" Paul asked. "I don't know anyone here yet. Is it appropriate for me to appear to be dating one of their eligible young women so soon after my arrival?"

"Most definitely, old boy!" his English cousin reassured him enthusiastically. "Most of your other guests will come as couples. This way you'll be sure of making a splendid show of it! A melding of cultures, and all that, you know. You'll be a sensation, you'll see … you'll make a huge impression on everyone!"

And quite an entrance it was. He walked down the steps of the grand staircase from his second-floor master bedroom with Sylvia McCracken of Maidstone clinging to his left arm. The room fell ominously silent. There were audible gasps, and a few giggles were heard.

Paul sensed immediately that something was wrong. He caught the eye of the butler, Carlson, just back from vacation, who motioned him discretely to a side room. He excused himself from Sylvia, already slightly tipsy.

"Lord Prescott," Carlson began. "May I be permitted to ask your lordship how you came to have Ms. McCracken as your date for this evening's celebration?"

"Why, it was my cousin, Willard," Paul replied. "In fact, since you were away on leave, he took the trouble of inviting her on my behalf. I just now met her. Is something wrong?"

"Yes, Milord," Carlson said. "I believe there is. I must tell you, sir, that Ms. McCracken runs the most famous, ah, how should I say it? Forgive me, sir … the most famous house of ill repute in Kent County. I can't imagine what in the world inspired him to do so."

"I think I do," Paul said, deeply embarrassed.

The spectacle of Paul and Sylvia descending the grand staircase arm in arm brought a bemused reaction from the assembled guests, and then brief restrained exchanges and polite silence. A few were unable to contain their amusement. Guffaws were heard. Others were chagrined. Most left early.

The next morning at breakfast, Willard could barely contain his merriment over the cruel trick he'd pulled on his American cousin … second cousin once removed, he corrected himself, wanting to put as much distance between the branches of the family as he could manage.

"Right! Just like the bloody hillbilly he is!" Willard laughed heartily to his wife Alice. They were having breakfast in the spacious kitchen of their two-story sandstone home surrounded by tall oak trees on the edge of Earnscliffe Estate.

Willard slapped the table with glee, reliving the night before. He was delighted with himself for embarrassing his "cowboy cousin". Alice was dismayed. She saw Willard's nasty trick as his immature way of venting anger over Paul having inherited the bulk of Lord Percival's estate. Willard was livid about the comparatively modest bequest their uncle had left him.

As the closest relative living in England, Willard assumed he was entitled to inherit virtually all the extensive assets. At the very least, he expected to inherit their home and a substantial sum of money. To his dismay, he couldn't find a lawyer willing to pursue the legal challenge he wanted. In Willard's opinion, the late earl had seen fit to leave him 'an insulting pittance.' In fact, his inheritance would provide him and Alice with a generous income and the use of the two-story, four-bedroom gatehouse rent-free for the rest of their lives. Willard also conveniently overlooked the fact that he and his family had already lived there rent-free for more than 25 years. During that time, Willard had dabbled in numerous failed pursuits, mostly financed by Percival who tried to get Willard to become self-supporting, to no avail.

"Well, you know," Alice said pleasantly, "We really must be civil to the young fellow, my dear. He is, after all, sort of our landlord now."

"Bloody hell," Willard exploded.

"Just imagine, us beholden to that uncivilized Yankee fool," he ranted. "Good god! He's a fucking cowboy for Christ's sake, Alice! It's a damned embarrassment to the family name, that's what it is! It's a bloody insult to England!"

Willard stomped out of the room and headed for his den, muttering. He had more immediate problems. Their trouble-prone son Reginald, better known as Reggie, was due for parole from prison. He'd been convicted of trying to sell valuable artifacts stolen from Earnscliffe Manor. It was Reggie's latest brush with the law.

As if I don't have enough deal to with, Willard grumbled as he dialed the phone on his desk. *On top of it all, we have a thief ... a criminal in the family. Bloody hell!*

"Blantyre House Prison, warden's office," a bored female voice answered the phone.

"My son is due for release tomorrow," Willard said. "I'm wondering what time I might pick him up."

"Has he completed his FLED?" the voice snapped back.

Her attitude did nothing to improve Willard's state of mind.

"His what?" Willard asked.

"His FLED. His FLED ... His Full License Eligibility Date— FLED," said the now irritated voice. "Prisoners must have that form filled out to be released."

"I expect so," a flustered Willard responded. The irony of the acronym escaped him.

"My son called me that he'll be released tomorrow morning on parole. Is there a scheduled release time?"

The voice replied curtly, "We start daily releases sometime after breakfast. I cannot tell exactly when a given prisoner will be freed. You'll just have to wait. Released prisoners exit through the front gate."

She hung up on him.

21

James Osborne

Two years earlier, police had found Reggie, their trouble-prone 22-year-old son, passed out drunk behind the wheel of his aging car. He'd driven off a country road into a ditch on the outskirts of Maidstone. Artifacts stolen from Earnscliffe Manor were in the back seat. Police and the news media, in Maidstone as well as surrounding Kent County, had been notified of the theft immediately by the curator at Earnscliffe, who hoped the thief or thieves would be intercepted before they got too far. It worked.

A police search of the vehicle also discovered a World War II Webley Mk IV revolver in the car's boot. Reggie professed surprise. He was unable to produce a license for the weapon or a permit to transport it. A records search of the serial number identified the owner as Reggie's father, who'd served briefly as an officer in the Grenadier Guards. When police arrived at Willard and Alice's home to inquire about the Webley, Willard explained that he had obtained the antique revolver as a memento while serving with the Guards. It wasn't being transported legally, and the police knew it. But at least Willard had registered it, as required by law.

Willard lied when police asked if he knew why the Webley was in the car. He told them he was donating it as a family artifact to the Earnscliffe Manor military collection. There was no such collection, but the police didn't know that. Willard also claimed he'd put the gun in Reggie's car to take it to Earnscliffe. He said Alice needed their car to keep a medical appointment in London. That wasn't true either. Willard lied again when he insisted Reggie didn't know the revolver was in his car, making a mental note to ask Reggie *what the bloody hell* he'd been up to with the gun.

Local police forces often looked the other way when persons connected to the nobility committed minor infractions, and they did so now for Willard and Reggie. They were unable to overlook Reggie's theft of the artifacts from Earnscliffe, however, since the theft was not minor, and all the local news media had already reported it. Police did follow procedure by recording the serial number of the Webley. Before returning the weapon to Willard, they also had the forensic lab at New Scotland Yard in London conduct ballistics tests and take photos of the rifling, the marks made on bullets by grooves inside the barrel. The rifling matched nothing on record but was added to the files anyway.

Chapter Six

Maidstone

In the years following his humiliating introduction to English high society, Paul made a determined effort to adopt the lifestyle expected of an English nobleman. He persevered but yearned for his life back in America.

The main reason he'd remained in England was Anne, whom he married less than a year after arriving. Paul had fallen in love the moment he saw the petite young beauty at a charity ball. London's social elite was there, including members of the House of Lords, where Paul would soon be installed. It was Paul's opportunity for social redemption after the disaster at the welcoming party contrived by his jealous cousin.

The attraction between Paul and Anne had been immediate, compelling, and mutual. Anne was drawn to Paul by his handsome features, engaging charm, and wholesome values. Paul found irresistible Anne's independent attitude, sense of fun and zest for adventure. And her extraordinary beauty left him breathless.

Anne's parents, Agnes, and Richard Watson were delighted when the couple began dating. Anne was a widow with a four-year-old son, Douglas. Her late husband had been a British army officer, killed in Iraq before Douglas was born. Agnes and Philip had insisted a very pregnant Anne move back in with them.

Richard, the vice-president of an import-export company, took an instant liking to Paul's laid-back manner and wry sense of humor. Most important for Agnes was that her daughter could become Lady Anne, the

Countess of Prescott. It would satisfy the longing for higher social status she had nurtured for decades.

But strait-laced Agnes was horrified when Anne and Paul announced just three months into their courtship that they wanted to marry almost immediately. Anne planned to accompany Paul on his upcoming annual summer visit to his growing business interests and cattle ranch in the far-away United States. To Agnes' way of thinking, a six-month engagement was barely acceptable. A year would be proper.

She put in a sleepless night. By morning Agnes had decided to confront Anne and demand her daughter's wedding plans be changed to 'a more respectable' timeframe. After breakfast, Agnes asked Anne to join her in the parlor. Anne had no sooner entered than Agnes demanded, "What on earth are you trying to do to us?" Agnes said, barely keeping an even voice. "Don't you realize you will destroy this family's reputation, our good name?"

Anne considered her mother's attitude tiresome. It seemed she'd not learned a thing since Anne's first marriage to Douglas's father five years earlier. They'd dated just a few months before marrying, within days of him going overseas. This was no different. Her mother didn't see it that way, wanting to emulate what she thought were the norms of the higher society she aspired to join.

"Mother, don't you see? Paul and I love each other," Anne began calmly. "We can't wait a whole year just because of some rules that have been obsolete for years. Like it or not, I'm going to America with Paul this summer. Doug is coming, too."

"I will not have it, Anne!" Agnes said. "I will not allow you to bring dishonor on this family! Never! Never!" Her voice rose almost to a shriek.

Anne clenched her teeth and left the room. She rushed up the stairs toward the three-room suite she shared with Douglas. Anne ran down the hall, around the corner and plowed head long into her father.

"Hold on there, Princess," her father said, gathering her to his ample mid-section. "What's got you all upset?"

"Oh, Daddy!" she answered through her anger, "Mommy and I had an awful fight. She wants Paul and me to wait a ridiculous amount of time before we're married. I don't see why. Paul's going to visit America this summer, and I want to take Douglas and go with him!"

"Come along," her father said gently. He led her back downstairs to his den. Closing the door behind them, he said to her, "Paul is a fine young man, my dear. Your mother and I like him very much indeed. It's also abundantly clear he's head over heels for you. Just tell me one thing, Anne. Do you really love him? Think now, are you absolutely certain?" he asked, looking into his daughter's eyes.

"Oh yes, Daddy! Yes!" Anne cried, her clenched fists unconsciously emphasizing her heart-felt reply. "I never thought I'd feel this way again. I love him with all my heart. I'd marry Paul even if he was a penniless chimney sweep."

"Hush now, Anne!" her father said in a feigned whisper, a twinkle in his eyes. "Please don't say that around your mother! Okay, my dear? A deal?"

"Sure, Daddy. Does that mean you approve?" she asked.

"Of course, Princess!" her father replied with a warm smile. "All I want is for you to be happy. For the record, Anne, your young man did come to me and ask for your hand. I approved, of course! Now, let's get to work on your mother."

Chapter Seven

Paul and Anne were in a secluded corner of her parent's back garden cuddled up on the soft pad of a wrought iron bench. He had come for dinner to celebrate their engagement. It was growing dusk. Anne was wrapped in Paul's strong, loving arms.

"Anne, I'm going to Brighton next weekend to take care of some business," Paul began hesitantly. "Would you like to come with me?"

"Do you really want me to, Paul?" Anne said, surprised and excited. She sat up so she could look directly into his eyes.

"You know I do, my love," Paul replied softly. A mischievous grin lit his face. Anne could see the love and yearning in his bright blue eyes. The attraction was overwhelming.

Anne nodded, smiling coyly.

"What about my little buddy, Doug?" Paul said. "Do you want to bring him along?"

"Of course not!" Anne replied, another coy smile lighting her pretty face. It was the reply Paul had hoped for.

"I'll ask my parents," she said. "They love to spoil Doug. They get along wonderfully, just like you and Doug do. He adores you. I'm so thrilled the two of you have hit it off so well."

"How will you explain your trip to your folks?" he asked.

"I don't know," Anne replied. "I'll think of something."

The prospect of being alone with Paul for a weekend sent tingles running through her lithe body. She could hardly breathe from the excitement growing within her. She thought for a moment, then said, "I won't lie to my parents, Paul. You know I can't do that. But they don't need to know everything either, now do they? Maybe I can get some girlfriends to go along."

"What?" Paul exclaimed. His eyes were wide with surprise.

"Just a minute, Paul," She chuckled. "Do calm down, my love.

"If they come I can tell my parents that I'm going to Brighton with some girlfriends. It'll be the truth. I'll go down to Brighton with them. You and I will meet there. My friends know when to make themselves scarce."

"Oh, aren't you the schemer," Paul chuckled. "I knew there was something about you that was ever so attractive."

"You," she said, pressing her body against his chest. She thrilled at the feel of his firm, muscular body.

The next day, Anne announced to her parents over breakfast, "A couple of girlfriends and I are going to Brighton on Friday to do some shopping. We'll be gone for the weekend. Would you mind terribly looking after Doug while I'm away?"

"My word, Anne, you can't be serious!" Agnes exclaimed. "What brought this on? Who's all going? Will any parents be along with you?"

"Of course not!" Anne replied. "We're all adults, you know. And, no, we won't need parents there either. Good heavens, Mommy, I'm a 26-year-old mother and a widow."

"Well, what about Paul?" Agnes asked. "What's he going to think about you going off by yourself unescorted to that … that loose … that libertine resort, Brighton? My God, Anne! Really!"

"Mommy, I'm not going by myself," Anne replied. "And besides, Paul is going to be away then too, so I might as well get away for a few days myself. What's the harm?"

"What's the harm?" Agnes shrilled. "What's the harm? A group of naïve young women all on their own, at that low-life resort? I can't bear this. I've heard that all sorts of terrible things go on there.

28

"I don't like the sound of this one little bit," Agnes fumed, turning to Robert for support. She didn't get it.

"Agnes," Robert said gently. "Anne is a grown woman. She's quite able to make up her own mind."

"Yes, she certainly is a grown woman, Robert," his wife answered stiffly. Thoughts of their only child's shapely figure ran through her mind. "That's just what troubles me."

"Oh, Mommy, you do worry so," Anne said, getting up from the table and heading for her suite with Doug scampering along behind.

Whew! Anne thought as she reached their suite. *I do hope that's out of the way now.*

She turned her attention to making plans for her very first time alone with Paul. The prospect exhilarated her, gave her goosebumps, and frightened her just a little. She began thinking about the shopping she needed to do for negligees and other lingerie.

I'll take Paula and Janet with me, Anne decided. She was confident those two girlfriends were far more 'experienced' at this than her. Besides, with her friends along, Anne could pretend the sexy garments she would buy were for them. She couldn't take the risk of word getting back to her mother from someone who might see her buying such things.

James Osborne

Chapter Eight

Brighton, England

"Welcome to the Lions Head Inn, Mr. and Mrs. Winston," a beaming desk clerk said as they checked in. It was early afternoon.

"Your suite is ready, folks," he added. "Overlooking the Brighton Pier and the Channel, as you requested, sir. We hope your stay is a memorable one."

"Thank you," Paul replied, picking up the key. "I'm very certain that it will be, indeed!"

Anne held his left arm close to her and squeezed it with both of her hands. When Paul had said "indeed!" she'd moved her petite body even tighter against him, stepping gently but purposefully on his left foot.

Turning away from the desk, she was barely able to suppress a giggle. They made their way soundlessly up the main staircase, carpeted in a deep maroon pile, Paul's big, powerful fingers gently wrapped around Anne's delicate little hand. At the third floor of the elegant old inn, they turned down a long hallway newly restored in light oak and royal blue. They came to Suite 3C.

Anne looked at Paul timidly. They smiled coyly at each other. Their excitement rose. Each was feeling apprehensive but determined. Paul slid the key in the lock and turned it. The heavy oak door opened silently into a luxurious suite. From the open doorway they saw an elegantly furnished sitting room. Beyond, through large windows, was a panoramic view of the English Channel.

Well, well, Anne thought to herself, just a bit smugly, as they walked into the room. *So, this is where we will consummate our engagement. What a wonderful place to do that!*

"What do you think, Anne?" Paul said quietly, breaking into her thoughts.

"Oh, Paul, this is absolutely magnificent! It's extraordinary!" She replied. She turned away. Her eyes filled. She was feeling both ecstatic and frightened at the same time.

"Are you okay?" he asked, feeling awkward, hoping for her approval.

"I, I think so," she said, wishing they'd stop making small talk. She yearned for him to pick her up in his arms and take her to bed.

Hmm, I wonder where it is? Anne thought.

"Over here, my love," he said, reading her thoughts.

His smile was at once shy and warm as he pointed to the open door of the bedroom to their right. They walked toward it hand-in-hand. The room was so large it dwarfed the sumptuous king-size four-poster bed, complete with canopy. To their left were more large windows, continuing the breathtaking view of the English Channel.

Paul reached for the coat Anne was carrying on her left arm. He draped it over the back of a chair beside the bedroom door. She stepped toward him. He wrapped her gently in his strong arms. He could feel his desire mounting. Her heart began to race.

Suddenly, there was a knock on the door of the suite. Paul looked at Anne and smiled before walking out of the bedroom, closing the door behind him, and crossing the sitting room. He cautiously opened the door to the suite.

"Your luggage, sir," a porter said. "You left it in the lobby. We assumed you wanted it brought up?"

"Oh, yes," Paul answered, trying not to look sheepish as he stepped back. "Sorry. Just leave it over there, beside that sofa."

The porter wheeled the trolley over and unloaded multiple suitcases. The two small ones were Paul's. The two large ones were Anne's.

"There you go," Paul said, handing the porter a £20 note. The porter's eyes opened wide. In 17 years as a porter, he'd never received such a large tip.

"If you need anything at all, Mr. Winston, anything at all, you just call on me, sir," the porter managed to stammer out. "My name is Jackson, sir. Jackson."

"Yes, thank you, Jackson," Paul replied. "That'll be all for now."

He escorted Jackson to the door, closing it after him and latching the security chain.

Paul walked back across the sitting room and opened the bedroom door. Anne was nowhere to be seen. He was startled for a moment. Then he saw light under a door he assumed was the ensuite. He took off his suit jacket and tie, placing them on the chair beside Anne's coat.

Next he walked over to the windows. He was pleased their first few hours in Brighton had been under warm sunny skies, not common in parts of England even in summer. He closed the heavy floor-to-ceiling drapes and turned off the lights.

The sound of the door to the ensuite opening drew his attention. Anne was standing in the doorway, haloed in the light behind her. She was dressed in a beautiful red waist-length negligee and bikini panties, under a matching filmy cover that ended just above her knees. The cover was held in place by a tiny red ribbon tied in a bow at her graceful neck.

Paul heard his breath catch in his throat. They walked toward each other. He kicked off his shoes just as he wrapped her eagerly in his arms. Their mouths found each other's. Their desires rose quickly. Paul pulled gently on the delicate ribbon holding Anne's cover together at her neck. It slipped to the carpeted floor.

He saw the outline of her erect nipples through the lace negligee. His desire rose higher. Anne fumbled frantically at the buttons of Paul's shirt, then with his belt buckle. Meanwhile, he passionately kissed her mouth, face, and neck, then down into the cleavage between her firm breasts.

They stumbled toward the bed. It was then that Paul noticed Anne must have turned down the bed. They fell gently sideways onto it. Their kissing grew more intense as they struggled to help each other out of their clothing. Finally, they were naked under the covers, pressing their bodies together feverishly, their arms and legs entwined.

Anne felt Paul's right-hand caress her back, then her shoulders, and then her neck. She willed his hand to move down to her left breast. It did. Her nipples had become acutely sensitive. She felt herself becoming more and more excited as his hand fondled her nipple, then continued to roam her beautiful, slender body.

Paul's hand slowly traced her delicate curves, finally working its way down her creamy smooth skin, finding her most intimate and sensitive areas. Frantically they sought each other's bodies. They became lost in the urgent ecstasy of their mutual lovemaking.

Later, they lay quietly in each other's arms. Their spirits were consumed with the wonder of the shared intimacy they had experienced.

"Oh, my God, my love," Anne managed. "That was so beautiful."

She looked deep into the bright blue eyes of her husband-to-be. She was overcome by the love she felt for this wonderful man who'd come into her life. He gazed adoringly at Anne. He was in awe of her ... of her beauty, physically and spiritually. Of her gentle, caring manner. He was amazed that this wonderful, gorgeous woman had agreed to be his wife. He was so very grateful.

Each drifted off into a contented sleep. Eventually, the lovers stirred and woke. They made love again, more leisurely this time. Then they languished in each other's arms for almost an hour. Finally, Paul got out of bed and stood up, starting toward the bathroom.

Anne began to laugh.

"What?" he asked, smiling awkwardly, enjoying the warmth of her laughter.

"What?" he repeated, struggling to keep himself from laughing with her over something he knew nothing about.

"Are you going to remove that before we shower together?" she asked through her laughter.

Anne pointed down at his feet.

Caught up in their wonderfully frantic lovemaking, he'd forgotten to take off one sock. There he stood awkwardly, stark naked except for a calf-length black sock that had slipped down around his left ankle.

Both chuckled, thoroughly enjoying the shared humor. He took off the sock, finished his trip and then climbed back into bed. They wrapped their arms tightly around each other, hugging naked. They decided to call it Bare Hugs. They would Bare Hug from that day onward every single night they were together.

Finally, the happy lovers showered together, thrilling again in the wonders of each other's body. Then they dressed and walked hand-in-hand out of the hotel and onto the street in search of a special place for their very first 'post-intimate' dinner together.

Chapter Nine

Earnscliffe Manor

A few weeks after announcing their engagement, Paul received his Writ of Summons – the official invitation to sit in the British House of Lords. Paul wanted to visit the office that he would occupy and to meet his late uncle's secretary, Clementine Shackleford. The office was in a centuries-old building that he'd inherited from his uncle, near the Palace of Westminster. Paul invited Anne to go along.

As they walked into the outer office, Mrs. Shackleford looked up, startled. It was obvious she wasn't expecting company. Paul had forgotten to phone ahead.

"I'm Paul Winston," he said, smiling across the office at the frumpy-looking middle-aged woman seated before them.

"You must be Mrs. Shackleford."

She catapulted her large size from behind her desk with the speed of a gazelle and the grace of a water buffalo.

"Milord!" the redoubtable Mrs. Shackleford blustered as she came to a stumbling halt before her new boss. "This is an unexpected pleasure!"

In her wake, everything atop her desk went askew. A mini-blizzard of papers fluttered down onto the royal blue deep-pile carpet.

"I'm honoured to make your acquaintance," she sputtered awkwardly. "I'm Clementine Shackleford. I had the honour of assisting your late uncle, may God rest his soul." Mrs. Shackleford bowed her head.

35

"And I'll be most honoured to assist you as well, Milord," she said brightly, recovering her composure.

"I'm pleased to meet you, Mrs. Shackleford," Paul replied, barely able to keep a straight face as he beheld the bizarre spectacle standing before him.

Anne looked away quickly, her eyes seeking desperately for a distraction to keep her from bursting out laughing.

Mrs. Shackleford was dressed more like a charwoman than the secretary to a Lord of the Realm. Multiple strands of grey hair were making a break for freedom from a bun held precariously in place by a scattered assortment of bobby pins. Her chin and upper lip sported multiple grey and black curly hairs long overdue for a trimming or plucking. Her shapeless print dress clearly hadn't enjoyed the benefits of an iron for some time, although it seemed intimately acquainted with mending needles employing randomly colored threads.

"I'm sure we'll get along just fine," Paul reassured her. He'd found notes from her in his uncle's files at the manor house. The notes had impressed him immensely about her knowledge and organizational skills.

Only God and Mrs. Shackleford know just how desperately Uncle Percy could have used her skills at the Manor, Paul thought, recalling the chaos of his uncle's Earnscliffe office.

And the spectacle before him served as a reminder that packaging often differs considerably from what's to be found inside.

"Might I be presumptuous, Milord?" Mrs. Shackleford said, glancing toward Anne. "May I enquire as to whom this beautiful young lady might be?"

"Forgive me," Paul replied. He looked at Anne fondly, bursting with pride. "May I introduce my fiancée, Anne Watson."

"He asked me to come along on his first day," Anne said with a mischievous smile. "I'm his bodyguard!"

36

For a split-second Mrs. Shackleford's face bore a stunned, questioning look. Then a booming laugh erupted from her unpainted lips.

"I can see, my dear, we're kindred spirits, if I may be so bold," Mrs. Shackleford said, with a loud chuckle.

"It's going to be delightful working with you!" she added, leaving no doubt that a two-woman conspiracy in pursuit of Paul's best interests had just been launched.

"Is there anything you would like me to do for you today, Milord?" she asked turning to Paul.

"No, thank you. We've just come by to meet you and to have a look around the office," Paul answered, still trying to keep a straight face. "I'd like to be ready when Parliament resumes next month."

"Right you are, Milord," Mrs. Shackleford said. "An aide will deliver a package for you shortly to Earnscliffe with all the information you will be needing. Now, if you'll follow me, Milord."

She led them to the door of Paul's office. Mrs. Shackleford stepped aside so Paul and Anne could enter. She closed the door softly behind them.

What lay before them left both in awe. The opulent, brightly lit office Paul would soon occupy was grand, to say the least. The ancient ceiling was at least 10 feet high. Stained glass windows graced the top half of the wall to their right. The lower half was covered in rich mahogany paneling like the other three walls.

Beneath their feet was a vast expanse of gleaming hardwood floor, accented by three huge deep pile area carpets. On their left, one of the exotic carpets lay beneath a circular antique meeting table surrounded by six matching straight-back chairs. Behind was a tall antique wood fireplace. On their right, a matching off-white carpet defined a formal seating area. There, a tan leather sofa and two antique leather armchairs stood guard around a large oval mahogany coffee table. Before them was the third huge carpet, the far end of it snuggled beneath an immense carved wooden desk, some 20 feet from where they were standing.

"My God, Paul," Anne said. Her voice was barely above a whisper. "I've never been in an office quite this grand!"

She held back, intimidated by the grandeur while Paul strode confidently toward the imposing desk. The sound of his shoes, at first ricocheting off the hardwood floor and paneled walls, went eerily silent as his steps reached the deep carpet. Paul made his way soundlessly around to the far side of the desk and sat in a high-back leather office chair that would soon be his.

"My goodness, Anne!" he said. "I've never seen a desk this big. It's huge! I'll bet you could land a 747 on it with runway to spare!"

Anne smiled, admiring proudly her soon-to-be husband. She loved his sense of humor, and especially how his disarming modesty kept them both well grounded.

Paul had committed himself to carrying out his responsibilities to the best of his abilities, but his status as a member of British nobility didn't impress him.

Chapter Ten

Paul and Anne were married six months after they met, the wedding the social event of the season for Kent County. Four-year-old Douglas was the proud ring bearer. Paul's cousin was not invited. Paul had banned Willard and his son Reggie from the Manor house until further notice. Both were furious and swore to get even. No one paid them any attention.

Anne took easily to life as Lady Anne, Countess of Prescott. She cherished her role assisting her husband with his political, social, and ceremonial obligations. Anne valued the influence that came with her title, particularly the boost to promoting social issues she cherished, including her favorite: single mothers in need. While Anne was kept busy also with settling her new family into their home at Earnscliffe Manor, Paul divided his working time between commitments as an Earl and learning about his newly inherited investments and properties listed in Percy's will.

What he thought would take weeks turned into many months as Paul waded through decades of accumulated, disorganized, and mostly outdated records in his uncle's home office. The situation was much less challenging in the House of Lords office, thanks to the capable Mrs. Shackleford. but the den at Earnscliffe Manor had clearly lacked Mrs. Shackleford's competent attention.

One afternoon, Paul decided to take a quick peek into one of the many filing cabinets lining a long wall behind his desk. Unlike the others, it was locked. He found a key in the desk that unlocked it. A file in the top drawer caught his attention.

James Osborne

For Ted,
Re: Your Personal Bank Account, London

Intrigued, Paul pulled the file and sat at his uncle's old scarred double pedestal desk. The only thing in the file was a brown envelope with his father's name written on it in neat block letters. It contained correspondence with a bank in London, Coutts & Co. There were no bank statements, as Paul expected, just some official-looking bank documents used to open the account.

An undated handwritten letter was attached to the correspondence. Paul was surprised by what it said, but not nearly as surprised as he would be later after learning the full implications.

My Dear Brother Ted,
As I anticipated, this file has now come to your attention. It contains my correspondence with Mr. Neville Henderson of Coutts & Co. regarding a personal account established some years ago. I have instructed Mr. Henderson that upon my death the balance of this account is to be transferred to an account I have opened in your name that awaits your signature. This account is rather different, as you will discover, from the other of my business and personal assets that you will have inherited.
May I say, Ted, in the absence of children of my own, I am indeed proud that you will carry on our family title and that your son, Paul, will one day inherit from you the title and all that goes with it.
As I am certain you will recall, for centuries it has been the tradition of the Earls of Prescott for the title and all associated assets to be inherited by the eldest child or, in the

absence of children, the nearest sibling. That will be you, in this case.

It gives me great comfort to know that you will become the principal heir to my estate, and that one day so will Paul. I am confident that each of you in turn will put the proceeds of the estate's assets to wise use and will be duly mindful of others deserving of assistance and encouragement. I leave this world knowing the Prescott peerage is in fine hands.

I remain your devoted brother,

Percival Winston

11th Earl of Prescott

Paul realized that his uncle's letter had been written before his parents' tragic deaths. He thought it fortunate that his uncle probably would not have known. Stapled to the bank documents, Paul found another note, also handwritten, with Henderson's name and a telephone number. He dialed the number. A voice came on the line.

"Neville Henderson here."

Evidently it was Mr. Henderson's direct line.

"Mr. Henderson, my name is Paul Winston. I'm the nephew of the late Percival Winston, the Earl of Prescott. I believe he was a client of your bank?"

"Yes, he was," Henderson replied. His voice sounded guarded and cautious. "How may I help you?"

"Just before my uncle died, my parents were killed in a plane crash. My father was heir to Uncle Percy's estate. Consequently, I've become heir to his title and the bulk of his estate," Paul continued.

"Oh, yes, Mr. Winston," Henderson replied, still noncommittal.

Paul continued, "I've just come across a letter in my uncle's files that directed my father, and now me, I suppose, to contact you regarding an account he had set up in my father's name at your bank."

41

"I see," Henderson said. "I would imagine, then, young man that you would like an appointment?"

Paul was relieved that Henderson had not used his new title. The English were very conscious of titles and social status, in contrast to Paul's more informal upbringing.

"Yes, Mr. Henderson," Paul replied. "When might you be able to see me?"

"I could see you tomorrow afternoon around 1:30, if that would be convenient," Henderson said.

"I'll see you then, Mr. Henderson," Paul agreed.

"Oh, Mr. Winston. Would you be good enough to bring along your uncle's correspondence you referred to? I must ask also that you bring along your passport and a notarized copy of your uncle's will. Might I suggest that you bring along your solicitor, as well?"

"I will see you tomorrow at 1:30, then. Good day, Mr. Winston." Henderson hung up before Paul could respond.

Paul was not surprised by Henderson's request to bring his passport for identification, and his uncle's will. It was proper business practice. But he was taken aback by the request to bring a lawyer.

Malcolm Witherspoon, his uncle's solicitor whom he'd met several times since moving to England, happily agreed to accompany him, even on such short notice. Paul had become impressed with the rotund lawyer's command of English law and with his commitment to serving clients fully.

Chapter Eleven

London

Paul had arranged to meet Witherspoon at 1:20 p.m. in the lobby of Coutts & Co. The imposing building with its historic facade was prominently located at 440 Strand, in the heart of the City of London.

"Good afternoon, Milord."

A portly Witherspoon struggled to his feet from a seat in the cathedral-like lobby of the Coutts & Co. head office. He greeted Paul with a smile and a pudgy right appendage that rivaled the size of Paul's large muscular hand.

"I've notified the reception desk of your appointment," Witherspoon managed to puff.

Within seconds a young man appeared, saying he was to escort them to see Mr. Henderson. They got off the elevator at the top floor and turned left, down a corridor. The right wall of the wide corridor was half a solid wall topped by windows overlooking an elegantly furnished area accommodating reception and clerical employees. The corridor ended in a richly furnished lobby.

They crossed to a plate glass door with lettering: 'Neville Henderson, Deputy Chief Executive, Global Retail Banking.'

Paul was taken aback. Malcolm let out a low whistle.

They'd be dealing with one of the bank's top echelons. The two men went through the glass doors into the reception area. Their escort had silently disappeared. An all-businesswoman glanced up as a tall middle-

43

aged man strode around her desk toward them. His gleaming head proclaimed its lengthy history as a hair-free zone.

"Mr. Winston? Good afternoon. I'm Neville Henderson. Good to meet you. Won't you please come in?"

Paul introduced Malcolm, and the three walked across the spacious outer reception area into Henderson's private chambers. The size of his office rivaled Paul's in the City of Westminster. Paul and Malcolm were seated on one side of an impressive maple desk while the impeccably dressed banker sat in a large, overstuffed leather chair across from them.

Henderson looked at Paul and said, "Did you happen to bring along a copy of Lord Prescott's Last Will and Testament and a copy of his letter that you mentioned on the phone?"

"Yes, we did," Malcolm said as he extracted from his briefcase a notarized copy of the will, passing it across the desk.

Paul opened his briefcase and produced the letter from his uncle he'd found in the file. Henderson turned to Paul and said, "Please forgive me, sir, but I must ask also for your passport. Did you happen to bring it along?"

Paul produced his passport. Henderson studied and returned it. Then he read slowly through the few pages that made up his uncle's will and his uncle's letter to his father.

Henderson surprised Paul by removing from a file on his desk what appeared to be a duplicate copy of his uncle's will. He was even more surprised when Henderson produced what seemed to be a photocopy of his uncle's letter to his father. Paul and Malcolm exchanged looks and raised eyebrows as they watched Henderson place the two wills side-by-side and carefully read through both. He did the same with Percival's letter. Then he astounded Paul by producing copies of his parents' wills.

Where in hell ... how in hell, did he get those? Paul thought.

"Well, yes, hmm, everything seems to be in order," Henderson said. "I hope you understand. We must be scrupulously careful about our clients' affairs."

He opened another file folder on his desk, looked up at Paul, and began, "It has been established to my complete satisfaction that you are entitled to inherit all assets held at Coutts & Co. on behalf of the late Lord Percival Winston, the 11th Earl of Prescott. Congratulations, Mr. Winston.

"The late Lord Prescott was a man of considerable means. You may not be fully aware of this, Mr. Winston, but your uncle was an extremely wealthy man."

"I am in the process of familiarizing myself with my uncle's estate," Paul replied. "I've spent the past several weeks tracking and itemizing his assets. You are quite right, my uncle's means are considerable, and I must say I am deeply humbled to be entrusted with his estate."

"Quite," Henderson responded, adding a typically English, "Harrumph!"

"Your uncle did share with me some information regarding his properties and his miscellaneous bank accounts and securities elsewhere."

Paul thought, *miscellaneous?*

There was nothing 'miscellaneous' about the cash and other liquid investments Paul had identified so far totaling almost £16.3 million. Then there was Earnscliffe Manor, plus the 750 acres it sat on, and the four downtown office buildings. Hardly miscellaneous!

Henderson continued, "Mr. Winston, your uncle honored Coutts & Co. with the responsibility of caring for the bulk of his liquid assets. I have here the necessary documents to transfer to you the personal accounts that he left in our care. Those accounts, Mr. Winston, contain the sum of approximately £237.83 million, not including today's interest. That also does not include those other accounts you may be aware of that

His Lordship set up for you and your two sisters in your names containing £2 million each."

Paul was stunned. He sat back hard in his chair. His head was reeling. He made a quick calculation. He estimated that at current exchange rates, the amount Henderson mentioned would be close to US $450 million! Even after taxes, the inheritance would be far beyond his wildest dreams.

"If you will sign these documents where I've indicated, Lord Prescott, we can proceed with the transfer from your late uncle's accounts to the account we have taken the liberty of opening at Coutts & Co. in your name," Henderson said.

Paul was too shocked at first to notice Henderson had switched to using his vice-regal title.

Malcolm took the documents Henderson passed across his desk, reviewed them quickly and then passed them to Paul, who signed where Malcolm indicated. Malcolm and Henderson witnessed his signatures.

"May I extend my heartiest congratulations and best wishes, Milord," Henderson said, standing and shaking Paul's hand. "I hope we can continue to be of service to you, as we have had the privilege of serving your uncle."

"I ... I don't see the need for any changes at the moment," Paul stammered as he stood up. He was still in shock. He had just become an exceptionally wealthy man. It all seemed quite surreal.

"I think it will be a few days before all of this sinks in," Paul managed to add.

"I'm sure it will, Lord Prescott," Henderson said, smiling while not quite suppressing a chuckle. "I'm sure it will."

Malcolm accompanied Paul down the elevator. The lawyer shook his head in wonderment as he leaned back heavily against the polished brass handrail inside the elevator car, paneled in light oak and smoked glass.

"Good grief, Milord, I've never been witness to a transaction quite like that one," Malcolm said. "I guess it's fair to say that sort of thing just doesn't happen every day.

"That's amazing!" he added. "As you will recall, the only reference to this account in your uncle's will was that innocuous term, 'The cash holdings in my bank accounts'. Quite a surprise! Quite a surprise!"

Chapter Twelve

Earnscliffe, Manor
August 27, 1999

Paul and Anne had been married for eight years.

Their love for each other and their zest for life and adventure, had grown as their family had expanded, with Anne's son, Douglas, now almost 13, joined by siblings Catherine, 7, and Michael, 5.

Each summer, Paul and Anne had returned to Colorado, first taking with them Douglas and then, as they arrived, the other children. Attending to Paul's growing business interests in the U.S. took most of a month in Colorado Springs, Los Angeles, and New York. The timing also coincided with early cattle roundups in the area. Paul participated eagerly. It helped keep his hand in, but more importantly it maintained the relationships he cherished with long-time friends and neighbors among the ranching community. Anne looked forward to each visit. Over the years, she'd grown fond of Colorado and its self-reliant people. The children loved America. The family vowed that one day they would return permanently.

While in Colorado, the family lived at Two-Dot Ranch. During Paul's frequent business trips, Anne would take the children and roam the ranch on horseback. She was drawn to the raw, unspoiled beauty of the fertile Willow Creek Valley that wound its way through the heart of the ranch.

Anne embraced with enthusiasm new experiences and challenges that few women of her generation were willing or had the opportunity to encounter. She was determined to overcome the aura of a privileged life. Accordingly, Anne worked hard to become an excellent shot with a .30-30 Winchester lever action rifle, and an accomplished western-style rider. Anne also learned to rope a calf and do her share of herding during a roundup. She even tried to learn how to curse like a cowboy, but she quickly found that much too distasteful and gave it up.

As each of their children reached school age, Paul and Anne were apprehensive about taking them out of school for the four to five weeks they would be away each year. But their teachers and the headmaster at the private school were quick to put their concerns to rest. They pointed out what a rare learning opportunity the annual trips provided for the three youngsters, but also sent the children along with lesson plans.

Most people would think their life idyllic. But Anne was troubled.

Her husband had grappled for almost a decade with the contradiction between the real Paul Winston, a successful businessman and rancher, and the persona of an Earl, whose life seemed dominated by meaningless pomp and ceremony and egocentric elitism. Anne knew Paul had moved to England to honor his late Uncle Percival's wishes and to satisfy his curiosity. But he had remained this long only because of her.

One evening a few weeks after returning from their latest trip to Colorado, Anne turned to him and said, "You know, in all the many times we've visited Two-Dot together, I never thought to ask you how the ranch got its unusual name."

Paul chuckled.

"It was Mom's doing, really," he said, smiling. "When my parents founded the ranch they simply called it the Winston Ranch. Their brand was a big "W" surrounded by an even bigger circle.

"Mom was determined to get involved with ranch operations. But something bothered her. Mom was troubled when she heard the calves bawling loudly while they were being branded. She asked Dad to come up with something more humane than our big branding iron to use on the calves.

"Dad went to the blacksmith shop and personally created a branding iron with just two small dots. And that's how the ranch got its name. All the ranchers for miles around soon recognized our brand, perhaps because of how simple as it was. On top of it all, the calves were hurt less, and Mom was happy. We use ear tags now. Much more humane."

"I have a question for you," Anne said.

"Sure, love," Paul said. "What is it?"

"When do you think we can move home for good, Paul?"

The question caught him off guard. It brought a shimmer to his eyes as he looked upon the woman he adored.

"As soon as we can complete the arrangements, my love," he managed, struggling to maintain his composure.

Paul and Anne went into Maidstone later that week and began making plans for their move 'home' to Colorado. They booked passage on a sleek new ocean liner, the Empress of Victoria. A sea voyage was the unanimous choice of the children. They'd not experienced an extended journey by ocean liner. Paul and Anne booked an upper deck with three adjoining outside staterooms, one for Catherine, one for them in the middle, and one for their two boys on the other side.

The family received regal deference during the voyage across the Atlantic. It made Paul uncomfortable. Each time a member of the ship's crew addressed him as "Milord", he responded graciously but cringed inwardly. Paul was relieved when they docked in New York. A few days later they began their trip across the country by rail in a private car. Paul and Anne chose rail so the children could fully appreciate the vastness of the new country they now called home. Previously, the family had traveled by air across the Atlantic and the U.S., so they could spend as many weeks as possible in Colorado.

The Maidstone Conspiracy

For the railway company, having a genuine earl and his family as passengers was a novelty, something to brag about. What's more, Paul was both a significant shareholder and a major customer. His large ranch shipped thousands of head of cattle a year to market on the railroad. Accordingly, the railway had provided them with a private rail car attached behind one of its trans-continental trains. The family enjoyed hours together on the rear platform of the private car marveling at the sights and sounds they passed while the train made its journey westward.

Douglas, Catherine, and Michael were in awe as they encountered high misty waterfalls, panoramic displays of thunder and lightning on the prairies followed by rainstorms and rainbows, vast fields of grain swaying in the wind, massive herds of cattle, towering forests, enormous flocks of birds, and then the magnificent Rocky Mountains from a distance on the prairies. It would be the first time they could fully appreciate the majesty of the Rockies. Previously, they'd flown to Denver and then to Colorado Springs, just a few miles from Two-Dot. The ranch was so close and high in the foothills that the full impact of those huge mountains could not be fully appreciated.

One morning, Anne led the three children to the railcar ahead of theirs. It was a restored car Paul had arranged to be attached between their car and the rest of the train. It was a former passenger car with most of the seats removed so the kids could use it as a play area. It had steps leading up to an observation area. Once called a dome car, the upper level offered a 360-degree view and had become a favorite viewpoint for the children. This morning, looking westward, the children were startled at how imposing the Rockies were, even from a distance. They were captivated by the sheer enormity, the snowy peaks reaching high into the sky, glistening in the radiant sunlight. The mountain range was so huge the train seemed about to find its way in among them yet was still more than 100 miles away.

James Osborne

The family's arrival at Union Station in Denver early that afternoon was low key. No dignitaries or official welcoming committees greeted them. Paul was relieved. As he stepped from their car and helped Anne to the platform, he happily noted that people in the station were going about their own business, paying little attention to them although mildly curious about the restored car from which they descended.

"Hey there, Paul! How the hell are ya! Welcome home!"

The rich baritone with a western drawl belonged to George Underhill, general manager of the Two-Dot Ranch.

"Hi, Anne," George's voice again boomed out as he made his way toward them, waving both arms. "Nice t'see ya!"

"Hey, who are these ragamuffins?" the burly six-foot rancher said, turning to the children. He crouched low, chuckling as he gathered the three startled children around him for a warm western group hug, ignoring their English reserve.

George stood, turning to Paul and Anne.

"We've got two pickups waiting outside," he said as they shook hands. "I'll take one of them with you two. Our foreman over there, Kurt Willis, will take the kids in the other, if that's okay with you.

"You both remember Kurt," George added, as the smiling foreman strode over and shook hands warmly with each of them.

"Great to have you both home," Kurt said. The four adults talked about the rail trip across the country, then Kurt gathered up the three children. He led them to their waiting pickup for the 70-mile drive south to Colorado Springs and then on to the ranch.

"Couple'a the boys brought along a van for your bags," George said as they walked out of the station behind Kurt and the excited children. A pair of cowboys was helping two porters load a large stack of luggage onto three trolleys.

A half-hour south of Colorado Springs, the cars turned off the paved highway and headed west for the remaining journey to the ranch headquarters. On either side of the wide gravel road, vast grasslands stretched as far as the eye could see. In all directions, large and small herds of cattle were scattered across the landscape.

The trucks reached the top of a hill, where George pulled over and stopped. The second pickup with the three children pulled up behind. Below was a wide, fertile valley with Willow Creek meandering down the middle. An abundant current in the creek made its way around oxbows that it had carved into the valley floor over many years. Ahead, the road dipped down, crossed a wide sturdy bridge over the creek and then climbed up to a vast bench of land where the ranch buildings were nestled.

"This has to be my favorite view," Anne said, turning to Paul. "Every time we've come here, it has taken my breath away. It's majestic, absolutely majestic … like no other place we've ever been."

Spread out before them stretched the wide green valley, and on their right were the home buildings of Two-Dot Ranch. In the distance, behind high, grassy foothills, rose the majestic snow-capped peaks of the Rocky Mountains. The cluster of buildings could have been mistaken for a small village. The focal point was a stately, 2½-story fieldstone ranch house, built years ago by Paul's parents. Wide verandas graced three sides of the big six-bedroom house.

Across an expansive lawn sat a classic two-story ranch house where George and his wife Elizabeth had lived for 30 years and raised their two children. Surrounding the wide, half-acre well-kept yard were barns, corrals, a one-room schoolhouse, a workshop, garages, and a blacksmith, plus a dining hall and bunkhouse for unmarried ranch hands.

George drove down across the creek and valley floor, and then up to the ranch buildings, stopping the car in front of the fieldstone house. The other car with the children was right behind. Douglas, Catherine, and Michael jumped out and scampered back toward a corral where five mares were tending to their weeks-old foals.

James Osborne

Paul and Anne followed George up the front steps and across the veranda. George opened the front door and stepped back quickly. His wife Elizabeth came rushing out, warmly hugging Anne and then Paul. Then she reached up and affectionately cupped her husband's cheeks in her hands, pulled his face down towards her and kissed him firmly on the mouth.

"Welcome, welcome!" Elizabeth cried happily, turning to Paul and Anne, her radiant face glowing with delight. "It's so wonderful to have you all home for good at last!"

She glanced past their shoulders like an alert grandmother to where Douglas, Catherine, and Michael were admiring the foals through the corral rails.

Paul scooped his petite giggling wife up in his arms and carried her across the threshold into the tastefully furnished living room, winking at George and Elizabeth.

"Welcome home," he said, his eyes bright with excitement.

"Yes, my love," she replied. A tear trickled down her left cheek. "Now we're really home!"

Chapter Thirteen

While Paul was in England, George had managed the day-to-day operations of Two-Dot Ranch. This left Paul free to experience his British peerage, and for he and Anne to pursue their growing investments and businesses. They managed these interests through the holding company he'd incorporated in America, the U.K. and Germany shortly before Paul moved to England, called Prescott Enterprises.

In that time Prescott Enterprises had expanded geographically, building, or buying commercial office buildings in the Pacific Northwest and across America, the United Kingdom and continental Europe, and it had been investing in a broad range of economic sectors, including financial services, oil and gas, and high technology.

Paul made certain Prescott Enterprises also allocated funds for speculative investments. He focused on areas of Colorado's economy where few conventional investors cared to venture, especially high-risk energy prospects, both conventional and renewable. During one of his annual visits, Paul had set up a meeting with a young petroleum engineer named Philip Tremblay. A few years earlier, Tremblay had started up an exploration company called Continental Oil and Gas.

A story in The Economist extolling the virtues of promising young entrepreneurs in the world's oil and gas industry had caught Paul's eye. Tremblay was listed among them. Also mentioned was a company called Del Rio Exploration, which had a reputation for identifying promising oil and gas plays in Colorado and adjacent states.

Paul met the young oilman for the first time in Continental's tiny two-room office suite. Within minutes, Philip had his visitor chuckling with stories about his experiences working between university semesters first as a roughneck in Wyoming and then for a wildcat well company.

Philip's relaxed openness and candor tweaked Paul's instincts. They told him that this was a man of substance, someone to be trusted. Paul also appreciated Philip's thorough knowledge of and optimistic outlook for the oil and gas industry in the western US. After some quiet background research, Paul decided to make Tremblay an offer.

"What do you know about Del Rio Exploration?" Paul asked the young oilman during a meeting over lunch at the Hilton.

"I went to school with Robert, Robert Leipert, the president," Philip replied. "We're both petroleum engineers. Both of us started up our companies at the same time three years ago. He sure can find oil and gas, but I hear he's in financial difficulty, sorry to say … too much debt. He's a good guy. Deserves better."

"I've been hearing that, too," Paul said. "Any idea what it would take to interest him in a merger?"

"Someone probably could do a merger for their debt right now if Robert were to agree. My guess is the debt is between 3.5 and four million," Philip replied. "If I could afford it, I'd make Robert an offer right now. The value's there."

"What if I helped finance things?" Paul responded. "Would you be willing to partner with me? How much could you put up?"

"I'm afraid all I can spare right now, Paul, is one and a half million," he said, "and that won't do it. I couldn't even meet you halfway. That's all the 'enterprise' cash I have to spare, and I might as well tell you I'm not going into debt either.

"The bank thinks my little company is worth about $10.5 million already, and our oil and gas leases are worth another $3 million. I dunno about the bank's appraisal, but I sure do like being debt-free. I like even more having a bit of cash on hand. Not many in the oil patch have that luxury."

"I agree on all counts," Paul responded with a smile. He liked what he was hearing from this young oilman.

"Philip, I've a proposal for you," he added. "If I put up $3.5 million and you put up $1.5 million, do you think that would do it, including all of Del Rio's equipment and drilling leases?"

"I expect so," Philip replied, "if Liepert agrees to come on board, and I think he will."

"Well, I'm willing to do it," Paul said. "How about you?"

"You're on," Philip replied without hesitation. Paul liked that. They shook hands. It was a deal. For both, a handshake was as binding as any signed contract.

Within three months Continental completed a merger with Del Rio Exploration, forming a 'junior' called Continental Del Rio Oil and Gas, with Prescott Enterprises holding a 20 percent interest. When America's financial community learned of the private deal, the consensus among analysts set the 'enterprise' value of the combined entity at more than $21.7 million, an immediate and handsome increase in value for all parties. Prescott's reputation didn't hurt one bit, either.

James Osborne

Chapter Fourteen

Paul and Anne's move to Colorado Springs was timely. George was turning 60 and had said on several occasions he wanted to retire early. He and Elizabeth were eager to pursue the traveling they'd been dreaming about for years. Paul knew he would miss being able to rely on George to manage the ranch, and he would miss Elizabeth's warm personality.

From a young age, his father had mentored Paul to be his successor. As events turned out, it was a good thing he had. Paul's parents had left him 40 percent of their estate. Ted and Catherine had reasoned that Paul would run the ranch and the family's business interests after they were gone. Paul's two sisters, Emily, and Roberta had both expressed little interest in either. Each held equal shares of 25 percent. In addition to the ranch and several businesses, their parent's estate included a block of virgin land, part of which later became a city block in downtown Colorado Springs.

In a shockingly short time after their parent's death, Paul's youngest sister Roberta had asked him to buy out her share of their inheritance. Paul didn't relish undertaking a transaction like that from England where he was living. He couldn't leave to come home. Anne had been about to give birth to their daughter, Catherine. He had no intention of being anywhere else except with Anne.

"Look, Paul," Roberta had told him by phone. "You have plenty of money. Just buy my share and that will be that."

"Of course, I could buy you out easily, but that's not a good idea right now, Roberta," he said. "First, Prescott Enterprises has made some

58

investments recently that could skyrocket the value of your holdings. Second, I really don't wish to do this with us being separated by the Atlantic Ocean. And third, most importantly, Anne is due within weeks with our first baby. I'm not going anywhere right now."

Roberta knew that with Paul's newly inherited wealth, he could easily afford to buy her out. She pushed to go ahead with it despite Paul's absence and pressed for an outrageous price not supported by three independent appraisals Paul had insisted upon. He reluctantly settled halfway between the average of the appraisals and her demands. It was his sister, after all. Growing up, Roberta had not been happy living in the country, away from the exciting array of amenities offered by city life. With the buyout, she could afford whatever lifestyle she chose, but still she was angry that Paul had not paid her what she'd demanded.

She wanted the money to help her establish a law practice and to buy a retail franchise for her husband, Stephen. Within a year, her small law practice merged with a large firm in Colorado Springs. Critics said the inexperienced attorney had bought a partnership, not earned it. Her husband, Stephen Hooper, became the operator of Master Tailor Men's Wear in Colorado Springs, part of a national chain. Roberta owned the franchise.

James Osborne

Chapter Fifteen

For decades, Elizabeth had been the social sparkplug in the adjacent ranching community, so it was only natural for her to be the prime organizer of a welcome home party for Paul and Anne hosted by her, George, Kurt, and his wife Susan. Paul and Anne insisted the event also be a celebration of George and Elizabeth's retirement. Business contacts, rancher friends and associates from far and wide were invited. Guests fully booked the Antlers Hilton in Colorado Springs weeks in advance.

Emily and Jeremy had confirmed they would attend. They were childless but trying hard not to be. Paul personally invited Roberta, Stephen and their two children since he felt strongly about family ties. A week before the party, Paul phoned Roberta again to confirm that they were coming. She assured him that she, Stephen and their two young children would be there.

On the day of the party, dozens of families from far and wide gathered to welcome the Winstons. Some ranchers even flew in on their private planes. Paul and Anne watched with pleasure as their children socialized with the other children from Colorado Springs and the surrounding area. He was relieved to be back home. Here he was known simply as Paul. No titles, no nobility, no peerage. He felt joy in rediscovering the sense of contentment he had missed while in England. Anne and their three children made that contentment complete.

As the party was starting to wind down, Paul looked around and asked Anne, "Have you seen Roberta, Stephen and the kids?"

"No, I haven't, Paul," Anne replied. "I'm surprised. Maybe they were held up with something."

Their absence renewed his feeling of unease. He knew something was still not right with his sister Roberta. He was certain she'd become reconciled with him declining to buy her out. But he felt something else was bothering her, and that worried him. If she was having trouble of some kind, he was determined to help her make it right. Paul decided he would drive into Colorado Springs on Monday and speak with her. He mentioned this to Anne after the last of their guests took their leave. The two of them were in the house, leaning against the kitchen counter and having a cup of tea.

She glanced at him with a strange look in her eyes.

"Okay, what's up, my love?" he asked.

"I wasn't sure when to tell you this, Paul, but maybe you need to know before you meet Roberta."

"What are you talking about, Anne?" Paul asked.

"I need you to promise me you won't do anything rash," Anne said.

"I promise. What's this all about?" Paul replied.

"I'm disappointed for you that Roberta and the kids didn't show up," she said. "But I'm happy Stephen didn't come."

"I guess you should tell me what that's all about," he said.

"Remember when we invited Roberta, Stephen and the kids over for supper, right after we arrived?"

Paul nodded.

"After supper, you were outside playing baseball with the kids. Roberta and I were cleaning up in the kitchen," Anne began.

"Yeah!" Paul laughed, remembering the experience with the children who ranged in age from Roberta's preschooler Jessica to Douglas, who'd just turned 13. "We've got quite the ball team there … the six of us kids," he said. Paul enjoyed including himself among 'the kids'.

"Well," Anne said, her attractive face clouded over with worry. "While you were out, Roberta went to the bathroom. Stephen came in from the living room. I thought he was heading for the back yard to be with you and the kids. Before I knew it, he grabbed me from behind. He tried to kiss me. Then he grabbed my breasts. I hit him with a big metal stirring spoon I had in my hand. The jerk went outside. Paul, I don't want anything to do with him ever again."

"That son of a bitch!" Paul said, his face flushed with anger. "I outta beat that son-of-a-bitch within an inch of his miserable goddamned life! I damned well would if that bastard wasn't married to my sister."

Paul's uncharacteristic outburst of coarse language surprised her. But it was the look in his eyes that frightened her most.

"I know, Paul, I should have told you right away," Anne said apologetically. "For a few days I thought maybe I should just let it go. I didn't want to spoil the evening. But on second thought, I knew I had no right to keep it from you. We've never had secrets. You'll have to decide whether to share it with Roberta. Remember now, you promised. Don't do anything foolish, okay?"

Paul nodded.

Chapter Sixteen

Monday morning, Paul arrived unannounced at Roberta's law firm, Fredrick Mendez & Hooper, to invite her for lunch. Now, with Anne's revelation, he had much more to discuss with her than he'd known about earlier.

"Can't do it," Roberta told him abruptly. "I have a meeting over lunch with a client."

She was cool and dismissive. There were no sisterly hugs or pecks on the cheek as had been the family habit.

"Well, what about later? How about after lunch?" Paul persisted. "I have some other business I can be doing in the meantime."

"All right," Roberta answered resignedly, looking at her schedule.

"Be back here at 2:30," she said curtly.

That was more than four hours away. Paul walked two blocks to a building where a friend and his personal attorney, Walter Stewart, had his offices. He invited Walter for a working lunch, then he walked the five blocks to a small office building owned by Prescott Enterprises.

Renovations on the three-story walk-up had just been completed, along with an eight-story adjoining tower. The original building had been built years ago by Paul's father, on the corner of a city block he'd had the foresight to buy years earlier in small-town Colorado Springs. Now, it was part of a project to redevelop that section of the downtown business district.

The top two floors of the tower housed staff for the international head office of Prescott Enterprises. Paul preferred the old building where he and Anne kept a small suite of offices on the third floor. Paul met with

Bill Daniels, Prescott's vice-president, development. Then he called his banker, Jack Richardson at Wells Fargo Bank, setting up a meeting for 4 p.m. to set up an efficient system for financial transactions between America and England.

Paul returned to Walter's office. The two long-time friends walked to the Antlers Hilton dining room. Over lunch, Paul asked Walter to contact Malcolm Witherspoon, his solicitor in England, and make the necessary legal arrangements for the transfers. Paul also asked Walter's advice on some potential investments – the development of commercial properties in cities around Colorado, and people he might contact to explore other investment opportunities. He also wanted to add to Prescott's portfolio a few speculative ventures, what the financial industry referred to as 'high-risk, high-return' investments, solar and wind power among them.

Chapter Seventeen

Just before 2:30, Paul returned to Roberta's office to find that she was not back yet. He was ushered into a small second floor meeting room where he sat at a round cherrywood table. Windows on one wall overlooked a main downtown street. Paul began reading a copy of the Wall Street Journal he'd picked up on the way over.

At 3:07 the door to the meeting room opened. Roberta walked in accompanied by her husband Stephen and a man Paul didn't recognize. He stood, waiting to be introduced. He wasn't. Paul looked at Stephen, barely able to contain his anger over what Anne had told him. He forced himself to look at the stranger, wondering who he was and why he was there.

Paul had planned to meet one-on-one with his sister, to see if something was troubling her and what he could do to help her. And he'd decided to discuss her husband's assault on Anne. He wasn't expecting a group meeting.

"Paul," Roberta began, sitting down. "We have some things to discuss. Please sit down."

We most certainly do, Paul thought.

"This is Albert Deslaurier from Los Angeles," she said. "I've asked him to join me and Stephen here today. Albert is an attorney who specializes in estate litigation.

"I've hired Albert to represent me and Stephen in an action we filed today against Two-Dot Ranch, Prescott Enterprises and you, personally."

Paul sat back in his chair in shocked disbelief.

"Roberta, what in the world are you talking about?" he said.

James Osborne

Roberta pushed a large brown envelope across the table at him. Paul folded back the open flap and pulled out a sheaf of papers stapled with a blue corner-piece on the top left corner. It looked very legal.

"Paul, you've been duly served with notice of this action. Albert and Stephen are my witnesses," she added.

"Have you any idea what you're doing, Roberta?" Paul asked, trying to recover from this stunning surprise. "What in hell is going on?"

"Paul, years ago after you inherited that enormous amount of money and properties from our late uncle in England, I invited you to buy out my interests from our parents' estate. You refused. Stephen and I have been thinking about you hoarding that inheritance all these years. We've decided all of that inheritance must be considered part of the assets of the estate our parents left us, since we believe Uncle Percy died before Mom and Dad were killed.

"If Dad were alive, he would have inherited Uncle Percival's title and estate. The three of us should have had claims to Uncle Percy's estate in the same proportion as our parents' estate was settled following their deaths. The inheritance from Uncle Percy should have been included in the settlement.

"Accordingly, Paul, we expect you to relinquish all of the assets you inherited from Uncle Percival for division on the same basis as our parents' wills."

"You can't be serious, Roberta!" Paul exclaimed. "After all these years? Why now?"

He was shocked by what he was hearing from his youngest sister. Until now, he had been accustomed to affectionately calling Roberta 'his baby sister.' That would no longer do.

"My God, Roberta, this is ridiculous!" Paul said. "The settlement of Mom and Dad's estate was almost a decade ago, and so was Uncle Percy's. They're final. And when we were discussing you selling your share, that involved only the cash, the ranch, and the business interests

66

they left us. Uncle Percival's will has nothing to do with their estate, then or now."

"Yes it does, Paul!" Roberta shot back. "Our complaint demands that you pay me a fair share of Uncle Percy's estate.

"You have the choice of honoring our legitimate claim and paying 25 percent of what you got from Uncle Percy, or we will take you and the ranch and Prescott Enterprises to court."

"You mean George factors into this claim of yours, too?" Paul said.

"Yes," she said.

"Does he know about this?" Paul said. "Does he approve?"

"No," Roberta said, a bit too quickly.

She gave Paul a hard look. Her eyes were cold and lifeless. Paul barely recognized the person across the table.

"Have a good day, Paul," Roberta said. She, Stephen and Deslaurier stood and walked from the room. As Stephen left, he shot a sarcastic look over his shoulder at his brother-in-law. Paul suppressed the temptation to take after him.

A feeling of sadness and foreboding washed over him. He knew their family would never be the same again. He wondered what his parents would have thought about what had just happened. He was much relieved they'd not lived to witness it.

Paul left Roberta's office in a daze. He walked back to his own office, struggling with feelings of sorrow and anger, but most of all with a sense of loss.

Why, after all these years, would she pull a stunt like this? he wondered. *If she's in need of money I'd have loaned it to her ... hell, I'd have given it to her.*

Then another thought struck him, *I'd better call Emily right away.*

He wanted to be absolutely sure Emily was not involved in this absurd litigation. He didn't think so. Emily had such a generous nature and didn't have a single greedy bone in her tiny body. Paul gathered up files for his meeting with Jack Richardson at the bank, returned a few business calls and then walked the few blocks back to Walter's office. He needed Walter's immediate help on this, and he also needed Walter to be a witness when he phoned Emily to find out where she stood.

"Oh! Hello again, Mr. Winston," a surprised receptionist said to Paul. "May I help you?"

She looked startled at Paul's return to Walter's office.

"Is Walter still in?" Paul asked. "I need to see him right away. It's urgent."

The receptionist hesitated for a moment, looking uncertain, then walked over and knocked on Walter's door, opening it to announce Paul's return visit. To his shock, Paul caught a glimpse inside the office through the partly open door. What he saw troubled him deeply.

Walter, his friend since high school and now his lawyer and confidante, was at a meeting table in his office apparently sharing a joke with Roberta, sitting with her back to the door and to Paul. With them were Albert Deslaurier and Stephen.

As Paul turned to leave, he saw Walter catch sight of him. Walter's face had a look of shock, and it turned red with embarrassment and dismay.

Paul walked out of his former friend and attorney's office for the last time.

Chapter Eighteen

Paul was devastated. Two betrayals! And by people he had cared about and trusted … both in one day!

He'd never experienced such intense disappointment. A swirling mix of feelings rocketed though his mind: surprise, shock, disappointment, sadness, and anger.

Paul barely remembered his walk to Wells Fargo Bank. Almost before he realized it, he was sitting in Jack Richardson's office half an hour early for his appointment. Paul relayed to Richardson as best he could a description of the events of the last hour. Jack was also a close friend, going back to their teenage years.

"Did I hear you right, Paul?" Jack said. "Roberta was in Walter's office just minutes after she told you that she was suing you and your businesses? And he's your personal and business attorney?"

"Yeah, he was," Paul answered, still trying to make sense of it all. "That would about sum it up.

"At first, I wanted to believe that meeting was all perfectly innocent," he added. "But hells bells, Jack, I know better than that, for Christ's sake! He's in cahoots with her!"

Paul took a moment to calm down.

"My first reaction was that maybe Roberta and Walter were working on some other business. All I could see was Roberta's back, but the look on Walter's face told the story. They were up to something, and it wasn't innocent. And Stephen and Deslaurier were there, too.

"Jack, I need your help with two things right now," Paul added.

"Of course, Paul," Jack replied. "What do you need."

69

"Obviously, I need to find a new lawyer, one I can trust. I'd appreciate your recommendations.

"The other thing I need to do right now is to call my sister Emily. I have to find out if she knows anything about this mess, and I need you as a witness on that call. I know it's way outside your line of work, but would you be okay with that?"

"Of course, Paul," Jack replied. He buzzed his intercom, and his assistant came into the office.

"Mildred, please bring me our file on law firms back east that Wells Fargo has used to handle litigations, particularly estate litigations."

She was back a minute later with a blue file folder and put it on Jack's desk.

While Jack was busy looking through the file, Paul dug into his briefcase and found Emily's phone number. He handed it to Jack, who picked up his phone and dialed.

"Hello, Emily? It's Jack Richardson calling." Jack paused while Emily recovered from her surprise.

"Yeah, it's me. Yes, I'm still at Wells Fargo here in Colorado Springs. You bet. We love it here. Yes, indeed, it has been years.

"Emily, I'm glad I caught you at home. Your brother's here in my office with me. He'd like to speak with you. Do you mind if I put this on the speakerphone? Paul will explain. Thanks."

"Hi, Emily," Paul said into the speakerphone, "How're you doing?"

Emily's voice echoed from the speaker. Her unease over this mysterious sounding call was obvious.

"Paul, this is a very strange call. You're in Jack Richardson's office? Why? What's going on, Paul? Is everything all right? Please explain."

"Emily, I'll explain in a minute," Paul replied. "But first I need to ask you a question. It's very important. Have you and Roberta had any contact recently?"

"Why, no, Paul," Emily said. "We haven't spoken for months. Is she okay? Is something wrong?"

"Well, that's the good news, sis. She's fine," Paul answered. "And yes, something is very wrong."

He filled his sister in on the events of the afternoon.

Emily interrupted occasionally with exclamations of surprise or anger or disappointment, and finally, "Well I'll be go to hell!" she exclaimed. "Oops, sorry, fellas. I usually don't use such language.

"Has Roberta lost her mind, Paul? I can hardly believe she would do such a thing. What on earth does she think she's going to accomplish? What's come over her? Greed! That's all it is. Senseless, mindless greed!

"Paul, you know what I think?" Emily almost shouted, getting more worked up as she went on. "I'll just bet that damn Stephen is behind all of this. I've never trusted that slimeball from the moment I first laid eyes on him. That good-for-nothing! I still don't understand why Roberta married that ... that ethically challenged lightweight."

Emily paused to take a breath.

"Emily," Paul responded, "I suppose it really doesn't matter who put her up to it. She's an intelligent woman and perfectly capable of making up her own mind. I'm sorry for their two little kids, though. They're not going to have much contact with the rest of the family from now on."

"You're right," Emily replied, "this family will never be the same. Mom and Dad would have been devastated, Paul. Our little sister has become a disappointment, Paul. Sad. So very sad."

He decided to tell Emily about Anne's experience with Stephen at their family supper.

"What?" she exploded. "That pathetic little son of a bitch! Pardon my language again. Don't you do anything dumb now, you hear? I know you, Paul. I want you to promise me!"

71

"I know, I know, and I promise. Much as I'd like to kick the shit out of that little jerk, and as much as he needs it, there's no point," Paul replied. "It would serve no useful purpose."

"Emily,' he went on, "we're going to give them one hell of a fight. One they'll never forget. I'll keep you posted, Sis. It was good talking to you."

"Oh, Paul, before you go," Emily said, her voice choking up. "I've got some marvelous news for you to share with Anne and the kids."

"Jeremy and I got the confirmation call this afternoon. I've been home waiting for it. We've just been approved to adopt a set of twins! A boy and a girl. It's perfect! Isn't that wonderful, Paul? We're so excited!"

There was a long pause. Paul could hear his sister over the phone sniffling as she tried to collect herself.

"They're babies," she managed, her voice cracking. "Just two weeks old. I'll FaceTime you and Anne tonight with all the details."

"That's wonderful, Sis! Congratulations! I'm delighted for both of you," Paul replied. It was the first time he'd smiled in hours. Emily and Jeremy had been trying for years to have a family. The couple had consulted numerous specialists without success. They both loved children and would be excellent parents.

Jack's voice broke into Paul's thoughts, "Ah, here he is," he said, looking at the file of litigation lawyers he'd requested.

"Tom and I were graduate students at Yale. He was in law and I in commerce. He's become one hell of a litigator. Never lost a case in court he's handled for the bank.

"His name is Tom Cameron. You should speak with him yourself, Paul. See what you think."

"Sure," Paul answered. "It's late now back east. Do you have his home number? Perhaps we can get him on the line. Would he mind?"

"Not if the call's from Wells Fargo," Jack said, and chuckled. He looked at the list in front of him and dialed Cameron's home number.

Jack explained the reason for his call and passed the phone to Paul.

"Hi, there, Tom. Paul Winston here. Yes, indeed I do. I just received notice about an hour ago that I'm about to be sued. We could be litigating over $150 to $200 million, perhaps more. Yeah, really. Let me give you a quick overview."

After Paul explained his encounters with his sister Roberta and with Walter Stewart, then gave Tom a brief description of his inheritance from his Uncle Percival, he listened briefly, then said, "Well, okay, Tom. I don't think it's quite that urgent, but yes, I'd welcome a face-to-face meeting with you. All right, Tom. See you in a couple of days, then."

Paul handed the phone back to Jack.

"Tom has something to wrap up, then he's going to head out here," Paul said. "Let's see. This is Monday. Tom said he'd be here Wednesday morning."

"Guess you got his attention," Jack replied, raising his eyebrows.

"Paul, about that new personal lawyer," the banker added. "I found a fellow the other day for another client. He's a young lawyer here in town named John Everett. Not very experienced, but evidently extremely bright ... top of his class at Harvard Law School. Sound good to you?"

Paul nodded.

"Opened an office here recently. With such an impressive resume, I can't imagine what brought him to Colorado Springs. A couple of my clients have used his services. They were impressed enough to mention him to me. You might want to check him out."

"Sure, Jack. I need someone locally," Paul replied. "I'll give him a call."

Jack opened the top left drawer of his desk. He pulled out a black notebook, copied a number on a pad and handed it with the phone to his client. Paul called and arranged to see Everett the next morning.

Paul returned home and brought Anne up to date on the disturbing events of the day. She was beside herself with anger that Roberta, whom

73

Paul once trusted and nurtured, had betrayed him. As for Walter, his behavior merely confirmed Anne's low opinion of attorneys. Most of all, she was sad for Paul that both a member of his family and a friend since boyhood had let him down.

When he'd finished and answered all of her questions, he said, "Oops, I almost forgot, Anne.

"Emily told me they've just been approved to adopt twin babies. Two weeks old. A boy and a girl, I think she said. What do you think of that?"

"What!" Anne exclaimed, "You waited until now to tell me! Good heavens, Paul! This is important. Such wonderful news! I've got to call Emily right away.

"Oh, you men!" she exclaimed as she went to retrieve her iPad from their shared home office. She wore an exasperated but loving smile on her face.

Anne and Emily had grown close over the years. Emily became the sister Anne longed for but never had. Emily in turn adored this strong-willed woman, her brother's life mate and partner, who'd brought him such joy.

Their friendship began during Paul and Anne's annual trips from England. The couple and their growing family took time when traveling between Colorado Springs and Maidstone to spend a few days with Emily and Jeremy in Somerville. The couple often remarked at how lucky Paul and Anne were to have three happy and healthy children. They yearned to be parents, and now they would be.

Despite the distance between them, the long absences disappeared when Emily and Anne got together. They texted and phoned often. Each time the two women met they picked up where they'd left off, carrying on as if no time had passed. It was a special relationship both cherished.

Chapter Nineteen

April 12, 2014

It was a morning he'd never forget. Paul arrived at John Everett's office fifteen minutes early for their nine-a.m. appointment.

The office was on the second floor of a two-story building above a clothing store, a downtown Colorado Springs landmark since Paul had been a boy. He walked up the long flight of worn and creaky wood stairs.

Just as he reached the top, Paul heard the street door close below.

A lanky young man jogged up the steep flight of stairs. The slender fingers of his right hand clutched two takeout coffees. Dangling from his left hand was a scarred old brown leather briefcase.

Everett tried juggling the coffees and briefcase in one hand so he could shake Paul's hand with the other when they introduced themselves. He gave up after Paul opened the door to the modest law office. They exchanged good-natured grins and shrugs. John was an athletic-looking thirty-something, about Paul's height.

In the outer office, an attractive young woman greeted them. Her long dark hair was tied back in a tidy ponytail. Her ear-to-ear smile lit up the room. She jumped up as they entered and opened the door to John's office. Paul noticed that she smiled coyly and winked at John as he led Paul into his office.

"My fiancée, Allison," John said introducing her, and answering Paul's unasked question. "We're going to be married next month. Allison's a paralegal, hoping to go back for her law degree. We moved together to Colorado Springs.

James Osborne

"Her mom and dad, Richard and Kathy Brownlee, are retired here," John continued, thinking hard to make conversation with a potentially very important new client.

Paul knew the Brownlees well. They'd been neighbors and good customers for years for the purebred Black Angus bulls that helped make the Two-Dot Ranch famous. They'd retired and moved into town. Paul thought highly of both. He vaguely remembered they had a younger daughter, an unexpected late arrival. Elizabeth and his mother, Catherine, had described the little girl as 'a lovely late blessing'.

"Allison's mom isn't well," John went on. "After we're married, we plan to have them move in with us. I'm building a suite for them. Mr. Brownlee isn't all that well, either. Bad heart. He needs help looking after Allison's mom. Not ideal for newlyweds, I know. But, hey, they're wonderful people and they're family. We'll get along just fine."

Paul was sorry to hear about the Brownlee's health issues. Listening to the way John talked and thought, Paul liked him. John plunked the worn briefcase on the floor beside his rickety swivel chair. He sat the coffees on the worn surface of the old double-pedestal desk, motioning for Paul to help himself. John chuckled, anticipating another question from Paul.

"Yeah, that briefcase's been around a while," John said nodding toward the well-worn flap-over case. "It belonged to my grandfather, who was a lawyer, and then my dad used it. He was a lawyer, too. Just retired. He gave it to me when I graduated. It has a long and honorable history. Kind of a lucky charm and a legacy in one, I suppose."

Paul was impressed by what he was hearing. He decided to try out this young man with the kind heart, respect for family and keen sense of tradition. The framed certificates on the walls didn't hurt, either. One proclaimed John had graduated cum laude from Harvard Law School, and another testified to his term as an editor of the prestigious Harvard Law Review.

76

"Now, Mr. Winston, if you'll please have a ..."

Paul interrupted. "Paul, please."

"Okay, Paul. Please have a seat. How can I help you?"

Paul recounted once again the events he had experienced on Monday. John's eyebrows raised a time or two as Paul described his considerable inheritance, and his meeting with Roberta. But John's strongest reaction came when Paul related his return visit to Walter's office.

"Good Lord! This may be a matter for the bar association, if not the authorities," John said. "We can look into that later. Have you spoken to Mr. Stewart about this?"

"No," Paul replied, "and he hasn't phoned me, either. At first I tried to convince myself Walter's meeting with Roberta was perfectly above board. Had that been the case, he'd have talked to me right away. And his reaction to them being caught together ... well, the look on his face ... he knew that he was offside. No question about it.

"John," Paul continued, "I want to retain your services. I'm going to fire Walter today."

He reached into his briefcase and pulled out an envelope. In it was a bank draft for $5,000 made out to John Everett Professional Corporation Inc.

"Here's a retainer," he said, putting the envelope on the desk. "You okay with that?"

John opened the envelope and pulled out the bank draft, then returned it to the envelope.

"Of course, Mr. Winst ... ah, Paul" John was saying. "But you need to know I've just opened my practice here in Colorado Springs. Most of my experience has been five years with a law firm back east, and I'm just working into the community here. That said, I'd be honored to represent you, but I need to lay this out for you in case you want to consider finding a more ... seasoned attorney."

77

"I understand, John," Paul replied. "Tell you what. This issue with my sister Roberta will give us a chance to see how we do. You'll be working with a senior lawyer out of New York. You cut the mustard, John, and you're hired. You don't, you're fired. How are you with that?"

"Just fine," John replied with a smile. They shook hands.

Paul explained to John about his conversation with Tom Cameron. Paul said Tom would lead the defense in the lawsuit that his sister had filed. He wanted John to work with Tom.

"I've heard about Tom Cameron," John said. "He graduated Harvard Law quite a few years ahead of me. Some of his work became case studies for classes I took. He has an impressive history. Hell, he's a legend, Paul. It'll be an honor to work with him."

Paul walked back to the bank and then to his office. He dictated and signed letters firing Walter Stewart as his and Anne's personal and company attorney. Then he and Bill Daniels prepared letters appointing John Everett as both his personal and company lawyer and directing Walter's office to deliver all of Paul's personal and company files to John. Copies of everything were addressed to Everett's office.

He arranged for a courier to pick up and deliver the letters. He was happy he had taken the time to have Jack Richardson arrange for the $5,000 bank draft. He sensed John could use it.

Then he called Anne to tell her he was on his way home. As always, he was excited by the thought of seeing her. He told Anne he was bringing home a letter he'd received from Earnscliffe that morning. His cousin Willard said he wanted to negotiate his departure from the cottage on the Manor grounds where he'd been living rent-free for over

25 years. He and his wife Alice were moving, 'retiring,' as Willard chose to describe it, to the Canary Islands.

Paul left his modest office in the three-story building, walked down to the street, and headed toward his pickup parked at the curb.

That short walk changed the rest of his life.

Chapter Twenty

Colorado Springs

Anne raced into the emergency department at Memorial Hospital, her spring coat flapping out behind her. Fifteen minutes earlier she'd received a call at the ranch from the hospital informing her that Paul had just been brought in by ambulance. The caller said her husband had been shot.

Anne was frantic, her face pale as a ghost. George and Elizabeth came running in behind her.

"My name's Anne Winston," she called out as she raced through the door. "My husband's here, Paul Winston. Where is he, please? I need to see him right now!"

An emergency room nurse and a doctor intercepted her. Anne struggled to get around them. She was almost hysterical.

"Where's my husband?" she cried, her voice panicky. "I must see him right now! Oh, please let me go, I need to see my husband!"

"Please, Mrs. Winston," the ER doctor said gently. "Please hold on. Your husband's in surgery. There's nothing you can do for him right now."

The nurse added, "We have a private room over there where you can wait, Mrs. Winston. Someone will come and talk with you just as soon as your husband is out of surgery."

George and Elizabeth came up beside her. Each took one of Anne's arms to support her. She swayed side to side, looking as if she might collapse at any moment. They guided her toward the private room off the emergency department waiting area just as two Colorado Springs Police officers arrived and took up positions on each side of the door.

Another doctor followed them to the private room. When Anne was seated, the doctor crouched down in front of her. She was dressed in operating room scrubs. The doctor reached for Anne's hand and said, "Mrs. Winston, I'm Doctor Lillian Moore. Your husband was brought in by ambulance about 25 minutes ago with severe gunshot wounds. We took him directly into surgery.

"I'll be honest with you, Mrs. Winston. Your husband's condition is extremely critical right now," Dr. Moore said quietly. "We're doing everything in our power for him. We need for you to try to be calm. I promise you I'll have someone come and talk with you just as soon as we know more. I'll get you in to see your husband just as soon as I possibly can. Okay?"

"Yes, okay, I suppose … Yes, I understand," a terrified and confused Anne managed to say, fighting to calm herself.

George followed the doctor as she walked out of the waiting area and down the corridor. He looked over his shoulder to make sure Anne was out of earshot.

"I'm George Underhill, an employee and close friend of the Winston's. I manage Two-Dot Ranch for them. Is there anything I should know? You know, maybe we should be helping Anne get, ah, get ready, I mean, get herself ready just in case, ah, for the worse?"

"Mr. Underhill." Dr. Moore said, stopping and turning toward him. "All we know right now is that Mr. Winston was brought in with three life-threatening gunshot wounds. As you heard me tell Mrs. Winston, his condition right now is very critical, grave in fact. One bullet entered his back and two entered his chest. The bullet that entered his back appears to have lodged near his heart. The other two fragmented when they hit and broke his sternum and some ribs and penetrated his right lung. That's what I told the police.

"As it happens," she continued, "we are very fortunate. An extremely talented surgeon is on a visit to Memorial. He's quite famous. Dr. David Shepherd is leading the team working on Mr. Winston right now. I'll see that you're kept informed of Mr. Winston's condition, Mr. Underhill. Now, if you'll excuse me, I must scrub up and get back in there."

"Yes, of course, doctor," George said. "Thank you."

Chapter Twenty-One

"So, what the hell are we supposed to do now?" Stephen Hooper asked Roberta.

"I guess we ought to send something," his wife responded coldly. "A card, maybe. After all, he *is* my brother; what will people think? I suppose we should do something. We gotta make it look good. Geez, this is damned awkward."

Emily had called to tell them Paul was in hospital and why.

Roberta and Stephen turned on the television. The shooting was the top of the news. A reporter at the scene said Paul had been shot by an unknown assailant. He was in critical condition and undergoing emergency surgery. An all-points manhunt was underway for the assailant in Colorado Springs and throughout the state.

The news report included video of a bloodstain on the sidewalk where Paul had been shot. Roberta watched expressionless.

"Listen, Roberta, I'll get someone at the store to buy a card. Nothing too soppy," Stephen said. "Do you want to sign it? I'll bring it home."

"Yeah, sure," she replied. "I guess. Suppose I, uh, we, should sign it."

"Okay, I'll get one tomorrow. Do you think we should get some flowers as well?"

"Are you serious?" Roberta shot back. "Of course not, you idiot!"

Stephen hoped he'd remember the card. He had other matters on his mind; a foxy salesgirl he'd just hired. Stephen was sure the new girl would entertain ways she could improve her career prospects at the store. He was looking forward to taking that matter up with her. He'd forgotten her name, Mabel or Mary or Margie something. He'd look it up when he got to work in the morning.

Chapter Twenty-Two

Livingston Valley

Doug didn't know his father had been shot and was fighting for his life in Colorado Springs Memorial Hospital.

The 14-year-old was thoroughly enjoying himself in a vast mountain valley southwest of the Two-Dot Ranch buildings. He was sitting under a tree beside a small pond, taking in the wonders of Nature. The lush valley was a tapestry of trees, bushes, grass, ponds, streams, and all manner of wildlife. He loved this wilderness place called Livingston Valley that his father had told him about.

The only access for miles north and south was through a canyon bisected by a narrow, swiftly flowing stream that meandered down to Willow Creek some six miles east. In prehistoric times the stream had been a river draining an ice-age lake, now Livingston Valley. The stream had carved a path creating the steep narrow canyon walls of brown and rust-colored rock.

There was just enough room on one side of the stream for Doug's horse to pick its way along a narrow gravel bank for 200 yards to the other end of the canyon. It opened into the wide lush Livingston Valley, where Douglas now sat contentedly. He'd found the valley while exploring the southwest corner of Two-Dot Ranch on horseback after his family moved from England.

Paul had told him about it and was delighted when his son had found the canyon and the valley hidden at the far end. It had been one of Paul's favorite boyhood places. Paul asked Douglas to herd any stray Two-Dot cattle he found there back down into Willow Creek Valley. Doug had done so a few times. That's why he'd begun taking Tippy along with him. The aging Border Collie's instincts for herding never seemed to rest.

Tippy had attached himself to Doug, and Doug to Tippy, named for the white tuft of hair on the tip of his black tail. They'd become a classic team of boy and dog. Tippy was too old now to work like the younger dogs on the ranch. His new job was to herd the few strays they encountered but mainly to provide a distraction if Doug needed help to escape a cranky wild animal. Tippy's nose and ears could pick up on the presence of any cougars, bobcats, wolverines, coyotes, or wolves in the area. The good-natured dog was going blind, but his keen sense of smell and hearing were working just fine.

This day, Doug sat with his back to his favorite tree beside a pond, on the edge of a small clearing. His unsaddled horse, Apache, was grazing nearby. A trickle of water from a nearby spring flowed past just inside the trees beyond the clearing, and then back out into the pond. Toads croaked in a marshy area. Dozens of tadpoles flourished in the shallow water at the grassy edge of the pond.

Doug had learned that if he sat quietly long enough, the flow of Nature would return to its normal tempo, unfolding before his eyes. Even Tippy was content to lay beside him with one of Doug's hands on his graying head.

With each visit, Doug became more enthralled by the interaction of squirrels, mice, rabbits, coyotes, marmots, beaver, songbirds, and birds of prey like hawks and owls, and by the bighorn sheep, deer, elk, and other big game that made their way to drink from the spring and the pond. He was impressed most of all by the respect one species seemed to show for others, and the peaceful co-mingling of birds and animals, except when a member of one species was being hunted by another for food.

The afternoon wore on. Doug dozed amidst the soothing, intoxicating heat of the sun flowing down from an almost cloudless sky.

His daydreaming ended abruptly when Tippy began growling deeply in his throat for no apparent reason. The dog's behavior was out of character. He seldom growled while seated beside Doug. Tippy normally would just sit up and point his snout when he sensed the arrival of birds or animals just passing by or preying on other birds or animals.

This was a growl of impending danger.

Doug's eyes scanned the area carefully. He couldn't see anything that would cause Tippy to growl like that. Apache also seemed unsettled. The paint gelding neighed loudly and nodded its head a few times toward a grove of trees. Doug looked over. He saw nothing unusual.

But Tippy's and the horse's unrest did cause him to notice that the shadows were growing longer. It was well into the afternoon. He had a long ride ahead to be home by suppertime. After saddling Apache and pulling the cinch tight like his dad and 'Uncle' George had taught him, he climbed up and headed for home.

The boy, horse and dog reached the stream and were about to enter the canyon. Tippy started to bark. Apache acted skittish. Doug spoke to the dog, trying to calm him, thinking the dog's unrest was causing Apache's unease.

Suddenly he felt a rope tighten around his lower chest and arms just above his elbows. Doug was pulled from his horse. He splashed down heavily sideways on the rocky bottom of the stream. The fall knocked the wind out of him. He struggled to get his knees under him while trying to pull the rope off, fighting to regain his breath. A dusty old gunnysack was pulled down over his head and shoulders. It smelled like a moldy old grain bag.

Doug felt a knee dig into his back. He was pushed back face down into the streambed. His head was underwater. Water poured into the sack. He couldn't breathe. His hands were pulled behind him roughly and tied together tightly. Doug heard male grunting sounds and heavy breathing as he was pulled back upright from under a foot of water, coughing and sputtering. Then he was lifted and pushed awkwardly up onto his horse. He could smell alcohol and tobacco smoke through the dark bag over his head and shoulders.

Tippy was barking and snarling protectively. Doug heard the dog's barks grow louder and more aggressive. Then Tippy yelped and yelped again. He heard angry sounds from the man who'd tied him up. Tippy whined for a few seconds and yelped some more. Douglas heard grunts from the man. Tippy resumed snarling and barking, more aggressively now.

Doug was startled by a loud bang. He knew it was a gunshot.

That man shot my dog! he thought. *Damn him! He didn't have to do that. What's going on?*

Doug heard Tippy crying pitifully. It almost broke his heart. Then there was another loud bang. Tippy was silent. There was a low grunt, and some mumbled words Doug couldn't make out. Through his fear and discomfort, he was seething with grief and anger.

"Who are you?" he managed to gasp, trying to make himself heard through the thick sack.

"What have you done to my dog?" he wanted to shout but managed only to croak out the words from his dust-filled throat.

"What do you think you're doing?" Doug added through the gunnysack, his voice weak. "My family will be out looking for me. It's late. I have to get home right away!"

No response.

Doug heard a horse blow out through its nose and rattle its bridle. Almost immediately he heard the sound of shod hooves on rocks in the streambed. Then Apache surged forward and started to walk. His horse was led down the stream and out of the canyon.

With his hands tied behind him, it took all the effort he could muster to keep himself in the saddle pressing his knees against both sides of his horse and thrusting his feet hard into the stirrups.

They seemed to ride for miles. It was dark when they stopped. Douglas felt they'd been riding downhill for hours. He was lifted down from his horse and onto his feet. His right arm was grabbed just above the elbow. He was propelled forward roughly. Doug heard a heavy wooden door latch rattle and then door hinges complain loudly.

He sensed being led inside a building, a small building. It smelled musty. Old hay or straw covered the floor and crunched under his boots. The hood was pulled roughly off his head and shoulders. It was dark inside. He was able to make out what looked like a rough-hewn shack. Doug saw the vague outline of a man. His nose and mouth appeared to be covered with a bandana. Still not a word. The man backed out of the small building, keeping a close watch on him. Doug's hands were still tied behind him.

The door closed. A latch rattled into place. Something made a thud against the heavy wood door.

It became quiet.

Chapter Twenty-Three

Colorado Springs Memorial Hospital

George returned to the waiting room to join Anne and Elizabeth. The two uniformed police officers stood beside the door. Another man wearing a suit spoke to them and then walked over to where Anne was sitting.

As George entered the room he overheard the man say, "Mrs. Winston, I'm Lt. Dan Lorente. I'm the head of homicide for the Colorado Springs Police Department. I need to ask you a few questions if you're feeling up to it?"

Anne jumped out of her chair, her eyes wide with fear. Her hands shot up to cover her mouth. She let out a strangled cry.

"Oh, please forgive me, Mrs. Winston," the detective said quickly, noticing the look of horror in Anne's eyes. "I'm not here about a homicide. I'm so sorry. I didn't mean to upset you further. I'm filling in for my counterpart from the Major Crimes Unit. He's out of town right now."

"Oh, my!" Anne managed, relaxing slightly. "That was an awful fright. What can I do for you?"

"Again, Mrs. Winston, please forgive me," the detective said, pulling a chair around so he could sit facing her. "If I may, do you know of anyone who might want to harm your husband?"

"Well, no," Anne replied. "Oh my, I can't think very well just now. Please give me a minute."

"Of course," Lorente said. "Can I get you a bottle of water?"

"That would be nice," she said.

When Lorente returned with the water, she sat for a moment, sipping the water, trying to compose herself. She reminded herself that Paul was in the best hands possible; she would force herself to be patient for just a bit longer.

"Paul is very well liked," Anne said.

Lorente knew all about Paul. He still had to ask the questions. Almost everyone for miles around knew of Paul Winston, their very own locally raised English nobleman.

"As I'm sure you know, he's very well respected in this community," Anne continued "In this whole area, in fact. He's a kind man; he's helped lots of people around here. You can ask anyone who knows him. We just moved back from England a while ago with our family. Paul grew up here.

Anne paused, realizing her fear had created a torrent of words.

"Do you have any ideas, detective?"

Ignoring Anne's question, Lorente asked, "Would you know of anyone in this area who speaks with, ah, an accent like yours, Mrs. Winston. A British accent?"

"No, I don't, detective," Anne said. "Why do you ask?"

"We have a witness, Mrs. Winston. The witness was parked a few cars away from where the shooting took place. This witness thinks the man who shot your husband had shouted something at him. Our witness couldn't see the man, but he's quite certain the assailant spoke with a British accent."

Anne thought for a minute, and then shook her head 'no'.

"Detective?" Anne said. "While you're here, can I ask you if there've been any new developments in the investigation about the deaths of Paul's parents? I know it's been almost 10 years. But have you heard anything, anything at all?

"I'm afraid not, Mrs. Winston," Lorente said. "CSP is in charge of that investigation, but I'd know about anything new. I wish I could be more helpful.

He asked her a few more questions, thanked her, finished his notes, and then spoke to the uniformed officers. One stood guard at the door to the waiting area. The other accompanied Lorente out of the emergency department. They drove away in an unmarked police cruiser.

*

"Mrs. Winston?"

Anne was startled by the voice at the door to the waiting room.

Lt. Dan Lorente stood looking at her. His expression was troubled.

Anne glanced at her watch. It had been less than an hour since the detective had left.

What's he doing back here? she thought.

"I'm sorry. I didn't mean to startle you again, Mrs. Winston. "I need to speak with you once more. Something else rather important has come up."

"Yes, detective. What is it?" Anne replied.

"It's about your son, Douglas, Mrs. Winston," Lorente said, walking over to where she was sitting beside Elizabeth.

Anne and Elizabeth both sat upright.

"Is Douglas all right?" Anne demanded, standing. "Is something wrong?"

"I have some troubling news. I'm sorry to have to tell you this, but it appears he's been kidnapped."

"What? Kidnapped? My Douglas?" Anne shouted, her voice barely under control. "You can't be serious! Oh, my God!"

Her eyes were wide in shock as she looked at Elizabeth and George. They returned her look of disbelief.

"How did this happen?" Anne asked Lorente, unable to get her mind to fully process this latest outrage. "What's going on?"

"Detective, how do you know Douglas was kidnapped?" George asked.

"A call came in while I was over here with you," Lorente said to all three. "A guy named Kurt Willis phoned in the report. He was trying to reach you, Mrs. Winston." In her rush, she'd forgot her cell phone at home.

"Kurt is the foreman at our ranch," Anne said. She was numb with shock. It was so unreal.

This can't be happening! she wanted to scream out. *Not now, for God's sake!*

"Kurt and his wife Susan agreed to stay with our children after we heard Paul was hurt," she managed. "What happened?"

"Mr. Willis told us Douglas went for a ride on his horse about mid-morning," Lorente replied. "Is that right?"

"Yes," Anne said. "I made him a lunch. He was going to one of his favorite places—Livingston Valley."

Your son's horse came back around supper time without him," Lorente said. "A note was tied to the saddle saying he was being held for ransom. The kidnapper or kidnappers are demanding $2 million and safe passage to Namibia in Africa. Apparently we've no extradition treaty with that country."

"Do you know where they're keeping Douglas?" Anne said. Her tone was desperate.

"We have some information we're working on, Mrs. Winston," Lorente replied, hoping to bring some comfort but knowing that he didn't really have any viable leads. "Our best people are on this. We also have a team that should be at your ranch by now.

"The FBI is involved, too, since this is a kidnapping. They've a team with a special tracking dog on the way from Denver. We're going to do everything we can, Mrs. Winston, to get your son back safely and as soon as possible."

Elizabeth put her arms around Anne. All Anne could do was draw strength from Elizabeth's abundance of comfort and struggle to keep her fear under control. It was just too much. She reached for George's hand.

"What can we do, George?" she asked.

"Anne, I surely don't know," he answered firmly. "But by god, I'm going to get to the bottom of this!"

Chapter Twenty-Four

Willow Creek Valley

Doug had barely slept. He woke just after daybreak in a dusty old shack abandoned decades ago by some prospector or rancher.

The latch on the heavy plank door rattled open. In walked the man Doug assumed had kidnapped him. In the gloom, he could see the man's mouth and nose were covered by a red bandana with a white swirling pattern. He was carrying a dented, old metal kitchen plate. Doug looked down at it. The plate held a biscuit of dubious origin, three shriveled sausages and two sad-looking fried eggs. On the plate was a tin cup half-filled with water.

The man bent over and set the food down. Doug saw a pistol tucked into the back of his belt.

That's probably the gun he used to shoot Tippy, Doug thought. He choked back grief and anger.

The man motioned Doug to turn around. He untied Doug's wrists so he could eat. The man said nothing as he handed Doug a large bent spoon.

He was sure he'd seen the man before. He couldn't remember where or when. He ate the food while the man watched from a distance, seated on an old upturned wooden bucket.

"Where is this? What's this all about?" Doug demanded, with all the determination a newly turned 14-year-old could muster.

The man just stared back at him, saying nothing.

When Doug finished eating, the man motioned him to turn around. He tied Doug's hands behind him again. The man pointed for him to sit on a wood frame with slats. It looked like it had been the frame for a single bed. Doug hadn't seen it behind him in the dark the night before. He sat. The man left.

He heard the door close and lock. Then something solid made a thud against the door.

A leather thong bound Doug's wrists. It was digging into his skin, restricting the blood circulation to his hands. He knew he had to do something, or his hands would soon become too numb from reduced blood circulation to function properly.

He thought of the jackknife in the left front pocket of his jean jacket. His Dad had given it to him saying all ranchers and ranch hands needed to carry one. His captor hadn't found it or seen the slight bulge in his pocket. Luckily, the pocket flap was unbuttoned.

Well, I'd better get on with it, he thought.

His plan was to get the jackknife out, open the main blade and then figure out how to cut the leather thong binding his wrists without cutting himself. But there was a problem. How was he going to get the knife out of his jacket pocket?

His captor had left behind the metal cup with some water. Doug struggled to his feet and walked over to the cup. It was sitting on the floor. The cup was more than half full. He eased himself down beside the cup, worked his way around so his back was toward it and then backed himself up. He felt around until his fingers found the cup.

Doug knew he had to be careful not to spill the water. He wanted to pour it on the leather thong, hoping the water would soften it enough to get free. But in his heart he knew he'd have to be content just to improve blood circulation. Maneuvering to grab the cup with his hands tied behind his back took several minutes of trial and error. Once he almost

95

tipped it over. Finally, he had it in his hands. He bent forward and to one side. The water poured over his arms and down onto his wrists.

A few minutes passed. He tried again, splashing the rest of the water on his wrists. Eventually he felt the thongs loosening ever so slightly. Blood circulation to his hands began improving. But there was no way he could pull his hands free.

It would be up to his jackknife.

Doug went back to the bed frame. Long boards formed the sides of the bed. Wood slats were nailed between the long boards. A plan formed in his mind to get the jackknife out of his breast pocket – he would lay backward over the edge and tilt his upper body upside down. Doug lifted one knee onto the slats, then the other knee. His right knee wasn't positioned properly on the slat. It slipped down between the slats. He fell onto his right arm and chest. The sound of him falling seemed as loud as a rifle shot.

He froze, holding his breath and listening for movement outside. None. Doug pulled his knee up and worked back off the bed. He walked to the door and peered through a crack in the thick, rough planks. Flames from a campfire were visible some 30 yards away. His captor was sitting by the fire, smoking, and drinking from what looked like a whiskey bottle.

Guess he didn't hear that, Doug thought.

A rusty pickup was parked on the left side of the campfire. To the right was a large new-looking tent.

He crept back to the bed frame. Being more careful this time, he walked his knees halfway across the bed. Then he eased onto his stomach. He gradually worked his body forward until he could lower his head facing down toward the ground. Doug wriggled farther forward, hoping to tip the jackknife out of the breast pocket of his jean jacket. It was too tight, holding the pocket closed. The jackknife stayed in place.

Pushing his forehead down into the dirt floor, Doug lifted his body up a few inches with his knees, and then wriggled forward again. This time the breast pocket billowed out slightly, but still the jackknife remained firmly in place. He wriggled backward and forward. Finally, the pocket loosened, billowing open even more. At last, the jackknife tumbled onto the dirt floor. It hit something and rolled under the bed out of sight. Doug's heart sank.

He wriggled his body forward and tumbled off the bed. He rolled onto his side so his fingers could touch the ground. He worked his way backward under the edge of the bed. After searching with his hands behind his back for what seemed like a very long time, Doug's fingers finally found the jackknife. He grabbed it and scrambled back out from under the bed.

Working behind his back, Doug felt around until he found the small groove in the main blade of the jackknife and pulled the blade open. Holding the jackknife in his right hand, he slid the blade under the damp leather thong around his left wrist, being careful to keep the sharp blade away from his skin. After some trial and error, and a few nicks to his wrists, he got the blade lined up. Its sharp edge cut easily through the thong.

His hands were free! He cut the thong from his right wrist and flexed his arms. It felt so good!

Doug snuck over to the door. Carefully he tried the inside slider for the door latch. It was firmly in place. He knew that if he tried to force it, he'd make a noise. Through a crack between the door planks, Doug could see a heavy log about 10 feet long leaning at an angle against the outside of the door. One end was in a shallow hole dug in the dirt while the other was jammed halfway down the face of the door.

He scanned the inside of the shack, as best he could in the gloom, looking for possible weak spots in the walls. A boarded-over window initially seemed to have possibilities, but the boards were nailed securely to the heavy window frame. There were gaps between the boards allowing him to see out, but he'd need a tool of some kind to loosen the boards enough for him to escape. On another wall, a few weak-looking boards seemed promising. The bad part, that wall was exposed to where his captor was sitting in front of the campfire.

Moments later, as Doug continued his search, he heard the pickup drive away. He kept looking around the shack for tools to help with an escape, but all he found were the bed frame, an old wooden bucket and some rusty tin cans thrown under the bed.

He tried to pull the bed frame apart. It was built too strongly. Sitting down on the floor facing the door, his back to the opposite wall, Doug tried to concentrate on an escape plan. Afternoon turned into evening and then to night. The man hadn't come back. Doug was cold and felt pangs of hunger.

For a second time, Doug shivered through the night. He was wearing only jeans, a light shirt, and his jean jacket. Like the first night, he huddled in a corner of the shack, sitting on the packed dirt floor, knees drawn to his chest and his arms wrapped around his legs, trying to stay warm.

He slept fitfully until awakened at dawn by songbirds. in bushes between the shack and the road where the man parked the truck. Doug walked over and peered through a crack in the door. There was no sign of the man or the pickup. The tent flap was closed.

Douglas could feel pangs of hunger again gnawing away at his stomach. All he'd had to eat was one small meal and part of a cup of water since he'd been kidnapped.

Chapter Twenty-Five

Memorial Hospital

Time moved slowly for Anne, Elizabeth, and George as they waited for word of Paul's condition and Doug's whereabouts. Anne and Elizabeth spent much of it sitting together holding each other's hands for support.

Elizabeth had been like a mother to Anne during Paul and Anne's annual visits from England. She'd looked forward eagerly to each visit and to the joy Anne brought, with her sense of humor and high-spirited personality.

George paced in and out of the waiting room, and up and down the corridor.

In the background, sirens wailed repeatedly, first far in the distance, growing louder and then stopping. The three of them were vaguely aware of doors to the emergency department opening and closing time and again, carrying in patients with urgent ailments. They barely spoke, hoping for the best and trying, but not willing, to prepare themselves for the worst.

A man in pale green operating room scrubs appeared at the door to the private waiting room.

Anne was deep in thought, yearning for Paul to be all right, and worried about Douglas' safety. He walked over and put his hand gently on her shoulder. She snapped alert and jumped to her feet.

"I'm Doctor Shepherd," the tall slim man managed to get out before a wide-eyed Anne pleaded, "Is my husband all right? How is he doing? Can I see him?"

"Yes, Mrs. Winston," Dr. Shepherd said, reaching out and gently taking hold of both her hands. He led her back to her chair and then told her:

"Your husband's out of surgery. But I must be honest with you, Mrs. Winston, he's not out of danger yet. He's in extremely critical condition. The next 24 hours are going to be pivotal.

"We'll be keeping him in intensive care overnight," Dr. Shepherd added. "You can look in on him now, but just for a few minutes. Okay? He's very weak and under heavy sedation. I'll send someone for you in a few minutes, after we get him settled.

"Mrs. Winston," Dr. Shepherd continued, "You should know that we were unable to remove one of the bullets. It's lodged next to your husband's heart. We did extract nine pieces from two bullets we found in his right chest and lung, but he was too weak to undergo further surgery. The bullets broke into fragmented when they hit his sternum and ribs. This required more extensive surgery than we expected. The other bullet will have to be removed later once he has time to recover from this trauma."

Anne looked at George and Elizabeth.

Her mind was swirling with conflicting emotions – relief that Paul had come through surgery, fear for Douglas, and dismay that a bullet was still in her husband's body, next to his heart.

*

A nurse guided Anne to the Intensive Care unit. She'd noticed with relief that a police officer was posted at the door. The charge nurse directed her to a small room where she put on a hospital gown and cap, booties over her shoes, and a surgical mask.

100

A specially gowned nurse took her into the ICU, to a room with curtains pulled tightly across the windows. Another guard was posted at the door. Anne was shaking with apprehension as she entered Paul's room. Her knees weakened when she saw him lying on his left side in a semi-fetal position, covered with a hospital sheet and blanket, his back to the door.

Beside the Stryker bed was an intravenous tree holding clear plastic bags with tubes connected to Paul's arm. An oxygen mask covered Paul's mouth and nose. His breathing was labored. Other tubes came from under the blankets that covered his hospital gown. They disappeared over the side and beneath the bed. Wires connecting Paul to screens and monitors emitted a symphony of electronic sounds.

"Your husband will be lying on his side overnight," the nurse said in response to Anne's alarmed gaze at Paul.

"We need to dress the sutures in his back and his chest. The less we have to move him for the next few hours the better. When we can, we'll try to make him as comfortable as possible lying on his back."

Anne struggled to hear the nurse. Her focus was on the man she so dearly loved lying before her, still in grave danger. She sat down beside the bed, facing Paul. His eyes were closed, and he lay so still it terrified her. He seemed to be barely breathing. Her emotions welled up as she watched him. She fought to keep her composure and lost. Hot tears coursed down her cheeks. They flowed into and around the surgical mask, down her neck and then disappeared beneath the gown.

She sat beside Paul's bed and tenderly took his right hand between both of hers covered with surgical gloves. His strength, that had given her such comfort over the years, was missing. She stroked the back of his limp hand gently, willing her strength into him, willing him to heal, praying for him to come back to her.

The ICU nurse walked back into the room and stood quietly at the foot of Paul's bed. She looked compassionately at Anne, who caught her eye. The ICU nurse nodded. Anne understood. Time to go. With a loving look at Paul, she stood and left the room, looking back again from the door, seeing him lying there so helpless. Anne covered her mouth with her left hand as she fought to maintain her composure.

Throughout the night, Paul's condition steadily improved. Teams of doctors monitored him continuously. They knew he was young and strong physically, but they were still amazed at the speed of his progress. They understood they were witnessing the product of his extraordinary will to live. By morning, Paul's condition was still serious but stable. Dr. Shepherd gave orders to move him into a private room under guard in a secure wing of the hospital.

*

An orderly came for Anne at 6:30 a.m. Minutes earlier, Paul had been moved to a private room.

For Anne, it had been a stressful night with little sleep. She felt helpless, unable to do anything for Paul. A police officer was posted at the door to the wing and another at the door to Paul's room. Anne was comforted, knowing her husband was under protection, while he lay helpless in the room beyond. The man who'd shot Paul was still at large. She remembered what Lt. Lorente told her. The assailant had not been identified. An interstate manhunt was now underway. Meanwhile, police were taking precautions to protect her and Paul's safety, the safety of their children, and the safety of Paul's sisters.

After gowning up, she entered the room. A nurse motioned Anne to a chair on the right side, next to Paul's head. The nurse left. Anne looked at Paul for a long time. Fear and worry and hope all swirled through her mind. She closed her eyes to concentrate harder, willing him to grow stronger and get better quickly.

Anne woke with a start. She glanced at her watch. It was almost 9 a.m. She'd slept for two hours. Anne glanced up. She was startled to see Paul watching her. His smile widened when he saw the woman he loved so completely return his gaze. Anne felt the warm glow of love and relief wash through her body and soul.

Paul's face was pale, his cheeks hollow. But his eyes had that familiar sparkle. She felt an enormous swell of excitement and tenderness.

"Welcome back, my love," Anne said tenderly.

She could see it was a struggle for Paul to keep his eyes open. He'd just been through a horrible ordeal and was under heavy sedation. Without a word, his eyes closed slowly, a hint of the smile remaining as he drifted back to sleep.

George and Elizabeth appeared at the door.

Anne motioned them to come in. It was the first time either had been allowed to see Paul since he'd been shot. As Elizabeth approached the foot of the bed, her hands swept up, covering her mouth.

"Oh, my!" she gasped quietly, her eyes filling.

Elizabeth looked at Paul and then at Anne. The expression on her face was a study of shock, pain, and fear, all in one. This was the man she regarded as a surrogate son, a boy whom she'd watched grow up into a wonderful, caring, successful man.

"He's not out of danger yet," Anne whispered. "But the doctors say he's getting stronger by the hour."

She walked over and put her arms around Elizabeth.

"They're very optimistic," Anne said softly, trying to reassure Elizabeth. "They're surprised at how well he's doing under the circumstances."

George walked over awkwardly and put an arm around Anne. She felt her strength suddenly desert her. Her knees buckled. George grabbed her. He and Elizabeth guided her to a chair. Elizabeth sat next to Anne, holding her close, while all three watched Paul sleep and heal. The nurses came in from time to time to check the IVs, occasionally changing one.

"Anne," Elizabeth whispered, leaning toward her. "You need to get some rest. You're exhausted. I've asked George to arrange a suite for you at the Antlers Hilton."

"But I can't leave Paul," Anne protested. "Not just yet, anyway."

"There's nothing you can do for Paul right now," Elizabeth argued, "except get some rest. Forgive me, Anne, but when Paul wakes up again, if he sees you the way you are right now, he'll be worried sick about you. He has more important things to concentrate on than worrying about you.

"Please, Anne," Elizabeth insisted. "George and I will take turns sitting with Paul while you get some rest. If there's any change, any change at all, we'll call you immediately. We have a room at the Hilton, too. The three of us can take turns being with Paul until he's out of danger."

"I suppose you're right, Elizabeth," Anne said reluctantly. "I just don't want to leave him alone. And what if we hear something about Douglas? I need to be here!"

"Anne, we'll call you. And you'll be no help to Paul or Douglas if you're out on your feet," Elizabeth persisted. "Oh, and I called your dress shop. They've put together a few complete changes of clothes for you in your size. They know what you like. The clothes are in your hotel room waiting for you."

"Well, all right, but what about Catherine and Michael?" Anne asked. "I want them in town. They have a right to know what's going on. They'll want to see their dad."

"I hope you don't mind, Anne," George said, "but I took the liberty of calling the kids to tell them that their father has been hurt. And I called Emily. She and Jeremy and their kids are flying here now, be here in a few hours. Emily offered to take over from Kurt and Susan looking after the kids and do whatever else you need done for the next few days."

Anne felt grateful to have around her so many caring people. She hugged Elizabeth and George tightly. Then reluctantly she headed for the door.

Elizabeth followed her. George stepped forward.

"Why don't you wait here, Elizabeth?" he said. "Anne needs rest right now. We need to take turns."

"I'll be right back, George," Elizabeth replied firmly.

"I want to see Anne to her hotel then I'll come back," she added.

George sat down, frowning. He hated being contradicted by anyone, including his wife.

Chapter Twenty-Six

Willow Creek Valley

Doug heard the pickup before he saw it through a crack in the door.

The old truck rattled and clanked its way up the dirt road in a cloud of dust, coming to a stop beside the tent thirty yards away. The pickup's door squawked on its hinges and slammed shut. His captor took something out of the back on the far side of the pickup, but Doug couldn't make out what it was. The man walked around the front of the pickup with a package in his left hand. Doug guessed it was food. The man headed straight for the shack. In the bright early afternoon sunlight, Doug saw the man's face for the first time. He looked vaguely familiar, but Doug couldn't place him.

Guess I'd better come up with something pretty damned quick, Douglas thought about his non-existent escape plan. He was amused by the pang of guilt he felt for using the strong language his mother so disliked.

Doug realized that as soon as the man went to untie him to eat, his captor would see the thongs were missing. It would be a disaster for any hope of escape. Doug heard the log the man had pushed against the door lifted away. The wood latch on the door creaked as it was slid back. The door opened. The afternoon sunlight beamed in. It was blinding. The man was wearing his bandana.

Doug realized the bright light would make it difficult for his captor to see inside, coming into the dark shack. As the man stepped slowly through the door, it was obvious he was peering around cautiously trying to find his prisoner. Doug got up off the bed frame where he'd been sitting.

"When are you going to let me go?" he demanded, allowing his captor to locate him by voice. A plan had formed in his mind.

Then he stepped forward, making sure the man could see his feet in the brilliant sunlight coming through the door.

His captor said nothing but walked forward. Doug stepped back, holding his hands behind his back as if they were still tied.

Doug slipped back around the head of the bed frame and got behind the bed, desperately trying to think of an escape plan. The man followed until his leg bumped up against the other side of the bed frame. He swore. Then man began feeling his way around the bed.

The man told Doug to turn around. His eyes apparently had adjusted enough to the darkness in the shack to make out Doug's outline but not many details.

Doug started to step forward then he bent over sharply and grunted, pretending to stumble. The man instinctively reached out to keep Doug from falling, thinking his hands were still tied.

Doug seized the opportunity.

He lunged forward, and then stood up quickly, forcing his head upward as hard as he could into the man's face. He heard a crunching sound. He'd broken the man's nose.

The man screamed and stood upright. He stumbled back, pulling the bandana away. Blood poured from his nose. As he backpedaled, the man's lower legs struck the bed frame. He fell backwards across the bed. His hips hit the far side of the bed frame. His shoulders and head snapped down sharply onto the hard packed dirt floor. His cry of pain was cut short. He lay there moaning without moving. The man was dazed.

Doug skirted the bed and ran for the door.

Outside, he swung the heavy door closed. Doug tried to slide the latch. It started to move then stuck and wouldn't budge. The slide and the latch were out of alignment. He wasn't strong enough to lift the door up in place and force the slide into the catch.

His captor started to groan. He was coming around.

Doug looked around frantically, remembering the gun tucked in the man's belt. He saw the heavy log his captor had used to block the door. He managed to get one end into a hole in front of the door. Just as he brought the other end down, the door shuddered. His captor had gotten up, stumbled over, and was trying to force the door open.

"You little bastard! Open this bloody door," came muffled shouts through the door.

"I'm gonna to kick your goddamned ass if you don't open it! Ya hear me? Open the fuckin' door!!"

Shots rang out as Doug raced for the pickup, hoping his captor had left the keys in it.

Chapter Twenty-Seven

Memorial Hospital

A police officer met Anne and Elizabeth at the desk in the ER department. He told them he was to escort Anne to the Antlers Hilton. Elizabeth explained she was planning to drive Anne to the hotel. The officer, who's black on silver nametag said 'Thornton,' told them it would be his privilege to drive both in his cruiser to the hotel and bring Elizabeth back. The women exchanged glances, knowing it was futile to argue.

Officer William Thornton held the door to the ER as they stepped out into the parking lot. He gestured for them to head toward a black and white police cruiser parked in a reserved zone. As they reached the car, Officer Thornton reached into his pocket for a set of keys.

As he bent over to insert the key in the door lock, a loud 'crack' rang out. Then another.

Rifle shots.

Thornton was spun around and thrown backwards, his eyes wide with surprise. He lunged forward immediately. Anne felt her body thrust backward into Elizabeth, then crushed between Thornton and Elizabeth, as the officer pushed them both to the ground. He covered them with his own body and reached for his weapon.

While falling backward, Anne saw a hole in the window surrounded by a spider web effect in the broken window glass. She was shocked to see blood splattered around the hole. Anne noticed another hole in the door of the cruiser.

Seconds later footsteps came pounding out into the parking lot from the emergency department, accompanied by shouts of alarm.

"Gun shots! Stay alert!" Anne heard a man shout.

"Over there! That way!" another voice shouted.

"Officer down," a third voice called out.

The footsteps paused briefly, and then came towards them fast amid more shouted verbal exchanges. She heard the wheels of a gurney clattering on the rough parking lot pavement. Then she saw two police officers with automatic weapons and other people dressed in hospital scrubs and white smocks.

Officer Thornton was lifted off her and Elizabeth. Anne saw a spreading pool of blood on the asphalt.

"Are you all right, ma'am?" The question was directed to Anne as she got to her knees on the pavement. She was relieved to realize that the question had come from Thornton.

Oh, thank God! He must be all right, she thought.

Thornton was sitting up, holding his upper left arm tightly with his right hand, looking at her closely. There was a bloody mark on her coat the size of a silver dollar. Thornton released the grip on his left arm and pointed to her coat.

"I'm okay," Anne said quickly before he could say anything more.

Then she recoiled in dismay as she realized the blood on her coat must have come from the wound in the police officer's upper arm, just below his shoulder. She was impressed at his concern for her wellbeing.

When he saw Anne was okay, Thornton turned quickly toward where Elizabeth was lying on her back, not moving. Elizabeth's eyes were wide open with surprise, and blinking. Thornton urgently waived the ER people away from him and Anne, directing them to Elizabeth.

The pool of blood Anne had seen was spreading from beneath Elizabeth's body.

"Oh, my God, no!" Anne shouted.

She realized Elizabeth was seriously hurt. Anne reached for Elizabeth's hand just as someone in a white smock bent over them.

"I, I think I've been shot, Anne," Elizabeth whispered, weakly grabbing for Anne's hand as she was lifted onto the gurney.

"It's going to be okay, Elizabeth," Anne said trying to reassure her.

"They're going to take good care of you right away," Anne told her with a desperate confidence she didn't feel. "Just hold on, Elizabeth. Please hold on."

The injured Thornton and two hospital staff rushed the gurney toward the emergency department. The two other police officers stood guard, rifles ready. Anne ran after them. As they approached the door to the emergency department, Thornton stumbled and fell. He didn't get up. A police officer guarding the door ran toward him.

Anne heard urgent shouts.

Four burly men in hospital scrubs ran out of the ER door toward them, pushing another gurney. Thornton was lifted onto it, guarded by another police officer with her sidearm drawn. They ran the gurney back into the emergency department.

Chapter Twenty-Eight

Downtown Colorado Springs

It was Thursday evening after closing when the door to Stephen Hooper's office burst open.

"Get the fuck out of here," a startled Stephen shouted at the man standing in the doorway. Stephen swiftly turned his back on the equally startled intruder, his body shielding the woman lying on her back on his desk, her knees wide apart.

"Oh, shit!" the man said, backing quickly out the door and closing it. He had a terrified look on his face, and it wasn't from catching two people engaging in sexual intercourse.

Stephen turned to the young woman lying lengthways on his large office desk. Her clothes were disheveled, brassiere pulled up revealing two youthful breasts, nipples erect. Her skirt was pulled above her waist, her panties dangling from her right ankle.

"Get dressed, Marcie," Stephen ordered, tucking his now-flaccid penis back into his pants. He pulled up his zipper.

"Margie," she corrected him.

Stephen made a half-hearted effort to tug down her skirt.

"You need to get outta here. I gotta see this guy. It doesn't look good."

"Yeah, okay, Stephen," Margie replied, trying to calm her breathing. "This is awful. Who is he? Is he from around here? Is he going to blab this all over town? Geez, Stephen."

"Christ, Margie, you don't have to worry," Stephen replied. "He's from outta town, actually outta state. He works for me. He's not going to tell anyone. Shit, I shoulda locked the fuckin' door."

"All right Stephen," Margie replied, hurriedly reassembling her clothes. "I sure don't want this getting out and back to your wife. Shit, she's a big shot lawyer, isn't she?"

"Yeah, she is. Christ, Margie, I'd be sunk, too, if that happened!" Stephen said. "She'd kill me. But it's gonna be okay, sweetie."

Margie gave him a quick kiss on the mouth, gathered up her panties and walked out of Stephen's office leaving the door open behind her.

Stephen had hoped to finish 'getting it on' with this one like he had with the clerk before her. He'd had lots of great sessions with that one until she'd got married and quit her job.

Stephen was putting his desk back in order when he heard a knock on the doorjamb.

"Okay if I come in now?" the man asked. He was clearly agitated about something.

'Yeah," Stephen replied. "Come in. Close the fuckin' door."

Reggie Winston pushed the door closed behind him then turned to Stephen.

"We're in deep shit, Stephen," he began in his upper-class British accent. "I, I really fucked up. I'm sorry, Stephen, I'm so sorry, man. I don't know how it happened. Oh shit! This wasn't like the other one!"

"Knock it off, Reggie!" Stephen interjected impatiently. "What the fuck happened? What went wrong this time?"

"I shot the wrong fuckin' woman," Reggie replied. "It was an accident. I don't know how it happened. I hit the woman who was with her. And Stephen, I shot a cop too."

"You WHAT? You shot a cop?" Stephen shouted. "What the fuck! You dumb shit! Are you fucking nuts? Did you kill him?"

113

Reggie started to explain there had been two women and a cop. Stephen didn't wait for further explanation.

"So, you've screwed up both jobs. Both. Did you know that? You didn't kill Paul either, you asshole. He's still alive, you goddamned idiot! He's going to make it," Stephen shouted.

"You're a pathetic screw-up. And you just had to use your dad's useless fuckin' old revolver for that job, didn't you! Now you've screwed up on his wife too. You were supposed to get her as she was leaving the hospital!

"What's so fuckin' hard about that?" Stephen raged on. "I set the whole fuckin' thing up for you! What in hell went wrong?"

Not waiting for answers, he continued, "Well, you better get the hell out of here right now and back to England. Where's the rifle? Did you get rid of it like I told you? And that old God damned revolver. You'd better get rid of it, too. You shoulda used a .45, or a .357. Christ, they'll stop a bull. I know where we coulda got hollow points. Never mind. Too fucking late.

"You're nothing but a fucking screw-up!"

Stephen stopped to take a breath. He was so angry he could barely keep from throwing something at Reggie. And now he had ample reason to worry, too.

Reggie was fuming mad from Stephen's verbal onslaught. He said nothing.

Jesus Christ, Stephen thought, *I shoulda known better than to hire this loser to do my dirty work.*

Roberta had told him about Reggie having been in jail. He'd tracked him down and talked him into doing the hits. Stephen could see now it was a mistake. But how he'd relished the idea of one Winston killing two other Winstons – a delicious irony! Reggie had thought so, too.

When Stephen discussed the job with Reggie, the Brit jumped at the chance to avenge his father. At least that's how Reggie saw things. He'd told Stephen his father had been 'cheated' out of inheriting his Uncle Percival's estate. Had his father inherited the money and property, he would have been very wealthy and his own pressing money problems would have gone away.

Stephen's biggest concern now was getting rid of Reggie. He had to get him away from Colorado Springs and on his way home to England as fast as he could. Otherwise, the cops would sure as hell follow a trail from Reggie straight to him. At this point, he would have not hesitated to kill Reggie to silence him if he could think of a way to do it without getting caught.

"Yeah, yeah," Reggie said, stinging from Stephen's rebuke. "I got rid of the rifle like you said. It's out in the dump and soon will be under piles of garbage and other shit. But I'm taking the Webley back with me. My old man might notice it's missing. He already did once. It's one of his prized souvenirs."

"Well, I guess you'd better tell me what happened," Stephen added, "But, fuck, if I had my way, I'd just as soon *not* know."

Reggie began, "I parked the car on the side street where you said. I waited 'til I saw Paul's wife come out of the hospital. Then I ran over to the row of bushes beside the parking lot where you told me you hid the rifle. I found it and did everything just like you said.

"After I got set, I looked up and there were three of them, for Christ's sake! The guy's wife was with some other woman. And a cop was with them, too. Instead of going to her car, the cop took them to a squad car. Shit! He was going to drive them in a goddamned squad car! How was I to know?" Reggie was almost whining.

"I was all set up to take her out at her car when she went to unlock it. So, I had to improvise … take the shot that I had. Well, I accidentally hit the fuckin' cop. Then I tried again for Paul's wife. I accidentally hit the other woman with that one. It was dark. Then I saw other cops with their guns out in the parking lot. I got outta there as fast as I could and went to the dump."

"Where've you been hiding?" Stephen asked, almost afraid to hear the answer. He had a crazy vision of a drunken and dazed Reggie wandering the streets of Colorado Springs, a rifle in one hand and an antique revolver dangling from the other.

"In the back of your storage room, like we agreed," Reggie answered. "Used the key you gave me. Hid in a big cardboard box behind the table back there. Don't you remember, you were supposed to leave me some food? I'm starved. I thought maybe you'd taken off and forgot about settling up with me."

"Oh, shit, yeah," Stephen said, calmer now and able to concentrate better. "Is that car I got for you parked out back like I told you?"

Reggie nodded.

"Well, look, I'll go get you something to eat," Stephen said. He wasn't enthusiastic. "Harvey and Margie can handle things. Coupla hamburgers. Okay?"

Reggie nodded again.

"Then I want you outta here, Reggie," Stephen said firmly. "Take those back roads I marked on the map until you're out of state. That should keep you away from the cops. Head for Salt Lake City, like we agreed. Leave the car at the airport. It can't be traced. You got your plane ticket, right?

"One more thing, Reggie," Stephen said. "We agreed on $30,000 for both jobs, and $5,000 for expenses. Yeah? But you didn't do the jobs I hired you to do. Right? You screwed 'em both up. I should pay you nothing.

"So, here's what I'm gonna do for you," Stephen said, using his best sales persona. "I'm gonna give you half. That's all.

"By rights, I should be demanding back what I've already given you. I sent you five grand up front. So, here's another fifteen. That's all you're gonna get, Reggie."

"Jesus Christ, Stephen," Reggie complained. "I tried my best. That's all I promised you … my best effort … nothing more. It's not my fault things didn't go like they were supposed to. C'mon, you can do better than that. Shit, most of the five grand is already gone. I had expenses."

"Yeah, you told me about the broad in Denver," Stephen replied. "That's your business."

"Stephen, you said I'd get five just for expenses, plus the thirty," Reggie pleaded. "C'mon, man."

"Look, Reggie, you got five up front, and now here's another fifteen," Stephen replied, handing him a large, padded brown envelope stuffed with $100 bills. "That's all you're gonna get! And I'm being damned generous giving you that much for jobs you fucked up.

"Goddamnit Reggie, you didn't do the fucking jobs!" Stephen shouted in frustration.

"Well, that's bloody well not how I expected it to go either, damnit!" Reggie shouted back, as Stephen walked out the door heading for his car and the fast-food drive-in.

Reggie was furious. Stephen had stiff-armed him over the jobs. He'd told Stephen from the beginning he'd do his best, no more … that there would be no guarantees. He'd never done anything quite like this before.

I gotta get out of here,' Reggie thought. *But this ain't the end of it. Not by a bloody long shot!*

He walked over to the shop's lunchroom to make a coffee for his trip.

An embarrassed Margie helped him and found a half-full bottle of whiskey in the bottom drawer of Stephen's desk. She asked him about his accent. Margie was surprised and doubtful when he told her that he was visiting from England. Reggie gave her some British coins from his pocket to prove he was from England like he said. Margie made him a sandwich.

Reggie headed for the car Stephen had gotten for him. He wasn't going to wait for Stephen to get back with his hamburgers. Nor was Reggie planning to use the return airline ticket to England that Stephen gave him when he arrived three days ago. He'd cancelled that American Airlines reservation and applied the money to one of the airline's flights to Melbourne, Australia.

Before leaving England, Reggie had sent a letter to Jason Burke, a fellow student he met years ago at the Sutton Valence School, a private senior school in Maidstone. Jason had been in England at the time with his diplomat parents from Melbourne posted to London. Reggie and Jason hung out together for two years as teenagers until Jason had returned to Australia with his parents.

Reggie thought hiding out in Australia for a while might help cover his tracks if the cops somehow came looking for him. But more importantly, he was going to ask his friend Jason in Melbourne to provide an alibi. They'd been kindred spirits – getting into trouble together as boys do, and sometimes getting into far more trouble than boyhood pranks.

Reggie knew he could use the leverage he had over his friend to persuade Jason to give him an alibi. While at school, Reggie and Jason were in a park after dark when Jason grabbed a teenage girl walking past them the other way. Jason had started to sexually assault the girl but was interrupted when an older couple had entered the park. Reggie had acted as the lookout, so he hadn't joined Jason in the assault. He was waiting his turn when they were forced to run to escape. The girl reported the incident to police but was unable to give a useful description of her assailants.

Now Jason was a high school teacher in Melbourne. Reggie was sure Jason would do what he needed him to do. After all, Jason wouldn't want stories about that episode coming to the attention of his family and superiors, now would he?

Chapter Twenty-Nine

"Hunter, Cameron, and Greenberg," said the cheerful female voice on the phone.

"Tom Cameron, please," John replied. "It's John Everett calling. I'm an attorney in Colorado Springs. Tom and I are working on a case here together."

"Yes, Mr. Everett," the pleasant voice said. "One moment please."

"Hey, John!" Tom's voice came over the phone. "Good to hear from you. I'm just about to head for the airport to catch my flight for Denver. Got a rental car waiting. When can we meet? I should be in Colorado Springs around 5 or 6 o'clock.

"Hold on, Tom," John replied. "We need to postpone your trip for a bit. Paul's in hospital here in Colorado Springs. Someone shot him."

"Did you say 'shot?'" Tom said. "What happened? How is he? Is he going to be all right? Who'd do such a thing?"

"Paul was brought in by ambulance in grave condition, Tom. Shot three times," John answered. "Paul underwent some tricky surgery."

Good God!" Tom exclaimed. "How's he doing?"

"The doctors say he should make it." John replied. "But it was touch and go through the night. It's going to take a while. Looks like he'll be a few weeks recovering."

"Okay, I'll cancel my travel plans," Tom said. "Do the police have any idea who did this?"

"No," John replied. "There's an all-points bulletin out. It's quite bizarre, Tom. I understand Paul got a look at the shooter but can't place him. He wasn't up to giving the police much more than that. They also have a witness who told them the shooter spoke with a British accent. That's about all the police have to go on right now."

"Keep me posted on Paul's progress, will you?" Tom said, and then added, "By the way, thanks for the briefing package you sent on Paul's case. An impressive job, John. Well done. When you think Paul's up for a meeting, let me know. I'll clear my schedule immediately. Paul sounds like quite the fellow. Looking forward to meeting him, and you as well."

"He sure is. Thanks, Tom. I'll let you know."

John hung up, elated. Working with one of the top civil litigators in the country on a case for an important new client like Paul Winston— well, he felt like pinching himself. He'd been dreaming of this day since he was a boy.

His excitement was tempered by his worry for Paul and concern over the stress Paul's family must be going through.

Chapter Thirty

"Douglas!" George shouted. "Good god! How'd you get here? Where've you been? Are you all right?"

Doug watched bemused as George stumbled through, over and around chairs in the hospital waiting room in his rush to reach him.

"We've been worried sick!" George said, grabbing the shoulders of the tall teenager and looking questioningly at the young police officer behind him.

"We heard you'd been kidnapped. How'd you get away?"

"It's a long story, Uncle George," Doug replied. "I got away and I've just come from the police. Can I tell you the rest later? Do you know where my dad is? How is he? I need to see him right away! Do you know where my mom is?"

"Okay, okay, Douglas," George replied gently. His face was etched in fatigue and worry.

"Slow down, son ... one thing at a time. Your dad is here. He's going to be okay. I just came from his room. Your mom is with him. I'll try to get you in to see them just as soon as I can. Okay?"

"Alright, Uncle George. But I have to see him right away. I've got something to tell him that he needs to know." Doug had no idea about the seriousness of his dad's injuries.

"Wait here a minute, Douglas," George said.

He went to the ER reception desk and spoke with a group of people dressed in white hospital smocks. While George was speaking to them, they kept looking over at Doug, their expressions alternating between understanding and admiration. George returned and sat beside Doug.

"They're tracking down the doctor who's looking after your dad. I'm sure she'll let you in to see your mom and dad. Now tell me what happened to you," George said.

"I want to know what's wrong with my dad, Uncle George. What's going on?"

"Okay, Douglas," George answered. "Someone shot your dad two days ago. And someone shot Elizabeth tonight."

Douglas's eyes grew as big as silver dollars.

"Whaaat?" he said. It was all he could manage.

"We don't know who did these terrible things," George continued. "The doctors say your dad's going to be all right. He was hurt pretty badly, but the nurses had him up and taking a few steps this afternoon. You'll get to see him in a few minutes. But while we're waiting, tell me what happened to you, okay?"

"How's Aunt Elizabeth?" Douglas asked, ignoring George's question.

"We don't know yet," the big rancher replied, worry etched into his weathered face. "She's in surgery. It just happened a couple of hours ago. I'm waiting to hear from the doctors. Now, tell me what happened to you."

Doug gave George a quick summary of how and where he'd been kidnapped. He described the shack where he'd been kept prisoner.

"Yeah, I know where it is," George commented. "It's down the valley, about eight miles south of the ranch turnoff. A prospector built it years ago. Hunters use it sometimes."

Doug assured him that Lt. Lorente also knew where it was, and told him a team of city police, CSP and FBI were on their way there.

"By the way, have you had anything to eat?" George asked. "Of course not. Just a minute, I'll get you something. A couple of your favorite burgers okay?"

Doug nodded, "Yeah, sure. That'll be fine. Thanks, Uncle George."

123

George walked quickly back to the reception desk. He spoke on the phone for a few minutes, and then returned to Doug.

"Someone will bring those burgers, fully loaded, and something to drink in a few minutes. Root beer, right? Gotta fill those hollow legs. Hey, I remember when I turned 14 … I was eating all the time."

Doug nodded. He knew the feeling, especially right now.

"Okay, go on," George urged Doug. "How did you get away?"

Doug explained how he'd escaped, and about stealing the pickup truck and it running out of gas.

"I didn't think to check the gas when I drove away. Anyway, I didn't have time. He was shooting at me. Besides it was late. When I started running across the field toward the highway it was getting dark. The highway was maybe a mile and a half away. I could hear coyotes yelping and barking.

"It kinda felt like the coyotes were trying to circle around me. When I got to that barbed wire fence along the highway, I was going to climb through it and try to flag down a car. But I couldn't see anyone coming. And that pack of coyotes was scary.

"So, I climbed up on one of the fence posts. Good thing those posts are so high. My new jeans got ripped, though. Mom's gonna be mad about that.

"It was kinda eerie," Doug continued, his voice distant as he recalled his encounter.

"After a while, a car came along. I waved my jacket at it, but it kept going. Didn't even slow down. Guess it didn't see me. It was getting dark.

"Then I saw the lights of another vehicle coming. I pulled off my shirt so I could wave it instead of my jacket. It's lighter. A man in a pickup saw me on the post. He drove right into the ditch and jumped out. Boy, was I ever glad to see him.

"You probably know Mr. Cordell, Uncle George."

"I sure do," George answered. "Randy Cordell's a neighbor," George replied. "He has a ranch a few miles from Two-Dot.

"Mr. Cordell said it was pretty funny seeing me sitting on that fence post, with no shirt on. When I told Mr. Cordell what happened, he made a U-turn right in the middle of the road. Took me straight into town to the police station. They asked me a bunch of questions. I was there for over an hour.

"They told me Dad was hurt and is here. Lt. Lorente sent me over with a policeman. That's the cop over there sitting by the door. He drove me. On the way over here, he told me he has to guard me no matter what. What's that all about? What's going on?"

"Well, Douglas," George said. "Looks like you've had a terrible experience. I'm afraid we've had an awful time of it here in town, too."

"Mr. Underhill? Douglas Winston?"

A woman dressed in mauve scrubs came over to where they were sitting. A nametag identified her as Carol Mackenzie, RN.

"Yes?" George said, preparing to get up. The nurse stepped over quickly to where he was sitting and put her hand on his shoulder. He sat back down.

"You're Douglas Winston?" the nurse turned to Doug, keeping her hand on George's shoulder.

Doug nodded eagerly.

"Can I see my father now?"

"Yes, you can," the nurse said. "I'll take you to him. I'm Carol Mackenzie. I'm an intensive care nurse."

She looked quickly down at George, taking her hand from his shoulder. Her eyes had a tense look.

"I'll wait here," George said, looking up at her. "My wife's in surgery. They know to find me here."

"Yes, Mr. Underhill," the nurse replied gently. "I expect someone will be along to see you in a few minutes."

125

Nurse Mackenzie led Doug down a wide corridor, and then turned right into a smaller hallway ending at a pair of stainless-steel swinging doors.

"Do you know how Elizabeth Underhill is doing?" Douglas said.

"I'm sorry, but I can't help you with that information," Nurse Mackenzie replied cautiously. "You'll have to ask Mr. Underhill or someone else."

Douglas knew she was not sharing all that she knew. He was worried about 'Aunt' Elizabeth and concerned about the look in the nurse's eyes. He decided to let it pass for now. He was focused on making sure his dad was all right. As they reached the doors, a uniformed police officer stood. He'd been sitting on a folding metal chair beside the doors. He recognized Nurse Mackenzie and nodded.

A sign on the wall beside the policeman said, "Authorized Personnel Only."

Doug walked beside the nurse past several rooms. Windows formed the top half of the walls. Curtains were pulled on some. Others were empty, curtains open, beds neatly made. The curtains were drawn on the last room. The door was closed. Another police officer was posted at the door. He stood and nodded.

Nurse Mackenzie stopped and motioned Doug to go ahead. He opened the door slowly, apprehensive about what he might find inside. His mom and dad were sleeping as he walked into the room. Douglas saw his mom in a chair on the far side of the bed occupied by his sleeping dad. He tried to close the door quietly behind him, but the latch made a loud click as it closed.

Anne opened her eyes and saw Doug. She leapt from the chair, sending it banging into the wall behind her.

"Oh, Douglas," she said. "Oh, my! Are you all right? How did you get here?"

She rushed around the foot of Paul's bed to hug Doug.

The commotion woke Paul. He looked over and saw Anne, surprisingly happy, hugging their eldest son.

"What's all this racket about?" Paul managed to ask good naturedly, looking at both, their arms wrapped around each other. A tired smile blended with the questioning look on his face.

"Sorry, Dad. How you're doing? What happened?"

"I'm going to be okay, son," Paul said. "But we're not sure yet what this is all about. I'll tell you more about that later. How'd you get here?"

Doug looked at his mother.

"Paul," Anne said. "There's something I haven't told you. Douglas was kidnapped the day you were brought here."

"What?" Paul said, trying to sit up. "What in hell's going on?"

"Easy, my love," Anne said, worried about Paul. "He's here now. Douglas is safe. Nothing to worry about"

"I was in Livingston Valley, Dad," Doug said. "Someone roped me, tied me up and took me to an old shack down by Willow Creek. I got away. I'm okay."

"Do you know who it was?" Paul said.

"He looked kinda familiar," Douglas said. "I told the police all about it. They're looking for the guy. Spoke with a British accent, sorta like us."

"Douglas, we've got to let your dad sleep," Anne said. "He needs rest right now. You're safe and that's all that matters."

"Okay," Doug replied, looking over at his dad fighting to keep his eyes open. He had a feeling of suddenly being much older than his 14 years.

As Anne and Paul were making their goodbyes, a voice at the door interrupted them.

"I got here as soon as I could."

They looked up as Emily rushed into the room. Her face was lined with fatigue and worry. She stepped quickly over to her brother bedside, grabbing Anne's hand along the way.

"How you doin'?" she managed, fighting back tears. "You seem to keep getting into the darnedest scrapes, now don't you?"

Anne smiled at Emily, "Yes, and he hasn't gotten any better in that department. Seems I can't leave him unattended very long."

The two women exchanged smiles and kisses and hugs beside Paul's bed, each with a grip on his hand. His face bore a weary smile.

"Look, Emily, I'll fill you in on all that's happened in a minute," Anne said, looking down at her husband, struggling to keep his eyes open. "We need to let Paul rest."

She and Emily kissed Paul again. Doug gripped his father's hand gently. The three left the room. Anne turned off the lights and closed the door quietly behind them. Paul was already fast asleep.

As Doug, his mother and his Aunt Emily walked back toward the waiting room, his aunt's arm around his waist, Doug asked his mother, "What have you heard about Aunt Elizabeth? Is she going to be all right?"

"What? Is something going on with Elizabeth?" Emily interjected, alarmed. "What happened?"

"I need to tell you about that," Anne replied. "There's quite a lot you need to know."

As they arrived at the private waiting room, two uniformed police officers stood up from chairs placed outside the door. Standing with them were two large men in sport jackets with bulges under their left arms, armed security guards from Global Security International. John Everett had taken the initiative and hired them and a team of their colleagues to guard the Winstons immediately upon learning Paul had been shot. He knew Paul had Global on retainer and decided if Paul wasn't happy about what he'd done, his firm would foot the bill.

"Hello there," Anne said to the two officers, gesturing to the room. "We're going to be here for a while. We need to get a few hours rest."

The room was equipped with chairs, a couch, two single beds, a bathroom, and a small kitchenette.

Anne, Doug, and Emily walked into the room. All were exhausted. Anne hugged her eldest son again, and then explained.

"Elizabeth's been shot also," Anne said when the others were seated. "It happened this evening. We were on our way to the Hilton. I'm afraid, Elizabeth's in a very grave condition. She's been in surgery for hours. I might as well tell you now, the police think whoever did it may have been trying to shoot me."

Doug and Emily's eyes blinked and grew big with shocked surprise. Both were speechless.

"Yes, I know," Anne continued. "Something terrible is happening here. And no one seems to know what's going on."

Anne summarized what she had experienced and what little she knew about both shootings. Then Doug told an incredulous Emily about his kidnapping. Ten minutes later Anne said, "Now, we'd all better try to get some rest."

"I have a room at the Hilton," Emily said. "I sent my stuff ahead there with Jeremy and the twins. I'll come back here in the morning, see you and Paul, and hopefully drop in on Elizabeth for a moment. Then I'd like to go out to the ranch and see Christine and Michael. Would it be okay, Anne, if I brought them here?"

"Oh, yes, please, Emily," Anne answered. "Thank you. I was hoping you'd do that. I've been talking with them all along. They're anxious to see their father. And will you bring Douglas some clean clothes, please? I have some for myself over at the Hilton."

After Emily left, Anne turned to her son.

"Is that a tear in your new jeans, Douglas?" she asked. "How did that happen? Oh, never mind."

129

"I'm okay, Mom," Doug answered wearily.

"Well, okay," Anne replied. "But take off those dirty shoes and socks, and those jeans and your jacket and shirt. You can sleep in your underwear."

"I won't look," Anne added with a chuckle.

Both smiled. The humor was welcome.

"Yes, Mom."

He thought, *Some things don't ever change with moms.*

Anne and Doug crawled into the single beds and were asleep by the time their heads settled back on the pillows.

While they slept, a team of doctors feverishly worked to save Elizabeth's life.

Chapter Thirty-One

The man was furious. He was sitting in the dark shack, a prisoner. The kid he'd been holding for ransom had got away. The man was so angry he failed to recognize the irony in the role reversal.

It was pitch black outside, with no moon to provide light. The man found it almost impossible see anything inside the shack, and he'd used up all his matches to light the last of his cigarettes.

He tried pulling the old bed frame apart to make a tool to break out. It wouldn't come apart. He was strong but not strong enough. In the dark he could find nothing else to use. The sturdy sidepieces of the bed frame would have made good battering rams to break down the door, or pound the slats nailed over the only window. But he couldn't get them apart.

That goddamned kid! he thought. *Shit! I've got to get out of here before he tells the cops where to find me. Geez ... hope the little bugger ran out of gas. That'll slow him down.*

The man gingerly felt his way back to the boarded-up window he'd been working on. Wood planks were nailed across the window into the heavy frame. He peered out through cracks between the rough-hewn boards. He could see only darkness. His shoulders ached from banging one shoulder and then the other against the door after the kid had locked him in. His knuckles were bleeding from trying to work a window board back and forth. He hoped the rusted spikes might eventually give way and he'd be out. That is, if he could stand the pain. It hadn't worked. All he got were additional raw and bleeding knuckles.

He sat down on the bed for a rest.

"Oh, for Christ's sake!" he said out loud, jumping up.

A thought hit him.

Am I ever dumb!

He looked down. *The slats on the bed*! *Of course!*

The rough-finished boards were heavy and about the size of 2x6s. They once held a mattress.

Shit! Why the fuck didn't I think of that sooner? he asked himself.

He tipped the heavy bed upside down. Then he climbed up and jumped down on a slat. After repeated jumps in his heavy riding boots, the slat began to loosen. After more repeated jumps it finally came loose.

Right. There you go, he said to himself, feeling his way over to the boarded-up window with the 2x6 in his hand. The slat was almost four feet long.

He took a long swing with the 2x6, hitting one end of it on the bottom of a board. Once, twice, three times. The fourth time the board started to loosen. The man kept banging at the bottom of the board, slowly loosening it. After more repeated banging, the nails finally loosened and gave way. He pushed the heavy board out and up, bending the nails holding it at the top.

There was a gap between the next two boards. He jammed the bed slat between the second and third board, prying it sideways at the bottom. One of the nails holding it bent and then broke. He banged at the board with the end of the bed slat until the second nail came loose, then he pushed the second board out and up. The man righted the bed frame and pulled it over to the window. He climbed up. He was able to wiggle his head and shoulders through the gap. Then he lifted and pulled the rest of his body forward until he tumbled out onto the ground.

He was free! He looked around. Now what?

The man estimated he was fifteen to twenty miles from Colorado Springs. He had to get to the highway. He could see car headlights going by in the distance. There he'd flag a ride. But he would head away from Colorado Springs … as fast as he could.

The kid might have got to town by now, he thought. *If so, the cops'll be here pretty damned soon.*

He wasn't happy about having to hike across open country in the dark to the highway. The sounds of coyotes yelping made him shudder.

Damn it! He cursed himself.

The man had used up all the rounds in his gun trying to stop the kid and the pickup. The rest of the ammunition was in the truck's glove box, wherever it was. He decided he needed weapon, and the bed slat would have to do. It had nails in both ends. He stomped down the nails on one end so they wouldn't poke into his hand. The four-foot slat would have to do as a weapon in case the coyotes came too close. He tucked the gun in his belt just in case he came across the pickup. He knew it had been almost out of gas. The truck couldn't have got far. That's why he'd brought a can of gas back from town. He'd take that with him, too.

The highway looked to be two miles from the shack. He would have to walk down to the creek, wade across it and then make his way through a field of wild brush and rock and shallow ravines in the dark to reach the highway.

It wasn't an inviting prospect.

What the hell, the man thought. *When I get to the highway, I'll hitch a ride. Then at least I'll be outta here for good!*

He allowed himself a grim smile.

133

Chapter Thirty-Two

Colorado Springs

Anne felt her shoulder being shaken. She struggled to emerge from a deep sleep.

Anne looked up.

It was Susan Willis. Susan had been trained to succeed Elizabeth as director of the home school program based at Two-Dot Ranch after Elizabeth retired.

It was obvious she'd been crying. Her eyes were red and swollen. Susan's distress shocked Anne wide-awake. A terrible thought flashed through her mind – Susan must have bad news about Paul.

"I'm sorry to wake you, Anne," Susan said, crouching low beside Anne's bed, barely able to keep herself under control.

"It's Elizabeth," Susan added, her voice cracking. She wiped her eyes then her nose with a tissue.

"I'm so sorry!" Susan broke into heavy sobs.

"We lost her," Susan managed, her voice barely more than a squeak. "She's gone, Anne! Elizabeth's gone. We lost her. She died on the operating table this morning."

"Oh God, NO!" Anne shouted, bolting upright in bed. "It can't be! I thought she ... I hoped she was going to be all right. Oh, no! Oh, no! Oh my god! This can't be!"

Doug was startled awake by his mother's anguished cries.

"What is it, Mom?" he asked, sitting upright in bed. "Is Dad all right?"

"It's Mrs. Underhill," Susan said gently to Doug, reaching over to put her hand on his shoulder, tears flowing down both her cheeks. "I'm afraid we lost her. She passed away a few hours ago.

"I apologize for not waking you sooner," Susan said, turning back to Anne. "You needed some sleep. I hope you're okay with that."

"Yes, of course, Susan," Anne answered absently though her grief. "There wasn't much I could do. Oh, Elizabeth! Oh, my god! Poor George!"

Doug slipped on his jeans and went over to sit beside his weeping mother on her bed, putting his arm around her. She put her head on his shoulder, weeping uncontrollably in great heaving sobs. Susan sat on the other side and put her arm around Anne's waist. The tears kept coming.

"Where's George?" Anne finally managed.

"He's with her now," Susan replied. "I left them a few minutes ago. They've moved her, uh, her body into a private room."

"I must go to him," Anne said.

Susan replied, "Maybe you should wait for a bit, Anne. When I left them, George asked to be alone with Elizabeth for a little while."

"Yes, of course. You're right," Anne said through her tears. "How can this be? She was talking to me as they brought her into Emergency. I just can't believe it. Oh, Elizabeth. Oh, my god!"

"Anne, Dr. Shepherd told me they did everything humanly possible," Susan said. "There was just too much damage.

"He told me Elizabeth was on a heart-lung machine for more than five hours while they worked on her. I'm sure they did the best they could. Dr. Shepherd said the bullet caused massive damage to her heart and shattered an artery. Then it tore a big hole in her lung and came out below her left arm," Susan added.

"The doctor said Elizabeth had lost a lot of blood even before they got her into surgery. Apparently Elizabeth had a rare blood type, B negative, I think he said. It's really sad. The hospital doesn't have any blood of that type. And it has no record of any potential donors.

"I'm so sorry, Anne," Susan added, "I'm just rambling on. This is the worst thing that's ever happened to me. Elizabeth was like a wonderful aunt to me. She was so much help when I had my miscarriages. Oh, my!"

Susan broke down sobbing again.

"Yes, please forgive me, Susan." Anne replied. "I'm so very sorry. I know how much you loved and admired Elizabeth, too. She will be a terrible loss to all of us."

After Susan had earned her teaching certificate, Elizabeth mentored her to take over the home-schooling program after she and George retired. It became an important focus for Susan after two miscarriages and a stern warning from doctors made it clear to her and Kurt that another pregnancy could threaten her life. Susan decided to have her tubes tied and devote herself to teaching. She became fully absorbed in working with the children attending Elizabeth's home-schooling program. When the day came for Susan to take over, it would end almost three decades of Elizabeth's leadership.

Elizabeth had founded home schooling for grades one to nine at Two-Dot Ranch long before the school bus program began. It simply carried on. The program originally provided an education for her and George's two children, for Paul and his two younger sisters, and for the children of area farmers and ranchers. A succession of students had followed.

She was like a favorite aunt to Paul's sisters and loved them like her own daughter Kathleen as all three blossomed from children into beautiful young women. She and daughter Kathleen accompanied Catherine when she took her daughters to be fitted for their first training bras, explained to them the facts of life, and listened with understanding and affection as each shared their own special tales of first loves and first heartbreaks.

She also tolerated with good humor the endless pranks that Paul and her son Chester had played on her and the girls while the kids were growing up. She was often exasperated and sometimes secretly amused by Paul and Chester's shenanigans, but she loved both dearly just the same. When Catherine was away, Elizabeth tended to the boys' medical emergencies as each somehow miraculously survived their exuberant boyhood, becoming young men to be admired. She was fiercely protective and proud of all five children.

Elizabeth knew the time had come for new leadership to take over. She had taken comfort in knowing that the home-schooling program she took such pride in would continue under the capable direction of her protégé, Susan Willis.

Chapter Thirty-Three

Colorado Springs Police Department

"Okay, folks, let's see what we've got here."

Lt. Dan Lorente was in the squad room of the Colorado Springs Police Department.

He was briefing a special task force investigating the murder of Elizabeth Underhill, the shooting of Officer Bill Thornton and the attempted murders of Paul and Anne Winston. Lorente had been filling in for his vacationing colleague, Lt. Nick O'Donnell, when the shootings occurred. Now with a homicide involved, he would continue with the case.

Lorente also briefed the task force on the kidnapping of 14-year-old Douglas Winston and how he had escaped. They knew that was a El Paso County case. He said the sheriff's department was working with the FBI on that investigation and would keep them informed.

Lorente told the investigators that from all appearances, the three shooting cases in Colorado Springs were linked. The trouble was they had no suspects and few leads.

"Based on what little ballistics we have to go on right now, we believe Mr. Winston was shot with an antique gun. Rifling marks on the bullet fragments are consistent with a weapon of that vintage. Mrs. Underhill and Officer Thornton were shot with a .30-06 rifle," Lorente added. "Home-made hollow point bullets were used in the second shooting.

"My guess is the two shootings are not a coincidence. Let's operate on the assumption that they are related ... same shooter, different weapons. In terms of motive, it appears likely that Mrs. Underhill and Officer Thornton were shot by mistake, that the perpetrator's target was Mrs. Winston. The ultimate motive of the shooter is unknown at this time.

"We also know that our prime suspect in the shooting of Mr. Winston is male, probably Caucasian, and speaks with a British accent. That probably covers a couple of hundred residents of the area, so you'd think that should narrow things down. So far, though, we've not been able to identify any person of interest that might fit that description.

"Also unfortunately, we don't have a solid physical description," Lorente continued. "Mr. Winston was able to give a partial description to the paramedics at the scene. Evidently he was down and losing consciousness by the time he saw the shooter. We have one witness, but he didn't see the shooter. He was in a vehicle parked three cars from the shooting."

Lorente said the witness heard a shot, and then a pause. Then he heard two more shots and a man's voice shouting something. It was with a British accent, possibly an upper-class English accent. The detective added that three shell casings were found scattered for two blocks along the sidewalk where Paul was shot.

"We think the shooter may have been trying to reload on the run as he was making his escape," Lorente said.

A civilian employee entered the room and handed Lorente a file.

"We've just received a preliminary analysis of the shell casings and the rifling marks," he said. "They indicate the gun likely is a Webley Mk IV revolver or something similar. They were issued to British and other allied army officers during and after the Second World War. They're popular with collectors. We're asking other police forces and the FBI whether such a weapon has been reported in other crimes. The FBI is also checking with law enforcement agencies in Britain.

"Enlarged photos of rifling marks taken from the fragments of bullets recovered from Mr. Winston are accompanying the request," he added. "We're not optimistic. The fragments are not in good condition."

Lorente said the bullets that hit Mrs. Underhill and Const. Thornton went through them. Fragments found in the police car confirmed they were crudely made hollow point bullets. Although they were amateurish they still were able to cause extreme damage. Those fragments were also being sent for forensic analysis and to be photographed.

"One last thing, folks. I don't need to tell you the Winstons and the Underhills are highly respected members of our community. We're under a lot of pressure to get some answers and get them fast. I had a call just before this meeting from the chief. He's getting pressure from the mayor, some members of city council and a few of our prominent businesspeople.

"Okay, folks, that's all for now. We'll meet back here tomorrow at 0800 hours."

Chapter Thirty-Four

While Paul was recovering, another scene was unfolding across town involving Philip Tremblay, one of Paul's most trusted business partners.

"I don't give a shit what you want from us!" a drunk Gerald Horner was shouting at Philip. "We're not selling you any fuckin' drilling rights to anything!

"Not one fucking acre!" Horner screamed at him. "Got that? Nothing! Now get the fuck outta here. Go home, goddamn it!"

Philip was meeting with Harvey and Gerald Horner in the Governor's Suite of the Antlers Hilton.

Gerald pushed himself up unsteadily to his imposing six-foot, three-inch height. He staggered drunkenly toward the door. Philip and Harvey stood and followed.

Without warning, Gerald whirled and threw a punch at the shorter oilman. Philip saw it coming out of the corner of his eye. He was able to duck and spin away just in time, throwing himself off balance. Gerald leapt forward with surprisingly agility, considering how drunk he was. He grabbed Philip from behind, pinning his arms to his sides. The tall rancher lifted Philip off his feet and started carrying him toward the sliding glass patio door to the 11th-floor balcony. The door was open.

"I'm gonna throw you ... you little fucker, right off that balcony and be done with you," Gerald growled.

Philip almost gagged at the nauseating odor on Gerald's breath wafting over his right shoulder. It reeked of liquor, cigar smoke and bad teeth.

"You don't want to do this," Philip protested, trying to get free from Gerald's steel-hard grip. "Put me down, you idiot! Put me down right now!"

Harvey moved quickly, placing himself between his brother and the patio door. Gerald was holding the slender five-foot, 10-inch Philip four inches off the floor.

"Hold on, Gerry," Harvey said. "I'm not finished talking with Philip. Put him down, damn it. Go back to our suite. Please, Gerry. Do it! I'll see you there later."

Although Gerald outweighed Harvey by at least 40 pounds, the commanding presence of his older brother intimidated him. Harvey was hoping his inebriated brother would return to their two-bedroom suite, pour himself another drink and either calm down or pass out.

Gerald reluctantly put a relieved Philip down on his feet. He staggered out of the room cursing obscenities, slamming the door as he left.

Chapter Thirty-Five

"Oh, Elizabeth," George said quietly. "I never should have let you go with Anne."

George felt deeply that it was his fault, that he was the cause of her death. He sat beside Elizabeth's body, facing her. They were in a private room provided by the hospital's palliative care unit for this purpose, for saying goodbye to loved ones.

Elizabeth's eyes were closed. Her lifeless face, elegant even in death, looked serene. George held her cold, limp right hand in his two big weather-worn hands. Her left hand rested on her chest, her wedding band still in place. He knew she wasn't there anymore, knew that somehow he had to accept that Elizabeth was gone. He was seeing a shell, but his emotions kept control, demanding that he not give himself permission to believe it. The void he was feeling was beyond his ability to fathom, beyond his comprehension. A black, bottomless pit of despair wracked his soul, leaving him desperately empty, adrift in a dark and fearsome void.

George wanted to scream, 'NO! NO! NO!' He knew it would do no good. It wouldn't bring her back. It wouldn't undo what had been done. The woman he loved and cherished for 30 years, the mother of their children, was no longer beside him. George blamed himself. For one thing, if he'd not let her accompany Anne to the hotel, Elizabeth would still be here. There was nothing he could do now to bring her back to him, but he could do something about whoever had caused her death. He swore that he would find them and deal with them, even if the police got there first. He'd find a way.

For now, would he ever be able to forgive himself? How could he ever expect their children to forgive him? He knew that he was going to anguish over Elizabeth's death every minute until the day he died.

Chapter Thirty-Six

"Look, Philip, I apologize for my brother," Harvey began. "I'm afraid he can get a bit out of sorts at times."

Philip was strongly inclined to agree as he struggled to calm himself.

Harvey's younger brother Gerald had just threatened to throw him off the 11th-floor balcony of a meeting room in the Antlers Hilton Hotel. Harvey had managed to talk his drunken brother into going back to their suite so that he and Philip could meet calmly. Philip wanted to purchase leases to explore for oil on the Horner property.

The Horner brothers' personalities could hardly have been more different, yet they were fiercely loyal to each other. Gerald was a hard-working, heavy-drinking, tough-talking, thoroughly unrepentant redneck. He operated the family's 2,500-acre ranch near Colorado Springs. His older brother Harvey was a kindly and highly respected family physician who led a highly successful medical clinic in Denver.

As the eldest, Harvey was their father's choice to succeed him, but Harvey was more interested in medicine. He'd convinced their father to mentor his younger brother instead. Gerald wanted nothing more than to raise cattle. He was forever grateful to Harvey. They inherited joint ownership of the ranch after their parents died. Harvey left most of the day-to-day operations to Gerald. Drilling rights and financial matters were among the few exceptions.

"Sure, Harvey," Philip said, as they both sat at the meeting table. "God, I'm glad you stepped in. Our landman, Martin Jacobs, told me Gerald got quite nasty during his visit. Threatened to pull a gun. I guess he gets worked up over oil and gas exploration and drilling around here."

"Yes, he does," Harvey admitted. "You've got to understand, Philip, we've had some nasty experiences with oil and gas crews. That's no excuse for threats like that, but it's a fact.

"Last summer, we lost a champion bull," Harvey continued. "Cost us $35,000. Gerald blames an oil service crew. They were driving their rigs across a corner of our ranch without permission. Cut a barbed wire fence twice. Thought no one would notice. Apparently the bull did. That crew didn't know it, but they were trespassing in a breeding field. Guess the bull didn't like anyone invading his harem. He could be very aggressive. Gerald found him with a bullet hole between his eyes."

"Good heavens!" Philip said. "I'm really sorry about that, Harvey. I'll admit there are some bad ones in our business. For what it's worth, that's not how my company does business. We get permits and we get permission. All my seismic or drilling contractors who enter land without permission know they will be fired. No exceptions. It's in all our contracts."

"I know, Philip," Harvey answered. "Look, let's see if we can get together on this. Jacobs did some good work for both of us, I think. You leave Gerald to me."

In three hours, the men had worked out an agreement that each considered a win-win.

Five weeks later, Continental Del Rio spudded its first well on the Horner brothers' ranch. It would lead to one of the largest crude oil discoveries in Colorado history.

The Maidstone Conspiracy

Chapter Thirty-Seven

The door to Paul's hospital room was open, and two large men in blazers were standing in the hall. They nodded as Anne and Doug walked in to find Paul sitting up in bed.

"Well, good morning you two," Paul beamed to the startled duo. "Come here, my love. I need a big kiss! It sure feels good to be sitting up. The nurses had me take a few steps a few minutes ago. We're on our way!"

Anne was relieved. It was obvious that he hadn't heard about Elizabeth.

Anne went over and gave him a kiss and a long careful hug. Doug gave his dad a gentle hug. Both were reserved. Anne searched around in her mind for a way to tell Paul about Elizabeth. She was dreading it.

"It's so wonderful to see you're feeling better," Anne said.

Her face was drawn, and her eyes red. Anne didn't know how to begin to tell him about what had happened to the kind and gentle woman whom he loved like a dear aunt for virtually all of his life.

Paul could see Anne and Doug were troubled. He took the initiative.

"Are you two all right?" Paul asked. They were clearly distraught about something more than his condition. He had to know.

"Has something upset you? What is it?" he asked.

"Oh, Paul!" Anne sobbed, breaking down. "There's something I've not told you. I'm so sorry. It's very bad ... it's horrible!

"Paul ..." Anne paused. "It's Elizabeth. She was shot here in the parking lot last night."

Paul's eyes conveyed his surprise.

147

"Is she all right?" he said.

"I'm ... I'm so very sorry, Paul." Anne's voice was a high-pitched croak as she struggled to get the words out. "Oh god, Paul. Elizabeth ... we lost her ... they couldn't save her ... she passed away early this morning."

"WHAT?" Paul was shocked to his very core. He looked at Anne in utter disbelief.

"This can't be, Anne! I can't believe this. There's got to be some mistake. There has to be!"

Anne sat on the edge of the bed and put her arms around Paul. She held him as tightly as she dared with his injuries. She ran her right hand gently over his head and down the back of his neck, trying to sooth his shock and grief.

"Oh, how I wish it wasn't so, my love," she sobbed.

"Oh please, Anne," Paul managed, his voice little more than a deep rattle, barely a whisper. He lowered his head. Wet spots appeared on the blanket. "This can't be. Oh, my god! This just can't be."

It was the first time Doug had seen his father cry. The sound of his father's grief almost broke his heart. Struggling for control, Doug sought comfort in what his dad had told him just last night ... that it was all right to show his emotions. It seemed so long ago now. Doug had been embarrassed about breaking down, telling his father about Tippy being shot.

"I want you to remember something, son," his father had told him. "Very few men have the courage to show their emotions. Most cannot. It's very hard for many men somehow. It's very sad, but they're slaves to that macho stuff."

Seeing Paul grieving, Doug's pride in his father rose higher than ever. They'd both dropped the stepfather/stepson thing years ago. Paul was his father, period. He understood once again why he wanted to emulate this man he'd come to admire and, yes, to love.

After a few minutes, Paul lifted his head and looked into Anne's grief-stricken face. His eyes conveyed utter devastation. She'd never seen him in such anguish. They were silent for a long time. The three of them each were caught up in their own grief and the grief of the other two.

"Anne," Paul said at last. "Can you tell me how this happened?"

"Okay, Paul, if you're feeling up to it."

He nodded.

She summarized the two shootings in the hospital parking lot.

"The police think the person who did it ..." Anne paused. "The police think the person who did this awful thing was actually trying to shoot me."

"WHAT?" Paul exclaimed, his voice almost a shout despite his weak state. "Good god, Anne! What the hell is going on? What are the police doing? To protect you, I mean. And the kids?"

"It's okay, Paul." Anne answered, trying to calm him. "The police have guards on this unit, and they're assigned to all of us. And John Everett has asked Global Security to provide 24-hour protection for all of us. Frankly, I don't like it one bit, but I suppose it's necessary until they find out who did this."

"Yes, it is!" Paul said

"Where's George, now?" Paul asked. "I have to go see him. He'll need us. Oh, my god, what a terrible thing! This is awful!"

"Douglas, please go see if you can get me a wheelchair or something, will you?" Paul asked. "And see if you can find out where George is. Okay, son?"

"I'm here, Paul."

George stood unsteadily in the doorway of the hospital room, leaning on the doorframe for support. Before them stood the personification of a man with a broken heart ... a broken man.

James Osborne

The big rancher's rugged face was drawn and haggard. It was stained with the tears that no longer came. Deep lines were etched into his forehead and cheeks, and around his eyes and mouth. His eyes were bloodshot. He had that vacant look of the lost; the light in his eyes was gone. George had aged 10 years overnight.

Anne ran over and put her arms around his midsection. She pressed her head against his large chest.

"Oh, George!" Her cry was muffled.

He put his hands on her shoulders and held her for a moment, looking over at Paul. The two men exchanged long silent looks, their faces displaying the abject devastation that racked their hearts.

George walked over to the bed. Paul struggled to get out of bed, still connected to IV tubes. George stopped him. The two men embraced awkwardly. Their eyes were full. Neither could say anything meaningful to comfort the other.

For each, Elizabeth's loss was incomprehensible. It was an indescribable tragedy too horrible for the words that both struggled to find and couldn't.

Chapter Thirty-Eight

The charge nurse on duty at the ICU unit recognized Anne from the previous day.

"Good morning, Mrs. Winston," the nurse began. "We're just delighted to hear that Mr. Winston is recovering so well.

"It's wonderful," she added. "You know his room is in the secure section?"

"Yes," Anne replied. "I've just come from his room.

"Thank you, ah, Nurse Hernandez," she added, glancing at the nurse's nametag. It said *Janine Hernandez, BSc RN*.

"Please call me Janine," she replied. "I want to tell you, Mrs. Winston, your husband has a very special place in my heart, in my family's heart, that is."

Anne looked at the nurse with a mix of surprise and curiosity.

"Eleven years ago, Mrs. Winston, your husband arranged for my son to go to the Mayo Clinic in Rochester," the nurse said, her eyes glistening with emotion.

"Ramon had a hole in his heart. He was 12. He would have died without the operation. We couldn't afford it. Mr. Winston heard about us and paid for the whole thing, even our travel, hotel and living expenses. Isn't that something?"

Anne was stunned. But that was her Paul.

It's so like him to do something like that, she thought.

"He made us promise to tell no one," Janine continued. "Oh, I want you to know we haven't said anything to anyone. Not a soul. And we won't. But I'm sure he wouldn't mind if I told you about it."

"I'm sure he won't mind at all," Anne assured her.

"Mrs. Winston," Janine continued, her voice dropping to a soothing tone, "I heard about Mrs. Underhill. I'm so very, very sorry. Please accept my deepest sympathies.

"I know you were very close to Mr. and Mrs. Underhill. Some of my colleagues had the privilege of knowing her too. They admired her very much. They say she was pretty special."

"Yes, she was. Thank you, Janine," Anne responded, fighting to maintain her composure. "That's … very kind of you.

"If you don't mind, I'd like to check on someone else in ICU, if I may. Can you tell me how Officer Bill Thornton is doing? He was hurt at the same time as Mrs. Underhill."

Anne's voice began breaking with emotion.

"Oh, yes, Mrs. Winston," she replied, sensing Anne's distress. "Let me have a quick look. Here it is. Officer Thornton's in Room 327. He's recovering quite well, and he's being discharged later today."

She looked up and smiled reassuringly at Anne.

"Thank you," Anne replied. "I'm so relieved he's doing well. Thank you very much."

"Oh, and Mrs. Winston," Janine added, "I want you to know you don't need to worry one bit about Mr. Winston's care while he's here with us. We're going to make sure we take extra special care of him. You can count on it!"

As she walked back toward Paul's room, Anne felt a warm glow from the nurse's comments. It helped ease the burdens weighing heavily on her heart.

She took a detour to Room 327. After a brief visit to deliver her heart-felt thanks in person to Officer Thornton, Anne completed her return trip back to Paul's room.

Chapter Thirty-Nine

Maidstone, England

Reggie Winston was drunk again.

Another of his frequent benders was underway. It was 9 o'clock Wednesday night. He'd been in The White Rabbit pub in Maidstone since noon. Everyone was curious where he'd been for the past two months.

When he'd arrived, Reggie claimed he'd just returned from a business venture. He offered no details except a few vague references about America and Australia. No one paid any attention. They did notice, and benefit from, the extra money he seemed willing to spend.

Earlier that evening, before Reggie became too inebriated, the pub had ceremoniously dedicated a bar stool in his honor, that is, in honor of the amount of money he spent there. A plaque with his name on it graced the backrest. Beneath his name was engraved, "A faithful patron. Bottoms Up!" It was all the excuse Reggie needed to launch into yet another bender.

The pub had located Reggie's stool strategically as far out of the way as it could. His stool was at the end of the bar, against a far wall. The lighting was dim, and the background music and sounds from other patrons tended to drown out his frequent drunken outbursts.

Reggie's sometimes girlfriend, Isabelle Raleigh, was passed out in a booth at the back of the pub. The owner had turned off the lights in that section. It was a quiet night anyway. Reggie eased himself off his barstool and made his way, staggering around tables, to the back of the pub to where Isabelle was asleep.

"Right. C'mon Izzy," Reggie slurred as he shook her roughly by her shoulder. "Itz time ta go 'ome!"

He stumbled out into the night. Isabelle made her way out behind him, still drunk and barely awake. His car was parked on a side street somewhere, but Reggie couldn't quite remember. He walked up and down a few streets looking for it, becoming more and more agitated. Isabelle followed, complaining.

"C'mon Reggie. Fer Christ's sake, I 'ave ta pee," she said. "Where the hell's your damn car?"

"Awe, shut the fuck up," Reggie growled at her. "We'll find the damned thing."

Finally, they came upon the car. A multitude of parking tickets flapped in the night breeze under the wiper blade.

"Bloody hell!" Reggie exploded when he saw the parking tickets. "Why can't those fuckin' assholes leave a guy alone for once?"

He grabbed the tickets, leaned back unsteadily against the car, and ripped them in half. He threw the pieces up in the air, scattering them on the street. Passersby looked at the disheveled couple, clearly intoxicated, some with amusement and others with distain.

Swaying back and forth, Reggie tried repeatedly to get his key in the car door lock. Finally, he succeeded and crawled into the driver's seat. He started the car and began pulling away. Suddenly an image leapt into the car's headlights. It was Isabelle. He'd almost driven away without her. And he'd almost driven over her.

At that moment a passing police car made a U-turn and pulled up beside Reggie's car, its blue and red lights began flashing.

Later, police records showed Reginald Winston had been an unruly 'overnight guest' in the Maidstone Police holding cells, also known less elegantly as the drunk tank, on more than one occasion. This time, while sobering up, he kept babbling something about an American owing him thousands of U.S. dollars and that he was going to get even.

During his ravings, Reggie kept saying it wasn't his fault the shooting in America didn't go as planned. The young constable on duty at the time naively assumed Reggie had been on a hunting trip to America, a pursuit popular among the gentry and other well-off residents of Kent County.

Chapter Forty

Colorado Springs

George paused for a long moment in front of the house he'd shared with Elizabeth for more than 30 years. Most of their life together had been centered here, and now it was over. He stood unsteadily at the bottom of the four steps leading up to the veranda, his mind in a vortex of emotional turmoil.

I have to do this, he told himself.

"George?" Paul said gently. "Are you ready for this? Why don't you come stay with us for a few days?"

George shook his head 'no'. His back was to them.

Anne stood beside Paul. She held his left arm firmly in her two hands. Paul shared the grief and emotional torment of this man he so admired and revered. He was beset with feelings of helplessness, wishing he could somehow ease the pain of the man who over the decades had become all but family. This man had been his father's friend, and since his own childhood had been a mentor, almost as close to him as his own father. George's grief broke Paul's heart.

"Yeah!" George sighed sadly. "Gotta do this."

He was okay with Paul and Anne being there. They gave him comfort. But he was also relieved they were standing behind him. He didn't want them to see how the grief and agony tearing at his soul kept bringing tears coursing down his cheeks. George took a deep breath, struggling for control. He unconsciously squared his shoulders, tightened his chest, and clenched his teeth.

"I'll be okay," he said over his shoulder to Paul and Anne, knowing he wasn't quite as confident as he sounded. "I'll be okay."

Four steps.

His feet were like heavy lead weights as he forced himself up the steps to the top, his left hand gripping the handrail. He made his way along the covered veranda to the back door, shadows concealing from Paul and Anne the wetness on his face. The doorway opened to the kitchen.

George pulled open the screen door first and held it with his right foot. Then he opened the wood door with the big window in the top half. The inside of the window was dressed with lacey curtains. His heart shuddered. Elizabeth had replaced those curtains just before Paul and Anne had moved back from England.

He remembered what Elizabeth had said to him at the time:

I just want to spruce things up a bit for them, George. You know, she'd said turning on her radiant smile and chuckling. Elizabeth had done the same 'sprucing up' for Paul and Anne in the big fieldstone ranch house.

That was just like Elizabeth.

George replayed again in his mind's eye her sweet endearing smile. It had warmed his heart every time she'd smiled at him. A turmoil of emotions tugged at his very being, making his eyes glisten again. It was all past tense now. George walked on into the kitchen. Elizabeth's apron was draped across the back of the chair she'd always sat in, just as she'd left it.

He remembered: The moment they'd got the call about Paul being shot Elizabeth had whipped the apron over her head. She threw it absently across the back of the chair as she rushed out the kitchen door to find and comfort Anne. That was so like her, too. She always felt compelled to bring her generous comfort to those who were hurting, even in her own moments of distress.

157

James Osborne

George sat down heavily in the chair where he'd always sat, across from Elizabeth. Now just her empty chair was there … and her apron, without the life and spirit of its owner. He took a deep breath. Then another. A terrible weight kept tugging at his heart. He took another deep breath. Each breath brought none of the relief his mind had kept telling him that it would, somehow.

I suppose this is the way it's gonna be from now on, he told himself. It brought no comfort. *I just gotta learn to deal with it.*

He repeated to himself, *I gotta do this. I just gotta do this.*

A mix of urgent emotions continued to swirl within him. He was enraged with the person who had done this to Elizabeth. Devastated that her life was cut too short too soon. Frustrated for being so helpless to save her. Grieving over losing the woman he'd loved for more than 30 years. He felt overwhelming guilt.

And he felt emptiness. There would be no life together in retirement, the life they'd planned for and had so looked forward to. Now she … they would never experience it. He also recognized the self-pity for his loss and over the lonely life that lay before him. He felt bewildered, confused, and terribly disoriented. He felt incomplete. Half of his life, half of his soul, half of his heart – their whole life as they'd lived it – had been ripped away in a nanosecond of insanity.

How are the kids ever going to cope? he asked himself. *How are we ever going to get through this? Will they ever forgive me?*

George remembered a friend who'd lost his wife once telling him, "The pain never leaves me, George. But I hope with time that maybe one day I'll learn how to manage it better." George didn't think time was going to help him much.

Paul and Anne remained at the foot of the stairs for a few minutes, just in case. They had watched with deep sorrow as George made his way laboriously into the house and closed the door.

"He needs some time alone, Paul," Anne said, her eyes filling. "This has got to be terribly difficult for him, but he needs to do this alone. Only he can do it."

"Yes, I know," he replied softly. "I wish I could do something for him, anything to help him. I feel utterly helpless."

"Paul, maybe just knowing you're here, knowing we're here," Anne said. "I'm sure it helps."

"When do their kids get here?" Paul asked.

He was referring to the arrival of George and Elizabeth's children for their mother's funeral. Their youngest child, Kathleen, was teaching human anatomy at the University of Colorado School of Medicine in Aurora, CO. Their son Chester was a chemical engineer working at a 3M research facility in Silicon Valley.

"Kathy will be here tomorrow morning," Anne replied. "I understand Chet's on his way."

Paul and Anne turned and walked toward their own house across the large, grassed yard where the welcoming party Elizabeth had organized was held such a short time ago. Their own three children stood on the veranda, watching their parents walk the distance between the houses.

Seeing their children, it occurred to Anne they could be a great help to George in the weeks and months ahead. Once the funeral and the gatherings of family and friends were over there would be a huge void. George would need something to focus on, to distract him from his grief. After Paul and his family had arrived from England, Elizabeth 'recruited' George to teach each of the children about horseback riding, ranching, and what they needed to know about the outdoors. Continuing this could provide George with a much-needed distraction.

Now, at the foot of the steps to their home, Anne looked up proudly and lovingly at their three children standing at the veranda railing, smiling uncertainly back down at them.

It pleased her that Catherine was already showing signs of becoming an accomplished rider. And she was proud of how skilled her daughter had become with a rifle. It amused Anne to contemplate what Catherine's grandmother in England would think of her eight-year-old granddaughter handling a Winchester rifle like a cowhand.

No daughter of mine is going to be content just to cook and have babies, she'd told herself many times. Anne frequently reminded Catherine that she had the right and the ability to do and to be anything she chose. Catherine seemed to have taken the advice to heart.

Michael was going to be the developer in the family. He was forever involved in planning or constructing corrals and buildings. When they needed to find him, Michael was either helping George and Kurt build something, writing up proposals or drawing plans on the drafting desk in his room.

And their eldest son constantly amazed Paul and Anne. They knew Douglas' teachers in England considered him gifted, and maybe he was. He was only 14, but he was already thinking and acting like an experienced rancher and entrepreneur. They could see also that Douglas had a shrewd mind for business.

Chapter Forty-One

London Metropolitan Police Service
(a.k.a., New Scotland Yard)
London, England

Superintendent Charles Archibald answered an unusual phone call from the FBI in the United States.

Someone named Special Agent Richard Gervais wanted The Yard's help with tracking down fingerprints lifted from a Winchester rifle and identifying labels on a coat the gun was wrapped in. Two boys had found the rifle and coat near a landfill, just outside a city called Colorado Springs in America

"Witnesses to a shooting in Colorado Springs lead us to believe the shooter had a British accent," Agent Gervais told him. "The forensic evidence isn't as good as we'd like, but the rifle is at the very least consistent with that shooting, and the labels in the coat are from a British company."

"Email us those fingerprints and a close-up photo of the label," Superintendent Archibald said. "Where did you say that was? Could you spell that for me, Agent Gervais? Yes, okay, Colorado."

"Got it," Archibald said. "Spanish, you say? How interesting. Means 'colored red'? Really? Right you are, then."

Archibald rather liked the sound of the youthful FBI agent on the other end of the phone. And he especially liked the opportunity, however accidental, of dipping his toe into a genuine investigation again.

"I'll have one of our inspectors have a go at these and get back to you," Archibald said. "We'll be in touch, Special Agent Gervais. Cheers!"

Chapter Forty-Two

Colorado Springs

Paul and Anne had completed their sad walk across the big yard from George's house. They knew George needed time to himself. Besides, Anne wanted Paul to rest before supper. He'd been out of hospital for only a week, staying at the Colorado Springs home they'd bought recently. He shouldn't have been discharged that early considering his injuries, but he'd been adamant. George had agreed to stay with them in case Anne needed help. Besides, Paul was determined to attend Elizabeth's funeral, and he did.

They were standing below the veranda greeting their three children when the front door opened. A woman Paul didn't recognize walked out. She smiled slightly and waved at Anne, and then stepped behind the children. The woman placed her hands affectionately on Catherine and Michael's shoulders. Douglas stood maturely to one side by himself.

Paul's first thought was the woman must be part of the Global Security detail that was still watching over all of them wherever they went. He admitted to himself that he was growing tired of being shadowed all the time but comforted that Anne and the children were being protected. George had adamantly refused any security.

"Oh, Paul," Anne said. "This is Elsie's first day."

"First day?" Paul asked. "Elsie?"

"Yes. Elsie's our new housekeeper," Anne replied, squaring her shoulders. Paul knew the look. Anne was up to something.

"I'm going to spend some time helping Susan with home-schooling, and most of all I'm going to help out managing our businesses like we discussed. You okay with that, Paul, now that George has retired?"

"More than okay, my love," Paul answered, his face lighting up with pride. "It's great! But what brought this on?"

"Oh, you know, we've talked about me getting more active in our business interests," Anne said. "And that way I'll be using my business degree. I've been thinking about what I wanted to do ever since Michael started school full time. After we moved here, well, it just became obvious what that was."

While pregnant with Catherine, Anne had completed a master's degree in management at the London School of Economics. At the time, Paul wondered what that was all about. Now he knew, and he was proud of his ambitious life partner.

"Anyway, I want you to meet Elsie," Anne said. "She's so sweet."

They mounted the steps. Anne introduced her as Elsie Solomon. The name sounded familiar. Before he could ask, he was distracted when Emily joined them on the veranda, wearing an apron over a gingham dress, and a big mischievous smile. Emily was carrying what looked like a freshly baked lemon sponge pudding. It was one of Emily's baking specialties. That was partly because it was Paul's absolute favorite dessert. Anne and Emily both knew it. Paul quickly realized he was the object of an in-house conspiracy, something to do with Elsie's employment.

Emily's dessert appeared just in time. She was leaving the next morning for Somerville, returning to her husband Jeremy, their newly adopted twins, and her elementary school teaching job. She'd spent the last 10 days doing everything she could to help Anne, the children and George, after Paul was shot and Elizabeth murdered. That evening, Paul, Anne, Emily and the three children had supper together. Paul thoroughly enjoyed his lemon sponge pudding. Elsie had returned to Colorado Springs and the apartment she shared with her husband Marvin.

Later, Anne explained her plan was for Elsie to work at the ranch house three days a week and two days a week at their home in Colorado Springs. She said Elsie came highly recommended by Richard and Kathleen Brownlee, former neighbors of the Two-Dot Ranch. Elsie had worked for the Brownlees as a housekeeper for the past eight years. Now they would be living with their daughter and her husband and no longer needed Elsie's help.

"Mrs. Brownlee's quite ill, you see," Anne explained. "She's suffering from Alzheimer's. Very sad. And her husband has a heart condition. Allison and her husband – they've just married – are moving her parents in with them so they can help look after her mom. Isn't that quite something for newlyweds to do?"

"Yes, indeed," Paul replied, trying not to sound too smug. "I know."

"What? How could you possibly know that?" Anne asked, surprised at her husband for being so up to date on local gossip.

"John Everett is Allison's husband," Paul confessed. "He told me all about it, love … before all this trouble started. Remember, I mentioned that I'd hired John as our new personal and company lawyer? He told me about Allison and her parents. John's quite the guy, I must say. I think we're going to like him a lot, and so will Colorado Springs."

Anne filled Paul in on a few things about their new housekeeper he didn't know. She told him that Elsie and her husband Marvin had been married for almost 15 years. They had no children. He'd been a rodeo cowboy, a bull rider, until 10 years ago, when he was injured. Marvin was gored in the lower back and groin after being thrown by a particularly cranky Brahma bull. The tips of its horns that should have been trimmed, but somehow weren't, punctured internal organs and intestines and tore into his groin area. Doctors were able to save Marvin's life, but the injury left him impotent. For a long time, Marvin was unable

165

to work and began drinking heavily. After subjecting Elsie to some difficult years, he joined AA two years ago. He now worked part-time detailing used cars for an automobile dealer in Colorado Springs.

"Yeah, I remember him," Paul said, recalling Marvin's triumphs and the rumors about his drunken exploits. "He took the national bull riding title three years in a row. Marvin was world champ the year he got hurt. Was he ever something to watch! I doubt anyone rode a bull better than him. Hell of a bull rider!"

Anne cringed at Paul's occasional use of four-letter words, however mild. "Backwoods language", she said.

"I'm glad to hear Marvin's finally getting his life turned around," he added.

Chapter Forty-Three

Paul was feeling stronger. It had been two months since he'd been released from the hospital. Physiotherapy in Colorado Springs and Anne's healthy diet at home were working their magic.

He was back to working full time, three days at their office in Colorado Springs and two days in their home office at the ranch. Today, Paul decided to play hooky. It was mid-morning on a warm cloudless summer day.

He was riding his horse, a spirited Appaloosa stallion called Keith's Pride, into the foothills southwest of the ranch buildings. He was heading for a favorite boyhood retreat on a ridge high above the rolling grasslands.

The ridge was reached from a trail that made its way up a winding ravine behind the ridge, ending at a 350-foot slope that rose sharply from the valley floor. The view was breathtaking, a commanding 180-degree vista from north to east to south, spanning the heart of the ranch.

Far below were the remnants of an ancient river, a long-disappeared by-product of retreating glaciers aptly called the Lost River Valley. Waters from retreating glaciers had carved the wide valley out of the foothills, leaving behind Willow Creek to wind its way down the center of a narrower valley within. Across the wider valley, much of the opposite riverbank to the east had been eroded flat over the centuries, creating a panoramic view of grassy foothills gradually diminishing into rolling plains as far as the eye could see.

Paul stopped his horse at the crest of the ridge. He leaned forward contentedly, his hands crossed on the pommel of his saddle, enjoying the magnificent view that lay before him.

Moments later, he heard the sound of approaching iron-shod hooves clanking loudly over rocks on the trail up to the ridge. Paul turned and watched with pleasure as Anne, astride a bay gelding she'd appropriately named Buckshot, rode up beside him, a warm smile on her face.

"Happy to be home, my darling?" Anne asked.

The sound of her soft English accent propelled delightful tingles up and down his spine, just as it had since the moment they met.

"You bet, my love," Paul smiled back.

"I'll never get tired of the view," he said, his eyes roaming the attractive contours of her body. "Or that one either," he added, turning, and pointing out from the ridge.

"Oh, you!" Anne replied with a giggle, pleased he still found her trim body attractive. She worked hard at keeping it that way. Anne was even more pleased he had regained his strength, and apparently his friskiness was returning.

"I was just remembering back, about one of my early visits here years ago with Dad and some visitors," Paul said. "I was 13 or 14, and like Douglas – full of piss and vinegar."

"Paul! Such language," Anne admonished her husband with a smile. "That's no way to speak about our eldest son. Someone might hear you."

"Well, I was, in those days, and so is Douglas now," Paul smiled back, not chastened in the slightest. "No one can hear us. And no one's going to hear when I drag you off that horse, my love, and have my way with you in the bushes."

"Paul!" Anne laughed. "Don't say such things! Well ... not unless you're going to do something about it!"

She slapped Buckshot on the rump. He galloped down the gradual slope behind the ridge leading to a shallow ravine.

Paul marveled proudly at what an accomplished rider she'd become.

Anne guided her horse toward a grove of trees, Paul following. Ahead was a small opening in the trees that led to a clearing surrounded by aspen and spruce trees. The clearing was carpeted with tall grass and low natural shrubs. Anne knew it to be a favorite romantic place. They'd been there before and made love on the grass.

As they entered the clearing, Anne, laughing happily, slowed her horse. Paul caught up and noticed the grass was flattened in several places, he assumed by sleeping cattle or deer the night before

Without warning Anne's horse reared up, uttering a shrill, frightened whinny, throwing Anne backwards. Paul's ranching experience sprang into action as instinctively he leaned out from his rushing horse, gripping it tightly between his knees. The reins were in his right hand as he threw his left arm around Anne's waist, swinging her smoothly up behind him.

Before he could stop his Appaloosa, it reared too. Paul dropped the reins and grabbed for the pommel of the saddle with his right hand. He held Anne with his left. His hand missed the pommel. Instead, he caught a coil of rope tied to the saddle. It came away. The leather thong holding it broke as Paul and Anne fell. They slid backwards over the horse's rump onto the grass. Paul was pleased to see that Anne's riding experience had kicked in, cushioning her fall with her knees bent slightly, and was relieved at how easily his still recovering body handled being bucked off. A few pains here and there but it had responded as needed.

Paul glanced around to see what had spooked their horses. Both animals were gone, no doubt racing for home.

There was no mistaking what had frightened them.

169

A large female black bear stood on her hind legs, less than 50 feet away, glaring at them. A pair of two-year-old cubs, almost as big as their mother, peered out from behind her. Paul realized the mother bear and her cubs had spent the night in the clearing, leaving the impressions in the tall grass he'd seen.

Paul cursed himself for being unarmed. He remembered while growing up that no one in the region left their ranches without a rifle. Bears, cougars, wolves, and coyotes were a constant threat to young calves and to those who tended them.

Fine time to think of that, Paul chided himself.

He was armed only with the rope he'd inadvertently pulled loose from the saddle. Not much help, he thought. Paul knew he and Anne couldn't outrun a black bear. Those animals could run more than 35 miles an hour. And they could climb trees faster and better than any human. Paul looked around for something, anything to use as a defensive weapon. Nothing useful.

He made a quick assessment of the trees around the clearing. Most were small aspens and spruce, thin and stunted, typical for mountain foothills. He spotted a few that seemed sturdy.

Anne stayed behind him, terrified. She watched as the angry mother black bear considered her next move. Without warning, the bear dropped down onto all four feet. She came rushing at them, snarling and growling.

Anne let out a shrill scream. The bear skidded to a stop in a flurry of twigs and grass. It was less than 20 feet from them.

"Look away from her!" Paul quietly urged Anne. The bear watched them intently as she slowly backed up, looking over her shoulder to where she'd been guarding her cubs before charging.

"Don't look her in the eye," he cautioned Anne. "She'll feel threatened and attack. Right now, she's just bluffing, trying to scare us."

"It's working!" Anne replied in a brave attempt at humor. She moved closer behind Paul. He looked down at the rope and began to unfurl it, estimating it to be 50 to 55 feet long.

"What are we going to do?" Anne asked.

"We don't have many options," he replied. "I'll try getting her to stand up again on her hind legs. If I can get a noose over her head and tie the other end to a big tree over there, maybe it will hold her long enough to give us a bit of a head start."

Paul knew it was a long shot. He eased the noose open. He had thrown nooses before over the heads of 1,100-pound horned steers while on horseback galloping over uneven rangeland. But that was years ago, and this was quite different. Now his challenge was to get a noose over the head of this 200-pound black bear while she stood on her hind legs, snapping her jaw at them, and pawing the air. And he had no idea what effect his still-healing gunshot wounds might have on his accuracy with a rope.

"I'm going to jump up and make a lot of noise to surprise and distract her," Paul said. "I want her to rear up. She might do that, wanting to see better what we're up to.

"When I jump up, you run to the left as fast as you can. Head for those trees and crawl into the middle," he said, pointing to a thick grove of aspen, spruce and scrub brush. "I'll run to the right and try to get the rope on her.

"Here we go," Paul said with more confidence than he felt.

He stood and began shouting at the bear, then cried, "Run, Anne! Run!"

Paul sprinted to the right. He stopped, then began jumping up and down again, waving his hat and the coiled rope, shouting at the top of his lungs to draw the big bear's attention. The mother bear looked stunned and backed up further the way she'd come.

171

James Osborne

Then suddenly she reared up on her hind legs. A loud roar came from her huge mouth. Her long white canine teeth sparkled in the sun. The big bear glanced back at her cubs and then dropped down again on all fours. He'd missed his brief opportunity. Things weren't going as he intended.

Without warning the bear charged at Paul. He threw the rope. The noose sailed toward her head. The bear saw it coming and instinctively swatted at the rope. She deflected it away from her head. The bear stopped. Paul's heart sank. There'd be no second chances. He saw his effort failing, putting Anne and him in serious danger. He expected the black bear to charge again, and this time it would be a real attack.

Then he saw the noose had caught around one front leg. It had slipped over the bear's right paw. Paul pulled the rope tight. It held. He ran for the stand of trees he'd seen earlier while trying to hold the rope tight. Quick as a rodeo calf roper, Paul threw the end of the rope around a stout tree and tied it with a double half hitch. Then he ran, circling the bear as wide as he could, to the other side of the clearing where Anne was hiding in the bushes.

The black bear lunged after him, snarling. Almost immediately the bear hit the end of the rope. Her momentum pulled her right front leg across in front of her body and then back, forcing the big animal's body to spin around. The bear lost her balance and rolled over. She scrambled back to her feet, shook herself and stood on her hind legs, letting out an angry roar. It was deafening.

Paul heard a loud 'Crack!' ring out. Then another 'Crack!' He recognized them with relief as rifle shots. But he didn't dare take his eyes off the bear to see where the shots had come from. He knew it would take more than a couple of those bullets to stop an angry adult black bear. The sounds were those of a light caliber gun, one normally used to hunt smaller predators, not the heavy caliber rifle needed to stop a black bear.

172

The bear showed no sign of having been shot. Instead, she chewed on the noose tightened on her right leg. Paul watched helplessly. He knew roping nooses were designed to release easily. For a few seconds she alternately chewed and tugged. The tree swayed. The noose held. Then she backed up. Using her full weight, she tugged her roped foreleg back and forth. The tree swept forward and back, like a fishing rod hooked to a scrappy stream trout. Then the bear tugged and pulled again … much harder this time. The tree hesitated then pulled out of the ground, taking with it a clump of roots and dirt.

Anne saw Paul running toward her. She scrambled from the thick brush. He grabbed her hand. They ran zigzagging through the dense trees, with the branches and brambles tearing at their clothes. The black bear charged after them. She snarled menacingly, hobbling, and dragging 25 feet behind her the uprooted tree tied to her right front leg.

The bear was gaining. Suddenly, the tree was caught between two clumps of young aspen trees. It stopped the bear short. The big female black bear was flipped over onto her back. She scrambled to regain her feet, and then let out another loud angry roar.

Again, a loud "crack!" and then two more.

This time, Paul looked past the bear. Kurt Willis, the ranch foreman, was carrying a .23-caliber rifle, smoke drifting from the muzzle. He walked sideways toward them, his eyes never leaving the black bear. It was still standing, a menacing look in her eyes, her right front paw still tied to the rope and the tree.

"I was sure those first shots went near her heart," Kurt said. "And I pumped three more into her. But you know it takes a lot to stop a full-grown black bear, especially with this varmint gun. I'll finish her off with a few more to her brain."

Anne turned away, cringing.

Oh no! her mind cried silently at the thought of the mother black bear being killed. Anne steeled herself for what came next. She heard another loud 'Crack!' Anne's body convulsed instinctively at the sound of the shot and what it meant. Then another 'Crack!' Her body recoiled again.

There was silence.

Anne turned reluctantly. The black bear was down. Its eyes were open and sightless. The bear was dead. The cubs were gone. A profound sadness swept through Anne's heart.

"Damn good thing you came along when you did," Paul said, breaking the somber mood. "How'd you know we needed help?"

"Your horses came back all riled up," Kurt replied with a grin. "That meant trouble. I thought you might've ridden up to your favorite spot. I was headed there when I heard Anne's scream over here."

"Will the cubs be okay?" Anne interjected. "Who will look after them?"

"They're going to be just fine, Anne," Paul replied. "They're old enough now to look after themselves. The mother should really have sent them on their way already."

"I'll send a couple of guys up right away to dress and skin the bear," Kurt said. "Might as well save the meat and hide."

"I sure wish we hadn't gone crashing into that bear's space," Paul said with genuine regret. "This wasn't her fault. She was trying to protect her cubs ... just bein' a mom. Damned shame!"

As they walked back toward the ridge, Kurt turned to Paul.

"Pretty fancy roping, boss. Guess you're ready to get back in the saddle."

"I dunno, Kurt," Paul replied. "I was trying to rope her head. Got her front foot instead. Guess I'm in need of some practice."

"We can fix that, Milord," Kurt chuckled.

Kurt whistled. His horse, a big sorrel mare called Lightning, came trotting up. Her nostrils were flared, and ears pulled back, sensing the presence of the bear. Moments later Doug rode up, leading Paul and

174

Anne's equally skittish horses. It pleased Paul that this son, born in suburban Maidstone, England, had become so remarkably adept and thoroughly committed to Colorado's rugged ranching lifestyle.

"What a story we have for the folks back in England," Anne said as she swung aboard Buckshot, smiling proudly at an equally proud Doug for having participated in his parents' rescue.

"They'll never believe it back home," she said to their son. "On second thought, I'll just bet your grandpa will."

James Osborne

Chapter Forty-Four

Paul decided to ask for George's help. The retired general manager had done nothing for months, and Paul hoped that getting George to take on some new responsibility would encourage him to get his life back together and to move on.

"George, I know it's only been six months since Elizabeth's service, but I sure could use your help with something. Are you feeling up to it?"

"Of course, Paul," George replied. "What do you need?"

Paul sat across the table from George in the kitchen that his mentor and Elizabeth had shared for over 30 years. Paul was careful not to sit in Elizabeth's favorite pressed-wood chair. Her apron was still draped over the back.

"I've run out of patience with the police investigation," Paul began. "It's going cold. I spoke with Dan Lorente at CSPD today. They've been doing what they can, but their tight budget's putting severe limits on what they can do."

"Yeah," George added quietly. "What do you have in mind, Paul?"

Paul hoped that it would give George a sense of purpose if he could get him involved with the investigations. What better motivation than helping to track down Elizabeth's killer?

"I've hired a team of investigators from Global Security," Paul replied.

"As you know, they've a good rapport with law enforcement. They've helped police catch some seriously dangerous dudes. In addition to their personal security work, Global also hires top investigative talent,

176

including retired senior FBI agents, and LAPD and NYPD investigators. They've even got a couple of ex-Scotland Yard people and a few senior retired Canadian Mounties.

"We're going to get to the bottom of all this." Paul said. "I can't believe that in over six months nothing has come to light about who murdered Elizabeth and tried to kill Anne and me. I'm hoping Global can come up with something, anything to get things moving again."

"I'm with you, Paul," George said absently. "Nothing's more important. Whoever did this is still out there."

"A guy from Global's investigation team will be here in a couple of days," Paul said. "You and I need to brief him. Lt. Lorente told me privately we will have as much cooperation as he can give us, but it'll be off the books, so it has to be done quietly. He said that he's prepared to meet privately with Global if it'll help. After we brief Global, would you be okay with being the point guy for a while, help them get whatever they need?"

"Of course, Paul," George said. "What're you up to?"

"It's that damn lawsuit of Roberta's. We're starting discovery hearings soon," Paul replied, "And we need to get ready. Since we're the defendants we need to be flexible about the scheduling. We could be called to testify on short notice. John Everett, my attorney, and I are meeting with our lead attorney from New York, Tom Cameron, while the Global fellows are here. It was the only time I could get. I'll be available from time to time, but mostly I'll be tied up with them.

"I was hoping we could get Roberta's lawsuit thrown out of court before it gets started, but Tom thinks it won't be quite that easy," Paul added.

"Oh, yeah," George said. "I forgot those meetings were coming up. Don't worry about Global, Paul. I'll handle things with them."

While George had agreed to take on the responsibility, Paul sensed a decided lack of enthusiasm. George seemed more and more absent minded lately and had become increasingly reclusive. He put it down to grief over Elizabeth's murder and the lack of progress with the investigation. George occasionally joined Anne, him, and the children for supper, but his responses to invitations were becoming less frequent.

Chapter Forty-Five

Paul's executive assistant, Sally Miller, knocked on the open door to his office in downtown Colorado Springs.

"Philip Tremblay is here to see you, Mr. Winston."

"Thanks, Sally," Paul replied looking up from his file on Continental Del Rio. "Please send him in."

"Good to see you, Paul," the young oilman said as he strode through the door. They shook hands warmly.

"Hey, Philip," Paul replied as they sat at Paul's large oak desk. "You still pokin' holes in Mother Earth?"

Philip chuckled but was restrained.

"Yeah," he replied. "It has its ups and downs."

It was Paul's turn to chuckle.

"Great office," Philip said. "Terrific location. First time I've been here."

"Thanks," Paul replied. "My father bought the property many years ago and built this on it. We've just finished renovating and adding the tower next door. We've got some vacancies right now. Should we put Continental Del Rio down for a lease?"

"Not at the moment," Philip responded.

Paul sensed tension in his voice.

Years ago, Paul had decided to invest in Continental when it was just getting started. He'd liked the bright young oilman then and still did. Under Philip's leadership, Continental had grown rapidly, making one promising discovery after another in Colorado and some of the six adjoining states. The value of Prescott Enterprises' original investment had increased by at least thirty-fold. Regardless, exploration was costly, and Continental still needed more high-producing wells to achieve stable profitability.

"I came by to let you know we had a major oil well blow out last night on the Horner lease," Philip said. "Two men were killed. We think someone else was involved, maybe hurt. Found some blood in the parking area nearby. There was an explosion, and it looks like it could be sabotage."

"Good heavens, Philip! I'm sorry to hear about the men," Paul exclaimed. "Your employees? How are their families doing? Is there anything we can do?"

"Thanks. I think we've got most things in hand for now," Philip replied. "Our crews are on the scene and hard at work. The two killed were employees. We've sent counselors their homes. We'll do whatever they need to support their families. We don't have an ID on the third guy. It's possible he might have some connection to the explosion. Don't know yet. The sheriff is investigating.

"Anyway, we've got a major oil spill on our hands," Philip replied. "It's going to be an expensive cleanup. The foreman on site tells me almost a thousand barrels of crude have gone into a creek valley.

"Fortunately, our on-site people were smart. They built a weir immediately to divert the crude away from the creek and into a holding pond they made by damming a tributary at one end. It's temporary at best.

"Paul, I need a first-class investigator to look into this explosion and to work with the sheriff's office," he said. "Employees on the scene are certain there was no way an explosion like that could have occurred accidentally. That confirms sabotage. Someone could be trying to damage the company and its reputation. I have no idea why.

"Can you put me in touch with that security firm you've used before? I think you called them Global Security. Do you think they'd have someone experienced in this area?"

"Yes, the company is Global Security International," Paul replied. "They have people who are savvy about the oil patch. Hey, as you know, before I first invested in Continental Del Rio years ago I had you checked out thoroughly, and Global did that job. As a matter of fact, I have one of their investigators here right now on another matter. I'll ask him to phone their chief investigator to call you directly."

"Thanks, Paul," the worried oilman replied. "I also should tell you we're looking at huge expenses as a result of all this that we didn't anticipate. We could face lawsuits we might not recover from. It could seriously affect your investment in Continental.

"I had been planning on going to the board next week with a proposal to list shares in the company on the stock exchange so we can raise some capital," Philip said. "I don't think banks will advance us what we'll need considering what we're facing."

Paul was surprised and dismayed.

"An IPO isn't going to be easy in the best of times. With this spill, there could hardly be a worse time to go public," Paul replied. "The purpose of going public normally is to raise growth capital. Besides, if you go public you'll lose a lot of control over your company. How much do you need?"

"Look, Paul, I'm not here to ask for money," Philip replied. "Prescott is a big investor already. But to be honest, I was hoping an IPO would raise at least $150 million, maybe $200 million, to get us through this. I'm sharing this with you because Prescott is our largest investor, after me, of course. As you know only too well, an IPO would dilute your holdings and the holdings of all our existing shareowners."

"Listen to me," Paul said, "You need to call the board, the shareholders and other stakeholders right away about the spill. It's going to be all over the news media within a few hours if it isn't already. Give them and the media the straight story before they start inventing stuff to fill in the gaps.

"Meanwhile, can you leave the IPO proposal with me for a day or two? I need you to hold off from doing anything more on an IPO until you hear from me. All right?"

"Okay, Paul, but like I said, I'm not here to ask you for money," Philip responded. "You ... well, Prescott ... is an important investor. I can't ask you to put more money at risk."

"That'll be up to me to decide," Paul replied firmly. "I'll be back to you within 24 hours. Meanwhile, please let me know the names of the men who died. Send me all the information you have on their families. And please have someone keep me posted on the cleanup."

After the oilman left, Paul called John Richardson at Wells Fargo Bank. Continental would get what it needed. There weren't that many oilmen around who were as smart and as responsible as Philip Tremblay. Paul was determined Colorado wasn't going to lose this oilman or his company for want of some short-term fallback financing.

Next Paul called Sally in and told her about the employees who'd been killed. He told her that he wanted someone to quietly keep an eye out for the families to make sure they got all the help and support they needed. They weren't to know the source.

Sally knew what to do. She'd handled plenty of similar assignments before. This is what she liked best about working for Paul Winston.

Then Paul called Emile Bilodeaux at Global Security.

"There's been a major oil spill near here, Emile. It was caused by an explosion and there's a suspicion that it may be sabotage," Paul began. "Nothing confirmed at this time. We've a big interest in the oil company involved. Have you heard from your folks here?"

"Sure did, Paul," Emile replied. "I've a call in to Philip Tremblay. I've got just the person for him. He recently investigated a case of sabotage on a platform in the Gulf of Mexico.

Chapter Forty-Six

Denver

A phone message was waiting for Richard Gervais when he arrived for work. The caller's name was listed as Superintendent Charles Archibald of New Scotland Yard.

It surprised the young FBI special agent.

A few days earlier, when he'd called New Scotland Yard requesting a favor, Gervais did not expect to speak with a senior police executive. He certainly didn't expect to hear back from him directly. He assumed he'd be hearing from a junior, like himself.

Gervais dialed the number.

"Good afternoon, Archibald here," said a deep British-accented voice at the other end of the phone.

It was 9 a.m. at FBI headquarters in Washington, but 2 p.m. at New Scotland Yard in London. Earlier, Gervais had asked Superintendent Archibald for help checking labels from a jacket and fingerprints found on a rifle recovered near a landfill. Local police believed the rifle might have been used in a murder. They were looking for a suspect that witnesses said had a British accent.

Archibald pledged the considerable resources of New Scotland Yard would go to work on the request. He'd gotten involved with the investigation by sheer accident. Archibald had been walking by an unattended ringing phone when he decided on impulse to answer it. Gervais was on the other end. The more he spoke with the young FBI agent the more impressed he'd become and wanted to help him.

The senior Scotland Yard executive was thoroughly enjoying the opportunity to step back into an investigation. *Why not?* he thought. He was senior enough that he could choose to do so, and besides, it offered a break from the mundane administrative matters that bored him to distraction day after endless day.

"Special Agent Gervais here, Superintendent. Thank you for calling back," the young FBI agent said.

After exchanging diplomatic pleasantries, he asked, "Well, Superintendent, do you by any chance have any news for us on those fingerprints and labels."

"Yes, m'boy, we have, somewhat," Archibald said, taking liberties with the considerable age difference he perceived between them. "I'm afraid we've struck out on the fingerprints. Not clear enough, but we're still working on them. Fortunately, I do have something for you with regard to the labels."

"What would that be, sir?" Gervais asked.

"It seems the labels were produced for a clothing manufacturer here in England," Archibald replied. "Sold their clothing all over the world. That includes the United States. What's so odd, Agent Gervais, is the company. It was called Rolling Mills. It's out of business. Has been for more than a year ... let's see, yes, for almost two years, actually. The last shipment of clothing to the United States that we could track down was 19 months ago, just a few weeks before they closed down. I can get you the exact day."

"Thank you, sir," Gervais replied. "That would be great. Would you possibly have any information on clothing agents here in America that handled the shipments?"

"I can do better than that, Agent Gervais," he replied. "My people will be emailing you a bunch of information. But I have here at hand the names and addresses of all the companies Rolling Mills shipped to all over the world, including addresses in the United States. It seems Rolling

Mills did not use an agent in your country but shipped directly to a few chains and even some individual retail stores. Probably trying to bypass the middlemen to save money.

"That information I'm sending you," Archibald added, "includes a list with 10 or 12 names on it. Two of the stores are, I think, in your neck of the woods, m'boy. Both are in Colorado. One city's your Colorado Springs, and the other's Denver. Are you familiar with Denver by any chance?"

Gervais chuckled.

"Yes, Superintendent. That's where I live."

"Yes, of course, m'boy. Quite so," a mildly embarrassed Archibald replied, clearing his throat. "Well now, the name of the company in Colorado Springs is called Master Tailor Men's Wear. Part of a national clothing chain in your country, I understand."

"Yes, Superintendent," Gervais replied, "I'm familiar with that company."

The Master Tailor Men's Wear store in Colorado Springs was a franchise operation, owned by none other than Stephen Hooper.

Chapter Forty-Seven

Colorado Springs

An FBI tracking dog found the body. It was lying beneath some bushes in a shallow ravine less than 200 yards from the highway, about 18 miles south of Colorado Springs. The body had not been there long. It was a horrible sight.

The corpse was missing flesh from its thighs, buttocks, and mid-section. The rib cage was half empty of inner organs. What looked like pieces of intestines and other human remains, as well as pieces of clothing, were scattered on the ground around the corpse. In the bright heat of the summer sunshine, flies swarmed around the corpse as two people from the coroner's office finished up their work and prepared to remove the body.

The location was a mile and a half east of the shack where Douglas Winston had been held captive. No link to the kidnapping had been established, but the FBI claimed jurisdiction just the same. Special Agent-in-Charge Frank Schuler argued it was their tracking dog that discovered the body. It was close enough to the kidnap shack there could be a connection. The El Paso sheriff's sergeant was less than thrilled, but he knew when he was overmatched.

Lt. Lorente had been called out as a courtesy by the El Paso County Sheriff's Office and happily conceded the body was outside Colorado Springs city limits. He had enough on his plate just now.

James Osborne

"There's no ID on the body," FBI Special Agent Milt Carson told Lorente and Schuler. The three were standing upwind from the body, their backs to the bright sunlight.

"We searched the area until you called us back," Carson said, looking at Schuler. "We did find a short length of 2x6 that had some recent scuffmarks. We're not sure what that's about, or even if it's connected.

"The coroner will lift fingerprints from the body," Carson added. "That's probably the only way we're gonna ID this one."

"Funny thing, though," Carson said to Schuler. "Some labels on the clothing are British. The shirt and the pants ... the labels say, 'Made in England'. Not much Brit stuff sold around here. Go figure. Might be helpful.

"As you know, the deceased was a male," Carson continued. "We figure the age of the deceased is around the mid-50s ... hard to tell, though. The autopsy will have to confirm that.

Carson, based at the FBI field office in Colorado Springs, also told them that over the years he'd come upon a few bodies like this.

"Sure looks like a coyote kill. Not often they go after humans," Carson said. "Must have been mighty hungry. The Achilles tendon on one ankle was severed. That's how coyotes make a kill. They hunt in packs. They cripple their prey, knock 'em down, and then rip out the jugular and the windpipe."

Special Agent-in-Charge Schuler didn't respond. He didn't have much to say anyway. He was a city guy, and all this country stuff was foreign to him.

County and Colorado Springs homicide detectives had come out to offer their help, but the senior FBI agent made it abundantly clear this was an FBI show, despite it being El Paso County's jurisdiction.

Chapter Forty-Eight

"Just put me through to him, will you please!" Philip Tremblay was almost pleading into the phone.

There was a pause.

It was late Friday afternoon, and the voice on the other end of the line was obviously tired, irritable, and devoid of patience or caring.

"Please, just tell him Philip Tremblay is calling. And tell him it's an emergency," Philip added. "Mr. Anderson knows me. My father and I worked for him in Texas and Oklahoma."

He listened for a minute then said, "Okay, here are my phone numbers." He recited the numbers and reluctantly hung up, discouraged.

Reg Anderson was the most expensive but also the best wild well fighter in the world. Philip needed his help urgently to cap their runaway oil well, and hopefully before it caught fire. But getting through to the legendary Anderson was no simple task.

"Who else can we get?" he asked Casey Meyer, his bright young vice-president of development. Philip was grooming Casey to be his successor one day.

"It's a pretty short list, Philip, and they're all busy," Casey replied. "There's Anderson, and then there's Well Companion, Oilfield Safety, and Wild Well Management."

"This is a first for us," Philip said. "Check around with some of the other companies, will you, Casey? Find out who they've used."

An hour later, Casey returned with a grim look on his face.

"All of the other outfits are booked solid too. Mostly overseas stuff," he told Philip. "But Delta Exploration gave me the name of someone. Never heard of them. Border Well Services."

"Okay, Casey," Philip replied. "Go ahead and call them. Guess we'll have to give them a try."

While they were talking, Philip's direct line rang.

"Philip Tremblay," he answered.

"Well, I'll be damned!" Philip exclaimed. "Good to hear from you, Mr. Anderson. All right, Reg, it is."

Philip grinned at Casey. He raised an eyebrow and a thumb, all the while smiling and nodding. The world-famous Reg Anderson was actually calling him back.

Philip and Anderson exchanged pleasantries.

In answer to questions, Philip summarized his career since leaving Anderson's employ some 10 years earlier. He told Anderson about how his father and mother were enjoying their retirement.

Then they got down to business.

Philip filled Anderson in on the wild well he was dealing with beside the South Platte River. Philip explained his concern about the potential for extensive environmental damage, plus the liability issues and uneasiness about using a company he'd never heard of to cap the wild well.

Anderson told him that Anderson Wild Well Services was booked solid for the next six months to a year. Philip's heart sank.

"Now, son, I haven't told anyone outside my guys about this yet," Anderson said. "But I'm about to announce my retirement. Been selling my interests to our key guys over the last few years. It's time for me to step aside.

"So, here's what I'd like to do, if you're of a mind to," he added. "Why don't you hire me as a consultant to liaise with Border Well Services for you?

190

"Don't you laugh, young man!" Anderson protested when Philip lost his struggle to suppress a surprised chuckle. "I'm serious!"

"Reg, you don't know how flattered I am," Philip replied, regaining his composure. "I knew Anderson and Company was booked solid, so I really was hoping you could recommend someone and help me get them. I just can't afford to hire both you and another wild well fighter."

"Can you afford one dollar?" Reg asked. "That's my fee for you, Philip. One dollar. In U.S. funds, if you please. Think you can manage that?"

Not waiting for Philip to answer, he went on, "Look, Philip, you and your dad did me some huge favors when both of you worked for my company. You may not know it, but I heard about what you two did for me. Saved me millions. I don't forget those things. I owe you both, big time. Really big! So now it's payback time.

"Will you give me a chance to square things?" Anderson asked. Again, he didn't wait for a reply. That was his style.

"Like I told you, one buck. Take it or leave it, Philip. And you damned well better take it, 'cause I'm on my way! My Learjet is warming up as we speak."

"It would be an honor, Reg," Philip managed to reply after overcoming his disbelief. "I don't know how I'll ever thank you for this."

"Oh, I'll think of something," Anderson laughed. "See you tomorrow morning. Seven o'clock sharp, your office. Be there!

"And Philip?" Anderson added.

"Yes Reg?"

"I prefer to be paid in advance, in cash, please." Reg chuckled and hung up.

Chapter Forty-Nine

Two-Dot Ranch

"Morning Elsie!" Anne greeted their housekeeper, bubbling with her usual enthusiasm. "How are you this fine morning?"

"'Morning, Anne," Elsie replied glumly. "I'm not so good this morning, I'm afraid. Would you mind terribly if I left early today? In fact, I'm very sorry, but I may need a week or so off. Would you be okay with that?"

"Of course," Anne said. "It's none of my business, but is there anything I can do?"

"Well, to tell you the truth, I'm worried about Marvin," Elsie said. "He's missing. Actually, he's been missing for over a month."

She decided to tell Anne the whole story.

"When he was drinking, Marvin would go missing for a few days, sometimes a week, but never this long. I can't stand it any longer. I've got to find out where he is. I'd rather not file another missing person's report. The police know all about Marvin. I want to go look for him myself first."

Anne realized the kind person standing before her had been living with the stress of her missing husband for weeks without saying a word to anyone. Her heart went out to Elsie.

The two women had grown fond of each other since Elsie began working for them. Anne liked Elsie's meticulous work and especially her fondness for the children. Elsie told Anne they were unable to have children of their own. Elsie was drawn to Anne's gentle caring manner and impressed by her can-do attitude. She felt she could confide in Anne.

"Marvin hasn't done anything like this since he joined AA two years ago," Elsie added. "I'm really worried.

"I don't like to ask for the time, Anne, but I need to look for him. He used to end up on the streets in Denver begging for money to buy booze. I've found him there a few times," Elsie added. "I hope he's not back drinking again. If I can't find him, then I guess I will have to file another missing person's report after all."

"Look Elsie," Anne said. "You take whatever time you need to look for Marvin. I can look after things here. Is there anything else we can do to help?"

"I sure could use the time. Thank you so much, Anne," Elsie replied, clearly relieved. "It could take a while, but I'll make it up to you. I promise."

Anne had no doubt that she would.

Elsie and Marvin were struggling financially, and Anne knew it. Elsie was the principal breadwinner, and Anne had every intention of ensuring Elsie would not lose any income. She just needed to make it look acceptable in a way that Elsie couldn't refuse.

After Elsie left for the city, Anne turned her attention to the children, who would be coming in soon from their morning chores. Anne would have to explain to them why Elsie wasn't there and might not be back for a few days. Each of the children had grown close to Elsie. She was like a popular aunt, much like Elizabeth had been, often preparing their favorite meals and unexpected treats for no reason at all except to please and surprise them.

Chapter Fifty

"Anne, I'm concerned about George," Paul said one evening. "It's been almost a year since Elizabeth died and he's still keeping himself cooped up in that house most of the time.

"He did that job for us helping Global Security. I was hoping it would get him going again. Help him move on. But that petered out quickly ... too quickly.

"Looks to me like all he's doing is grocery shopping and wandering the fields. Just like before the Global job. He hasn't been on that horse of his for months."

"Yeah, sadly," Anne said. "I was hoping the lessons he was giving the children would help him ... give him something to concentrate on. He seems to have lost interest in that, too. I think the children have given up on him."

"I went over this afternoon," Paul said. "The house is a mess.. He isn't eating well, and his personal hygiene leaves a lot to be desired. He hasn't shaved in over a week. It's just not like him.

"One good thing, though. He told me he was thinking about going away for a few months. I encouraged him. Maybe if he just got away for a while. It's not good for him to stay cooped up day after day, all alone with his memories of Elizabeth.

"Would you talk to him, too, Anne?" Paul said. "He'll listen to you. A trip could make a big difference for him. Maybe you can get him to make a decision."

"Sure, Paul," Anne replied. "I'll go see him tomorrow."

Chapter Fifty-One

Bill Radford was in charge of the Winston account for Global Security as well as their lead investigator. He arranged to meet Lt. Lorente one evening in Paul's high-rise building, away from inquiring eyes. They spent the next four hours going over all the evidence from CSPD, El Paso County Sheriff's Office and the FBI on the shootings and even added in the NTSB file on the plane crash years earlier that had killed Paul's parents.

"Thanks for the material, Dan," Radford said finally to Lorente.

"Sure, Bill," Lorente replied. "Just make sure no one else knows you have it or where you got it, okay?"

"Of course," Radford agreed. "And Dan, I want to give you a heads-up. I will be interviewing a few people in town and doing some looking around. How do you folks feel about that?"

"My guys already know you're here," Lorente replied. "They're okay with that. Everybody's frustrated by the lack of progress and the tight budget. We'd welcome any help, anything Global can dig up. Just pass it along to me quietly, okay?"

"That's good to hear," Radford replied. "Anything I find comes directly to you first. Just so you know, Dan, I'll be going back over all the work here, including the FBI's. Appreciate you're not sharing that with anyone there."

"No problem, Bill," Lorente answered. "We're not too fond of their head guy in Denver."

Radford told Lorente he'd be checking out the street location where Paul was shot as well as the parking lot where Elizabeth was murdered, and Officer Thornton shot.

Next morning, the former LAPD homicide detective was scouring a median in the parking lot at Memorial Hospital, trying to locate where the gunman had been when he shot Mrs. Underhill and Officer Thornton. Radford got bearings from statements in police reports from Mrs. Winston, Officer Thornton, and other police officers on the scene. Together they directed him to a row of shrubs in the parking lot.

He walked toward the center from one end of the median and then the other, narrowing the area down to a section about 10 yards long.

Landscape stone around the shrubs had been disturbed. He assumed it was by the CSPD evidence gatherers – new recruits usually – and by landscapers. Radford donned rubber gloves, coveralls, and kneepads. Picking up a hand garden fork, he began working his way along the section of shrubs. Around each bush he dug down and under, bagging everything suspicious as he went.

Twenty minutes later, beneath one shrub, Radford saw a tiny reflection. He dug deeper carefully into the landscape stone. There it was, a shell casing. The muted shine normally on shell casing like this told him it had been there for a few months. He recognized it as the distinctive Remington .280 caliber shell casing.

He carefully inserted a twig into the open end of the casing and placed it in an evidence bag. Less than two minutes later, he found another shell casing beneath the same bush. Same caliber. He placed that one in another evidence bag.

Inexperienced evidence gatherers, he thought, shaking his head.

Bill hoped both shell casings would yield fingerprints. He was willing to bet they would be the prints of the shooter who had murdered Elizabeth Underhill and shot Officer Thornton.

Radford used his cell phone to call Lorente. He told Dan what he'd found and said he would bring the evidence to Lorente's office. He would let the newly minted deputy chief – still head of CSPD homicide – explain to his colleagues how the two shell casings had suddenly appeared.

Chapter Fifty-Two

Dr. Lillian Moore carefully scanned Paul's x-rays for the third time. He and Anne were in her office at Memorial Hospital.

"The x-rays show the bullet is lodged very close to your heart," Dr. Moore said. "And frankly, I don't like the look of it one bit. You need to know that removal can be tricky depending on where it is precisely. We won't know for certain until we go in.

"I have to tell you, Paul, the alternative is worse," the head of the hospital's cardiovascular unit told her patient. "Leaving the bullet there presents a serious risk that I consider unacceptable. There could be damage we can't see on the scans and x-rays. Besides, this type of bullet contains lead, which is toxic. It can have serious negative effects on your organs, especially your heart muscle."

Dr. Moore looked closely at Paul and Anne.

"It's not an easy choice, Paul. Are the both of you still absolutely certain you want to go through with it?" she asked.

He looked at his wife and said, "Yes, Dr. Moore. It's been a year now since I was shot. You've told me I'm in as good a shape right now as I'm ever going to be. So, I guess there won't be a better time."

Anne looked down at her hands, clenched tightly together. She and Paul had discussed their options and the risks. They'd made the decision together. Amid her worry, she heard Paul continue:

"Besides, the authorities need that bullet," he was saying. "I'm hoping it will have better rifling marks on it than the other two. Can you be careful when you're removing it? As you know only too well, those other two bullets hit my ribs and sternum and fragmented. This one could provide important evidence."

"Paul, my job is not to help police recover evidence," the surgeon replied, bristling just a bit. "My only concern is your well-being. But I will do my best.

"I know you and Anne have considered the potential risks. But I'm obliged to forewarn you anyway, Paul, there is an outside chance you won't come through this. It's remote, of course, but it's still a risk. You need to have your affairs in order, just in case."

He appreciated Dr. Moore's candor, although he was concerned that it was increasing Anne's already heightened fear.

Paul and Anne looked at each other for a long moment, then went ahead and booked his surgery. It would be in three months.

Chapter Fifty-Three

Lt. Lorente's phone rang. It was Frank Schuler from Denver, Special Agent in Charge of the FBI's Colorado operations.

"Lorente," an arrogant-sounding Schuler said without preliminary courtesies, "Is Ralph Hinds with you?"

"As a matter of fact, he is," Dan replied, glancing across his desk at the El Paso County SO detective. Hinds was investigating the death of the as-yet unidentified male found on Two-Dot Ranch grazing land near Colorado Springs.

"I'm calling about that body we found a little while ago," Schuler said.

"Yeah, how could I forget," Dan replied, trying not to sound too sarcastic. He put the call on speaker.

"Well, we have a lead." Schuler carried on, missing Dan's sarcasm.

"Got a call from New Scotland Yard in London. The British labels on clothes we found with the body could possibly be from clothes sold right here, perhaps in Colorado Springs, in fact. Do you know a store there called Master Tailor Men's Wear?"

"Yeah, Frank," Dan replied. Hinds nodded. Both had been buying shirts and pants at that men's store for years.

The call reminded Dan he had intended to phone Schuler but had kept putting it off. He was planning to tell him about the leads uncovered by Global Security linking the body to the kidnapping of Douglas Winston. Ralph and Dan knew they should have passed that information along before now, but neither wanted to speak with the arrogant FBI Special Agent.

Both preferred to deal with Schuler's bright and cooperative subordinate, Richard Gervais, but Schuler insisted all contacts go through him. They suspected Schuler would take the credit for Gervais' work. What's more, the FBI Special Agent in Charge had all but excluded El Paso County and Colorado Springs detectives from the investigation.

Schuler had made it abundantly clear the FBI was asserting jurisdiction over the kidnapping. It was standard operating procedure and good practice for law enforcement agencies to include other agencies connected with cases, but Schuler had a reputation for ignoring those basic courtesies.

"As a matter of fact, Frank, I had some people go back to the scene," Hinds said. "We've come up with a few things that might interest the FBI."

Hinds decided to share with Schuler the evidence that Global Security had recovered from the grazing land near where Douglas Winston had been kidnapped.

"We have a 9mm Smith & Wesson Model 39, recovered from under a clump of sagebrush at the scene," he said, choosing his words carefully. "It was found using a metal detector, about ten yards from where the body was discovered. Must have been missed when your people did their area search. And, by the way, the gun appeared to have been fired recently. Forensics did some other studies; they believe the weapon could have been fired in a time frame compatible with the kidnapping."

Hinds continued: "It's the same caliber as the shells your guys found in the glove box of that pickup linked to the kidnapping. We've matched two bullets with the gun. One match is partial. It's a damaged bullet recovered from inside the pickup. The other is a solid match to a bullet recovered from the skull of the Winston boy's dog killed in Livingston Valley. Identical rifling."

Before he could continue, Schuler interrupted, "What the hell do you think you two are doing?" he demanded.

"This is an FBI case!" he said, shouting over the phone. "Our evidence. Our investigation. It's an FBI kidnapping case. Remember? You should know better than to hold back evidence."

"Frank," Dan shot back, "for one thing, until this very minute you had no evidence connecting that body with the Winston boy's kidnapping. We just gave it to you.

"Second, you personally signed off on the pickup, remember? It was stolen. The owner had to get a court order returning it to him after someone at the FBI office in Denver dragged his feet. The owner gave us permission to search the pickup. We found the bullet and got the match. It's evidence your guys let go!

"And just so you know, Frank, Douglas Winston told us the man who kidnapped him also hit his dog and then shot it. There was no mention of that in the FBI report. I was there when he told you about it, Frank. Well, young Douglas wanted to go back to Livingston Valley to bury his dog. Ralph sent someone along to make sure the boy would be all right and look for evidence."

Lorente and Hinds didn't bother telling Schuler the man who found the evidence was a Global Security investigator.

"We thought someone should go," Hinds continued, glancing over at a nodding Lorente. "The perp or an accomplice could've still been out there, Frank. The FBI hasn't made any progress at all on this case to date, much less made an arrest."

Dan and Ralph enjoying the opportunity to rub it in.

"You will remember," Ralph continued, "after the Winston boy was kidnapped, you didn't want to be bothered checking out the valley. Well, when they got there the dog's body was in bad shape; animals had been at it. But our guy recovered a bullet from the dog's skull. It gave us a match and the solid connection.

"Full circle, Frank," Dan added.

"It looks like that male corpse near the highway was your perp, your kidnapper," Ralph said. "It looks like us country hicks got a little bit lucky … did the FBI's work for them."

The phone went dead.

Schuler had hung up.

Chapter Fifty-Four

Paul drove to Colorado Springs from the ranch for a meeting in John Everett's office. It was early Monday morning.

John and Tom Cameron, the renowned New York attorney, were already seated at a well-worn table. Both looked somber. John motioned Paul to a chair.

Cameron was leading the defense in a lawsuit Paul's sister Roberta had brought against him, Two-Dot Ranch and Prescott Enterprises. She was claiming 33.3 percent of his inheritance from their late Uncle Percival in England.

The case had taken months to come to trial, and more months to complete. Paul felt the evidence was overwhelmingly in their favor and had been presented masterfully by Cameron with John Everett's capable support.

John looked unhappily at Paul. He said, "As I told you on the phone, Judge Swanson just released an advance copy of his ruling. He's going to announce his decision tomorrow morning in court.

"Paul, I didn't want to tell you this until we met face-to-face. The news is not good. The judge has ruled against us. We're both astounded.

"While Roberta didn't get the 33.3 percent she demanded in her statement of claim, the judge did order the portion of your uncle's inheritance you've transferred to America be divided between you and your two sisters in the same proportions as stipulated in your parents' will, after George Underhill's inheritance, on the basis of 40 percent to you and 30 percent to each of your sisters."

"He can't be serious!" Paul sat bolt upright. "I wouldn't begrudge either of my sisters one cent, if that was how Uncle Percival wanted it. But he made his wishes clear. I'm legally and morally bound to respect his intentions. This makes no sense.

"This is bloody ridiculous," Paul exploded. "What on earth was he thinking?"

"That's not all," Tom added. "Swanson has ordered a freeze on all of your assets in America until this is settled, and that means *all* of your assets."

"Good Lord, is Swanson bereft of his senses?" Paul asked. "There's got to be something else going on here. John, Tom, I want you to file an appeal immediately!" Paul's voice was uncharacteristically loud and angry.

"And I want you to apply to have that stupid bloody decision stayed pending our appeal. I'm going to bring in a first-class investigator to do some hard digging. This whole thing stinks to high heaven. Besides, what makes a U.S. judge think he can overturn a will that was made in England? This is nonsense. Uncle Percy's will was written in England and probated in England under English law. It's final and I believe the probate in the UK is just as valid in America as there, correct?"

"That's right," Tom said.

"At least that goddamned yahoo can't affect what's still in England. And that's the vast majority of Uncle Percy's estate," Paul said, struggling to calm down.

"Glad to hear you feel that way," John said. "Tom and I both are of the opinion that something's not right here."

"Who are you planning to bring in, Paul?" Cameron asked.

"Global Security," Paul replied. "They've done some other work for us. Do you know them?"

"Sure do," Cameron replied. "They have an office in New York. As a matter of fact, we've used them. Great choice."

Chapter Fifty-Five

Denver

Gervais knew he was stepping out of line. He did it anyway.

Gervais had spoken with Superintendent Archibald at New Scotland Yard several times, trying to link a British clothing label and a rifle found at dump near Colorado Springs to a series of shootings there, including a murder.

This time something else was bothering him. That 'something else' had arisen from an unofficial 'back-channel chat' with Dan Lorente of CSPD, Ralph Hinds of EPCSO and Bill Radford of Global Security.

They told Gervais that the two bullets taken from Paul Winston's chest almost certainly came from a British-made Webley Mk IV revolver. They based the conclusion on firing pin impressions found on shell casings recovered from the sidewalk leading away from the scene. It was all they had. There were no usable fingerprints on the shell casings. Bullet fragments taken from Paul's chest were so badly damaged it would be difficult to get a match with a specific weapon, even if a suspect revolver of that type could be found. A search of the crime scene at the time had failed to locate a weapon. CSPD had concluded the perpetrator must have dropped the casings while reloading as he fled the scene.

The young FBI agent found the coincidences irresistible. First, the English clothing labels, and second, the authorities had linked the shooting to a perpetrator with a British accent. The trouble was that the shooter was unknown, and the weapon was yet to be found.

The Maidstone Conspiracy

Frank Schuler refused to let Gervais send to New Scotland Yard photographs of the rifling on the fragments of the two Winston bullets. Schuler said the FBI had better things to do and so did New Scotland Yard. Besides, the other evidence was so inconclusive sending it to The Yard would be a waste of time and money.

Gervais thought otherwise.

He was convinced the evidence and coincidences were too significant not to be followed up. He decided to stick his neck out. He called Archibald and explained that he was investigating another case and was playing a hunch. After listening to the explanation, Archibald was intrigued. The superintendent agreed to check whether a Webley Mark IV revolver had shown up in any London Police reports in recent years.

Three days later, Gervais' phone rang just as he was preparing to leave for the day. The distinctively deep British baritone voice on the line bellowed, "You're brilliant, young man! You deserve a promotion!"

It was Superintendent Archibald.

Gervais smiled to himself as he checked his watch. It was well into the evening in London.

"Thank you very much. I'm flattered, sir," Gervais replied laughing self-consciously. "But may I ask what would put such a pleasant – and may I say, entirely accurate – notion in your mind at this late hour of your day?"

They both chuckled. Archibald became serious.

"We found it, young man!" he said. "Imagine that! We found it! Your hunch was correct, m'boy. A few years ago, one of our constables reported a Webley being transported without a permit. It was found in a car involved in an accident."

"Well, well," Gervais replied. "What a break!"

"Yes, a break it most certainly is, thanks to you, m'boy!" Archibald said. "I must say, there's something else here that's curious, though. The

207

revolver is registered to a man with the same last name as your Mr. Paul Winston. The owner of the Webley is someone named Willard Winston. Any relation, do you suppose?"

"I don't know," Gervais replied. "But I'll check it out. Our Mr. Winston is a prominent Colorado businessman and rancher.

"Oh! I just thought of something, sir," Gervais added. "I remember seeing on the news a while back about my Mr. Winston inheriting a lot of money from a relative in England. I think he got some sort of title and a big old house, too.

"Tell you what, Superintendent," Gervais continued, "I'll give Mr. Winston a call. Would you mind checking things out further at your end? We can talk later if that's okay with you, sir."

"Of course, m'boy. Of course," Archibald answered, smiling to himself. He liked the way this personable young FBI agent took the initiative.

"One last thing, Gervais," Archibald added.

"Yes, sir?"

"Our forensic people are also going to compare the photos of the rifling marks – the photographs you sent and the ones we took. I'm afraid, though, the photos of the rifling you sent are iffy. The bullet fragments are quite small. Not sure we have enough detail to get a match. But we'll work on them and have a close look."

"That's all we have, sir, I'm afraid," Gervais replied. "Both of the bullets were in multiple pieces. As you know, they hit Mr. Winston's ribs and sternum and fragmented. Lucky for Mr. Winston, though. I suspect this was an amateur hit."

"What do you mean?" Archibald asked.

"Would you agree, sir, a professional hit man probably would have used military-grade hollow points with a heavier load of gunpowder? These were amateur attempts at making hollow points from regular bullets," Gervais responded. "That weakened the bullets and probably made them less effective rather than more effective. Besides, a professional would have used a heavier caliber weapon, and likely would have had much better aim. Two of our suspect's shots missed vital organs by quite a bit. Those hollow points, amateurish as they might have been, did do a lot of damage, mind you. The most accurate seems to have been the first one, when he shot Mr. Winston in the back."

"I agree with you again on all counts, Agent Gervais!" Archibald said. "Good for you!"

"And Superintendent, we just might have an opportunity for a better rifling match," Gervais continued. "Mr. Winston still has that first bullet inside of him. He wants it out and so do his doctors. The bullet is lodged next to his heart, so they're worried about damage they can't see. And the bullet is lead. His doctors are concerned about the effects of lead on his heart muscles and other surrounding tissue.

"I've heard that he'll be having it removed in a couple of months," Gervais added. "We'll be there, along with other law enforcement agencies to collect the evidence."

Archibald enjoyed listening to young Gervais. The young man was thinking like an accomplished investigator.

Looking forward to retirement in a few years, Archibald was confident law enforcement would be well served in the future so long as the leaders of agencies like the FBI and The Yard were smart enough to recruit bright young people of Gervais' caliber.

People with initiative and audacity—that's what's needed, Archibald told himself.

Chapter Fifty-Six

Two Months Later

"That son of a bitch belongs in jail," John Everett exploded. He was commenting on a report from Global Security International on their investigation into the court decision involving Paul and Anne's assets.

Two months earlier, Judge Clifford Swanson had ruled against Paul and Anne in a lawsuit brought by Roberta demanding that a large portion of his inheritance from their late Uncle Percival in England be divided among her, Paul, and their sister Emily. In an affidavit, Emily had opposed the suit and had sided with Paul.

Despite a brilliant defense by Tom Cameron and Everett, and Emily's affidavit, Judge Swanson had found in favor of Roberta, and ruled that Paul and Anne's assets in America be divided. He ordered that his decision would apply to all assets in America linked to Paul's inheritance from his uncle. The judge had also ordered that all of their assets in the U.S. be frozen pending settlement or appeal.

Paul was enraged. He'd instructed his lawyers to file an immediate appeal and a stay pending the appeal and hired Global Security to fast track a private investigation into the circumstances surrounding the decision. The stay had been granted by the Superior Court. Global's report was to go directly to Everett and Cameron. The investigation uncovered much more than Paul expected.

John and Tom had just finished going through the report and the accompanying photographs and videotapes. They were in John's office sharing the report with Paul. The key finding: Judge Swanson and Roberta were having an affair.

And that was not all the videos revealed.

"I'm sorry, Paul, that you had to find out like this about your sister's involvement with the judge," John said. "These pictures and videos that Global took are revealing and, frankly, disgusting."

Paul declined to look at them.

Global Security used a hidden camera to secretly videotape Judge Swanson on four occasions having sex with Roberta. Three of the graphic videos were taken through the window of a Colorado Springs motel room, the other on the back deck of the judge's home while his wife was away. The audio gave ample reason to believe their affair had been going on for some time.

The Global videotape also included a segment showing Roberta in Judge Swanson's car handing an envelope to him, who then was seen counting the contents. Using high-tech sound recording equipment, the segment recorded Roberta and Judge Swanson's encounter confirming an agreement that she would pay him $150,000 in return for a favorable ruling.

"This is explosive stuff," Tom added. "We should have no difficulty getting Judge Swanson's ruling set aside immediately.

"Here's how I suggest we proceed."

Chapter Fifty-Seven

Colorado Springs

Paul answered the direct line in his office personally, as he usually did.

"Hi Paul, this is Emile Bilodeaux. We finally have some solid evidence on the Continental Del Rio explosion.

"What've you got?" Paul said to the lead investigator for Global Security."

"Philip Tremblay asked me to bring you up to date. Based on the evidence we've gathered the Continental oil spill was definitely sabotage. We've got solid evidence the explosion was deliberately set."

"Just as we feared," Paul replied. "We didn't believe the explosion was an accident. Philip runs a first-rate operation, too good for it to be accidental. Any evidence who might be responsible?"

"During our investigation, we found a complete blasting cap that evidently was dropped by accident, as well as some pieces of a blasting cap we think detonated several sticks of dynamite, along with a few tag ends of fuse," Emile said. "We and the police suspect that the dynamite used was most likely the same stuff that's marketed to the agriculture industry for blasting rocks and tree stumps."

"Yeah, sure," Paul said. "Two-Dot Ranch uses it all the time. The guys keep it locked up in the main horse barn. Any idea where it came from?"

"Yeah. Well, we have a good idea, at any rate," Emile answered, and then paused. "Paul, it looks very much like it came from a box of dynamite sold a while ago to Two-Dot Ranch."

"You've got to be kidding me!" Paul said. "Are you absolutely certain?"

"I'm afraid we're as certain as we can be, Paul," Emile replied. "We checked and rechecked. We've been working with local and state authorities on this, so you need to know they have all of the evidence we've come up with. They're already poking around the ranch as we speak."

"Good Lord," Paul sighed. "I can hardly believe someone at the ranch was involved in the explosion, the deaths of those two rig workers, and that godawful oil spill. I don't understand this. Any idea who might be involved?"

"Neither the police nor we have any suspects at the moment," Emile answered. "But it sure looks like the dynamite came from an order delivered to Two-Dot early last spring from Ace Hardware here in Colorado Springs.

"The police have already interviewed George and Kurt Willis, among others. Both said they're the only ones who have keys to the storage room in the workshop where the dynamite is stored. Is that right?"

"As far as I know," Paul replied. "Even I don't have a key. And I'm absolutely certain George or Kurt would not let any dynamite out of their sight unless they were absolutely certain it was going to be used properly."

"Do you know if inventories were done when the dynamite was shipped from Ace and when it arrived at Two-Dot?" Emile asked.

"You'll need to ask Kurt or George about that," Paul replied. "I haven't had much to do with day-to-day operations for a few years.

213

"We need to get to the bottom of this and quickly, Emile," Paul added. "If we have a loose cannon out there, we need to stop him and do it soon. He might target someone else. The shootings and this bombing are not reassuring in the least."

"As you know, the police and county sheriff are handling this case," Emile answered. "They're very concerned that you and Anne could still be targets. El Paso County has asked me to stay involved. You okay with that?"

"Of course," Paul replied. "And you can tell your head office you're still on contract with us. As far as I'm concerned, you're one of the best investigators I know of, and we sure could use your ongoing help on this case."

"Thank you, Paul," Emile said. "That's much appreciated. If you're okay with it, I want to interview George and Kurt again as well as some of your other employees who might have had occasion to use the dynamite. Maybe some went astray or was lost. People forget."

"Of course," Paul said. "You're welcome to stay with us at the ranch if you want to. I'd just ask you to tread carefully with George. As you know, his wife was murdered a little over a year ago, and he's still not over it. Maybe you could get him to help you with this. It could be a distraction for him."

"Sure, Paul. I'll think about it," Emile replied, clearly reluctant to bring an amateur into a criminal investigation. Emile was a retired chief superintendent for the Royal Canadian Mounted Police in Montreal and was meticulous about conducting his investigations. He agreed to keep Paul up to date as the investigation progressed.

214

Chapter Fifty-Eight

John Everett's Office

Both of Paul's attorneys were licensed to practice law in Colorado. Everett and Cameron flipped a coin to decide who would take the lead filing a complaint with the Colorado Commission on Judicial Discipline against Judge Clifford Swanson. John won the toss.

Within 48 hours of receiving the Global Security report, the Commission undertook a preliminary review of the complaint. Copies of videotapes and photographs supplied by Global Security were included with the written report. The Commission promptly recommended that the Colorado Supreme Court suspend the judge pending a full investigation into his conduct regarding the civil case brought by Roberta.

Chief Justice McMillan then consulted quietly with his colleagues, who recommended that the District Court expedite hearing an appeal by Paul's attorneys. They agreed and the appeal set aside Swanson's decision. In his ruling, the Chief Justice of the District Court, Judge William Hamilton, was livid that the state's judicial system had been misused in this way.

Justice Hamilton described Roberta's lawsuit as "an egregious abuse of a vital civic system established to bring fair and just resolution to legitimate differences, and not to be misused for the purpose of avaricious or capricious actions as was the case in this instance." He added, the lawsuit "lacked even the slightest grounds for legal action" and called it "the most baseless case in my seventeen years on the bench."

The Colorado Bar Association's Disciplinary Committee voted to suspend Roberta's license to practice law immediately pending a full review, possible criminal charges, and referral to the Colorado Supreme Court for subsequent disbarment proceedings.

A few weeks later, Paul's former attorney, Walter Stewart, was called before the Disciplinary Counsel to explain his collaboration. In return for full disclosure of his involvement and his confession to an obvious conflict of interest, the sterner action that many fellow lawyers had called for against Stewart was limited to a public warning by the Supreme Court. It also posted a notice of their decision in the bar journal, which was picked up by the Colorado Springs Gazette, the Colorado Springs Independent and the Denver Post.

The action against Stewart was the top news story in the local media for almost a week. The publicity prompted a steady flow of letters from former clients into his office cancelling his services. A few months later, with his law practice virtually dried up, Stewart closed his office and moved out of state.

Chapter Fifty-Nine

Stephen was in the den when Roberta arrived home. Their two children were with her. Jessica was five and in kindergarten. Joel, seven, was in the second grade.

"You're home early," Roberta said matter-of-factly as she stood at the door to the den.

She noticed her husband was holding a water glass filled with ice and what she suspected was white rum and ginger ale. His usual. The blurry look in his eyes told her it wasn't the first.

"Heard how your lawshuit turned out ... and why," Stephen said, his voice slurring. "Thought you were shmarter than that."

"You kids go outside and play," Roberta said to the children. "I'll call you when supper's ready."

After the children left, Roberta turned to Stephen.

"You're a fine one to point fingers, Stephen," she said. "You've been fucking damned near every young clerk that's worked for you ever since I set you up with that goddamned franchise. Worst thing I ever did. Don't think for a minute I haven't been fully aware of your shenanigans. And who knows how many other whores you've been doin' over the years."

"Ish that why you've been balling that fuckin' judge?" Stephen challenged. "Jusht to get even? Christ, Roberta, surely you could have been a bit sluber... ah, sutler... ah, a bit subtler about it. I can't believe you'd let that old prick get inta your pants."

"What the fuck do you care, Stephen? At home you sure as hell haven't been the big stud you seem to think you are at work," Roberta

217

shot back. "Stephen, I think it would be a good idea for you to move out for a while. In fact, maybe we should make that permanent."

"You're damn right," Stephen replied, thinking of the apartment he was renting downtown for his evening trysts … where he 'entertained' girlfriends, telling Roberta he was out playing poker with the boys. She knew the truth.

He staggered out of the den and upstairs to their bedroom with the twin beds Roberta had insisted upon. He threw into his big travel suitcase a bunch of suits, jackets, pants, and shirts. Into a smaller carry-on he stuffed underwear, toiletries, socks, and some shoes. He knew that he could get any other clothes he needed at the store. He never paid for anything.

With an angry look over his shoulder, Stephen charged down the stairs, out into the garage and drove away in the brand-new Jaguar he'd picked up last week, on Roberta's credit, although much against her wishes. He didn't know it yet, but she'd arranged to have the car repossessed by the dealer.

Chapter Sixty

Denver

"Gervais! My office right now!"

The voice and tone on the intercom were unmistakable. Frank Schuler, the special agent in charge of the FBI's Colorado field office, was angry again.

Gervais walked down the hall to Schuler's office. He'd no sooner got through the door than Schuler began shouting at him.

"What in goddamned hell do you think you're doing, Gervais?"

"What do you mean, Frank?" Gervais replied with a calm air of innocence. He knew exactly what his boss was upset about.

"Look at this!" Schuler ranted. "Just look at this, will you? It's a bill, a phone bill ... for calls to London, England. They're from *your* local. Who the hell authorized you to make these calls? Why wasn't I informed? What were they all about?"

"The Colorado Springs shootings," Gervais said.

"Our job is the kidnapping," Schuler said. "That's it. We've no obligation to do anything to help those guys in Colorado Springs!"

His voice had an unmistakable demeaning tone.

"And I told you to butt out of that investigation!" Schuler said.

"Frank, I was following up on leads about the shootings," Gervais said. "I'll pay for the calls if you want."

"Gervais, that's insubordination!" Schuler shouted. "You're suspended from duty as of right now. And I'm going to see about getting you fired! Don't you know that insubordination is a firing offence? Now get the fuck out of my sight, you useless prick!"

"Just so you know, Frank," Gervais answered calmly, "my contacts at New Scotland Yard, and in CSP and CSPD, and I, have come up with some key answers in these cases. We might just have solved them.

"Have a nice day," Gervais added as he wheeled around and walked away from Schuler's office toward the sixth-floor elevators.

Schuler shouted after him, "What do you mean? Are you telling me you've solved these cases? Where do you think you're going? Get back here!"

Gervais continued on to the elevator, and then turned. "I've been suspended from duty, Frank. Remember?"

He stepped on the elevator as the doors closed.

Schuler ran to the elevator and pounded on the buttons while other special agents and staff watched in ill-concealed amusement.

They glanced away trying to keep straight faces as Schuler's angry eyes scanned the room.

Chapter Sixty-One

Colorado Springs

The distinctive chocolate-brown UPS van stopped in front of Master Tailor Men's Wear on Main Street in downtown Colorado Springs. The driver took a parcel to the checkout counter.

"Are you Stephen Hooper?" he asked.

"No, I'm Robert Ericson," Robert said. "I work for Mr. Hooper. Here, I'll sign for it."

"'Fraid not," the driver said. "This one has to be signed for by Stephen Hooper. Says right here, addressee signature only. Is he in?"

"Okay. Just a minute."

Robert pushed the intercom. "Stephen?"

"Yeah, what the fuck is it? I'm busy, goddamn it!" the irritated voice shouted back.

The loud, rude voice caught the attention of the driver and the only customer in the store. Their startled eyes focused on Robert.

"There's a parcel here for you, Stephen," Robert began. Before he could explain further, the voice interrupted.

"Well for Christ's sake, Robert, you know what to do. Sign for the fucking thing!" the condescending voice on the intercom shouted back.

"The driver says you've got to sign for it," Robert replied, struggling to keep his patience.

The intercom went dead.

Robert looked up as the customer walked out the door.

221

James Osborne

Business had been falling off. Robert understood why. Stephen had become increasingly irritable. His outbursts of bad temper were spilling over into his dealings with customers. So was his heavy drinking. Robert thought their decreasing business was also a result of the scandal over his wife's affair with the judge and her suspension by the Supreme Court. They were the talk of the town. It had been all over the news media.

Some of their best customers hadn't been in for months. He knew they were shopping elsewhere ... he'd seen them ... even though Master Tailor carried all the top-quality lines of men's wear such as Brooks Brothers suits and other premium brands like Ralph Lauren, Bugatti, Armani and Bally.

Stephen stomped up to the counter.

"Where the hell is it?" he demanded.

The UPS driver glanced at Robert with a questioning look. He handed Stephen the electronic clipboard and stylus. Without a word, Stephen signed, grabbed the package, and headed for his office in the back of the store.

Stephen closed and locked the door to his office and then sat at his desk. He tore off the wrapping and opened the shipping box. On top was a typewritten note on letterhead stationery. The return address was Professional Uniform & Linen Supply, 3482 E 46th Ave, Denver, CO, 80216. The note read.

Dear Mr. Hooper;

In response to your enquiry, Professional Uniform & Linen Supply is proud to be included in the plans by Master Tailor Men's Wear to diversify its product offerings, and for your store to become our exclusive authorized agent in Colorado Springs.

We are pleased to enclose, as samples, one full set of hospital operating room scrubs, size medium, including cap, top, trousers and booties. We have also included a sample package of surgical masks, as requested.

Our Company manufactures all of these items, except for the surgical masks, which we can arrange for a third party to supply your store at an attractive price. Please note we produce only the finest quality of hospital uniforms and accessories.

We look forward to a long and mutually beneficial relationship with you and Master Tailor Men's Wear.
Sincerely,
Harold Simpson
Vice President, Business Development

Stephen smiled to himself as he tried on the pale green hospital operating room scrubs. They were a bit large but fit well enough.

He told himself that the next time he'd be putting them on he'll also be wearing street clothes underneath, so he can remove and dispose of the scrubs. It would ensure a clean getaway.

Chapter Sixty-Two

Denver

"Is that man daft?" Superintendent Archibald exclaimed.

Richard Gervais, the suspended FBI special agent, was on the phone to the London police executive with information about how Paul Winston of Colorado Springs, was related to Willard Winston of Maidstone.

Two weeks earlier, Archibald told Gervais that police in Maidstone had recovered a military-type revolver from a car involved in an accident a few years earlier. Coincidentally, it was the same make and model as the weapon believed used in the attempt to murder Paul Winston half a world away in Colorado Springs. It had raised a host of questions.

Gervais was returning the call from his home in a Denver suburb. Archibald's outburst came after Gervais revealed that Schuler had suspended him.

"Blimey! We're bloody well going to see about that!" Archibald added angrily. "Don't you worry about it one bit, m'boy. Ordinarily, I'd never think of interfering with the internal matters of a fellow law enforcement agency. But this is the most nonsensical thing I've heard of in a very long while.

"This most certainly is *not* the FBI I know," the English police executive fumed. "I have a few friends at FBI headquarters in Washington, m'boy. And by Jove, your Mr. Special-Agent-In-Charge is going to face some tough questions, I can assure you of that.

"Now, what about your man, Mr. Paul Winston?" Archibald asked, making an obvious effort to calm down.

"Believe it or not, sir," Gervais replied, "My Mr. Winston, when he's in your country, happens to be known there as Lord Winston, the 12th Earl of Prescott. And he owns a big house called Earnscliffe Manor. Do you know it by any chance?"

Gervais heard a low whistle from the other end of the phone.

"Yes, indeed I do," Archibald replied with obvious surprise. "That big house, as you describe it, m'boy, is indeed big. You might call it the first cousin to a castle, what with its four floors, 12 bedrooms and eight bathrooms, plus servants' quarters downstairs. Yes, it's a big house, all right!"

"Oh," was all a stunned Gervais could manage in response, smiling at his own inability to come up with anything more to say.

Archibald knew about the sprawling 750-acre Earnscliffe Manor estate. It was a few miles from his home in Gillingham. Years ago, he and his family had visited the medieval Manor with its large moat and lush rolling fields of grain and hay. Paul and Anne had opened the carefully restored Manor years go to provide for public tours. Donations from visitors went to local charities.

"Yes, sir," Gervais continued, "and my Mr. Winston's also a member of the House of Lords in your Parliament. Besides that, he and his wife Anne, an English lady, have a wide range of investments, including quite a list of properties here, in England and on the European mainland. According to our research, the Winstons head up a private holding company called Prescott Enterprises that's worth more than $3.7 billion. They're one of the wealthiest and most respected families in the western United States."

It was Archibald's turn to be impressed.

"Sir, your man Willard Winston," Gervais continued, getting to the main point of his call, "is a second cousin to my Mr. Winston. He told me their grandfathers were brothers. Paul Winston said that Willard and his wife have been living for some 25 years in a rather nice cottage on the Earnscliffe estate. A gatehouse, he called it."

Gervais continued, "You'll be interested to know, sir, Paul also told me that Willard and his wife Alice have an adult son, Reginald, better known as Reggie, who lives in a town called Maidstone. Apparently that's not far from Earnscliffe. I got the impression that Reggie may have a history of encounters with local police. Not sure there's a connection but perhaps it's worth looking into."

"Yes, indeed. Yes, indeed! Thank you," Archibald replied. "Quite a coincidence, I should think. I know Maidstone. I live not far from there. Well now, we seem to be making progress, Agent Gervais. Yes, indeed, we do seem to be making progress."

Archibald was thoroughly enjoying this break from administrative work – being involved again in an investigation. And he especially enjoyed working with this promising young FBI agent.

"Oh, and by the by," he added. "I'll let you know later about my calls to FBI headquarters in Washington."

"As you wish, sir," Gervais replied, thinking he had nothing to lose by Archibald's well-intention intervention. "Thank you, sir. Thank you very much."

"Cheers, then," Archibald said and hung up.

Gervais did not know that a very senior FBI executive, Joseph Foster, had been seconded 12 years earlier to New Scotland Yard to help investigate a terrorist network being formed in London. Foster had worked with Archibald, then head of The Yard's anti-terrorist unit, later merged with Special Branch to form the Counter Terrorism Command. Right from their first meeting, the two law enforcement executives had struck up a warm friendship based on mutual professional respect. They'd kept in touch over the years. Foster was now the Assistant Director in charge of the FBI's National Security Branch.

A few days after talking with Gervais, Archibald spoke with Foster on the phone.

"And that just about sums it up, Joe," Archibald said finally. "I know this isn't your bailiwick, but this Gervais fellow is a jolly good young lad, you know. Very promising if I may say. Hate to see him treated this way. Hell, I'll hire him if you guys let him go."

Archibald had briefed Foster on the cases he and Gervais were working on and the circumstances of Gervais' suspension.

"Not a problem, Charles. I really appreciate the heads up," the FBI executive replied. "Leave it with me. Gervais seems like just the kind of young agent we need more of, need to encourage."

"My thoughts exactly, Joe," Archibald said.

"I'll have someone deal with Schuler," Foster added. "I've heard rumors about that guy before. This isn't the first time his behavior has come into question. It could be this is one time too many."

They made their goodbyes and hung up.

Chapter Sixty-Three

Colorado Springs

Just after 7:30 p.m., Dan Lorente knocked on the door of Elsie Solomon's apartment near downtown Colorado Springs. He'd deliberately waited until early evening. Dan wanted to give Elsie time to get home from work and have her supper.

Lorente would have preferred to be doing almost anything else, but someone had to do these jobs. Although he was now deputy chief of police, he would continue to be responsible for homicide until a new department head was appointed. CSPD procedure normally would mean two uniformed officers making these calls. He'd decided to go solo. Tonight's unpleasant job was up to him.

"May I help you?" Elsie said as she opened the door, a pleasant look on her attractive face.

She tried to conceal her surprise at finding herself attracted to the handsome middle-aged man standing there at her front door, well dressed in a custom-tailored suit and matching tie.

"Are you Elsie Solomon?" he said.

Officially, he had to do that. He already knew who she was. He'd been drawn to her radiant good looks when he'd seen her several times at the supermarket and while shopping downtown. He'd asked around. Elsie nodded hesitantly, a mixture of apprehension and uncertainty springing to her eyes.

"My name is Dan Lorente. I'm with the Colorado Springs Police Department," he said. He felt using his new title might be intimidating and would be too ostentatious. "May I come in?"

Dan noticed Elsie's eyes narrow, and the muscles of her kindly face tighten slightly. He could see that Elsie had experience with visits from police, no doubt as a result of her husband, Marvin. She stepped back, holding the door open.

"Yes, please come in," she replied.

Lorente walked into a sparsely furnished living room. It was tidy and immaculately well-kept. Elsie motioned him to a clean but aged armchair. Lorente sat down as Elsie walked over and sat on a matching sofa.

"I'm here about that missing person's report you filed on your husband, Marvin Solomon," Lorente began.

"Yes, Detective," Elsie replied anxiously. "Have you found my husband? Do you know where he is? Is he all right?"

"I'm terribly sorry, Mrs. Solomon," Lorente replied, "but I have some very bad news. It's my duty to inform you that your husband, Mr. Marvin Solomon, is deceased."

A cry, almost child-like, escaped from behind the hands Elsie had instinctively clasped over her mouth.

"I'm sure you remember hearing about a body found in a field a while back?"

Elsie nodded.

"I'm sorry to inform you that it has been positively identified as that of your late husband," Lorente added.

Elsie remembered news stories at the time. She'd refused to believe what her instincts had been telling her – that it might be Marvin. She wondered what in the world he could have been doing there. Tears flowed down her cheeks and over hands still held tightly over her mouth.

229

James Osborne

God, I hate this part of my job, he told himself, looking at the distraught woman seated in front of him. He resisted the urge to step over and put his arms around this kindly woman to comfort her.

"How did it happen?" she said. "How did he die?"

"We're still trying to establish an exact cause of death," he said. It was only a partial lie, he told himself, sparing her the gruesome details. Telling Elsie that Marvin had been killed by wild animals and his body partly eaten would serve no useful purpose.

Lorente went into the kitchen and found a glass in a cupboard. He filled it with water and returned, handing the glass and a box of tissues to Elsie. He gave her a few moments to collect herself before he continued.

"I'm sorry we were so long in identifying your husband's body," Lorente continued. "For some reason the FBI took their time sending us the fingerprints to check against with our fingerprint file. When they did, Mrs. Solomon, we were able to confirm the identity of your husband. He was fingerprinted here a few years ago after being arrested for drunk driving."

Elsie felt dazed, and yet was not surprised. Marvin had been missing for almost than a year. Not a word. It was not like him. Even in the days when he went on his drinking binges, she would get occasional calls from him. She'd listen to him babble on the phone, often for up to an hour.

Sometimes she'd find him on the streets in Denver, where he had been living for months, begging for money to buy booze. There'd been no calls this time.

"Your husband apparently had a British accent," Lorente said. "Is that correct?"

"Marvin does have … did have an accent," Elsie replied. "Marvin was born in England. Came here with his parents when he was six or seven. For some reason, he tried to hide his accent. I don't know why. But his accent became quite noticeable when he'd been drinking or was upset. Oddly enough, he favored clothes made in England. Sort of a contradiction, I suppose. Anyway, when he had any extra money, he'd buy shirts and pants at a men's store here in town that carries British-made clothes."

"There are a few ... other things I have to tell you," Dan said.

Elsie looked at him. He could see she was steeling herself for more bad news.

"Just before he died, we believe someone may have paid Marvin to set an explosion at an oil drilling site near Fort Collins. Two men were killed, and the explosion caused a major oil spill."

"How could that be?" Elsie said. "What makes you think he was involved? How could he get there? He doesn't own ... ah, didn't have a vehicle. My old car is the only one we have."

"Investigators found a coat at the scene with British labels," Dan said. "They found a few blood stains on it. DNA matched the blood with your husband's."

"Oh," Elsie said. She felt confused.

"Do you have any idea how he could have become involved in a scheme like this?" Dan said. "I'm very sorry, but I have to ask."

"No, I don't have any idea," she said. "And yes, I understand, sir."

"Please, call me Dan," he said.

"Yes, Dan," Elsie said easily. "And Elsie, please."

Dan noticed that using their first names seemed to calm her.

"There's something else I have to tell you, Elsie," Dan continued. Reluctance showed on his face.

"Yes, what is it?" she said, looking him in the eye.

"Again, I'm very sorry, but, well, there's no way to tell you this gently. We've confirmed that your husband was responsible for the kidnapping of Douglas Winston."

"WHAT?" Elsie exclaimed, leaping to her feet. "That can't be. It just can't be! Please tell me it's not true."

231

"I'm afraid it is, Mrs. Solomon," Lorente replied calmly. "We have evidence linking Mr. Solomon with … with the kidnapping of the Winston boy. We have his fingerprints on a stolen pickup that he apparently used to travel to the Fort Collins well site, and to kidnap the Winston boy. I'm afraid it was the kidnapping that took him to the location where he died."

"Oh, my god!" Elsie said. "How could he do that to Douglas … to the Winstons? They're such nice people. I just don't understand. Are you quite sure, Detective?"

"Dan, please. And yes, we're very sure. Our evidence … are you sure you want to hear this, Elsie?" When she nodded, he went on. "The evidence places Mr. Solomon in Livingston Valley where the Winston boy told us he was kidnapped and in the shack where he was held. His fingerprints were found on the stolen pickup and on a handgun recovered from the scene where his body was found. It's been positively identified as the gun used in the kidnapping."

"I really am very sorry," Lorente added. It occurred to him that he kept telling this kindly woman how sorry he was … and was meaning it.

Elsie was in shock. It just wasn't like Marvin to do something like this, at least not since he'd joined AA.

"But why?" Elsie said. She felt betrayed and bewildered. She feared that Marvin might have learned something from her about the Winstons that might have helped him kidnap Douglas.

"The motive appears to have been money," the detective replied. "We found a shopping list in the pocket of his jeans. The writing matches a ransom note attached to the saddle of Douglas Winston's horse, which showed up at the ranch without him the day he was kidnapped."

"This must be a terrible shock for you," she heard Dan say. "I wish I could make this easier for you. Is there someone I can call? Someone who can come and be with you?"

Dan knew they had no children or any other relatives in Colorado Springs.

Elsie shook her head 'no'.

"I … I'll be okay," she managed.

Dan admired the strength of the woman he saw before him. Elsie reminded him of his late wife Helen, killed five years ago in a car accident and leaving him with two children to raise – a daughter and a son – without their mother. The other driver had been drunk and was able to walk away from the accident. Dan felt this kind person deserved better. His heart went out to her.

He stood to leave. Elsie got up and walked him to the door.

As he opened the door, he reached out and put his right arm around her shoulder, giving her a gentle hug. He felt her lean ever so lightly toward him, relaxing just a bit beneath his embrace. The gesture was against regulations, but he was pleased the human contact might have helped ease her distress.

Lorente knew Elsie worked for Anne and Paul Winston at Two-Dot Ranch. Despite the late hour, he went back to his office and called the Winstons at the ranch.

Anne answered the phone, and Dan explained what had happened. In minutes, Anne was in her car, heading for Elsie's apartment.

Chapter Sixty-Four

Anne and their three children accompanied Paul to the surgery department at Colorado Springs Memorial Hospital. It was early evening. They tried to not show how nervous they were about Paul's operation the next morning to remove the bullet lodged next to his heart.

Anne was still reeling from learning two days earlier that the body of Elsie's missing husband, Marvin, had been found. She was shocked to hear that Marvin had kidnapped Douglas. And she remembered Paul mentioning the explosion at the Continental Del Rio drilling site. Her sympathies went out to Elsie.

After Marvin disappeared, Elsie had confessed to Anne there'd been little affection between them for years. That had done little to ease her pain now. Elsie told Anne that under the circumstances she felt it best to quit her job. Anne refused to consider it. She finally talked Elsie into agreeing that the best thing she could do was to keep working at the job she enjoyed and did so well. Everyone there loved her and had come to depend on her.

"Mr. Winston?"

The surgery receptionist broke into Anne's thoughts. Paul walked to the desk. The receptionist handed him a clipboard.

"Please fill out these forms and sign where indicated, then return them to the desk. I'm off duty now, but someone else will be at the desk."

Paul and Anne went over to the area where the children were waiting. They were scuffling and taunting each other as children do. Paul settled them down with his usual good nature, then he filled out and signed the forms.

Nurse Janine Hernandez was waiting for them when they returned to the reception desk.

"I'm going to be looking after you, Mr. Winston," she told a surprised Paul and Anne.

She smiled proudly at them. They returned warm smiles but were curious. Seeing Janine helped ease Anne's fears. She'd told Paul what Janine had shared about him helping Ramon, the nurse's son. Paul was embarrassed as much by forgetting to tell Anne as he was about having his secret generosity revealed.

Janine explained:

"I've just completed my accreditation as a cardiothoracic surgical nurse. I'm assigned to the hospital's vascular and cardiac department now."

"Well, congratulations," Paul said, genuinely happy for her, taking her delicate hand gently in both of his. "We're very pleased for you. How is Ramon doing?"

"Oh, he's doing very well, thanks to you, Mr. Winston," she replied. "Thank you for asking. Ramon is finishing his master's degree in computer science at the University of Wyoming in Laramie. He's going on for his doctorate. Can you believe that? We're going to have a doctor in the house!"

The proud mother chuckled at her own humor.

"If you'll both follow me, please" she added, smoothly reverting to her professional persona. "We'll get you settled, Mr. Winston and ready for the morning. I'm off duty overnight but I'll be seeing you at 5:30 tomorrow morning. Dr. Moore has you scheduled for 6 o'clock.

"No more food or drink from now on, right?"

"Yup," Paul answered, not happy being reminded of how hungry he was already. He'd skipped supper.

Here we go, he thought.

Paul turned and hugged each of their children and then looked at Anne, reaching for her hand. He knew how stressed she was about the surgery. He wished there was a way to ease her fears.

"You'll look after things for me, won't you, son?" he said to Douglas, whose chest swelled with pride over his father's show of confidence in him.

"It's going to be just fine, my love," he said turning back to Anne.

"I know, Paul. Just a routine operation, right?" she added with gentle sarcasm, leaning her head against his broad chest.

They both dreaded spending nights apart, but this was much harder. It seemed worse than when he'd been shot. That time their separation was not by choice. As they turned and walked down the hall, he put his arm tightly around Anne's shoulders. The three children watched them go, each sharing their mother's apprehension.

Paul was wakened at 5:30 the next morning. Nurse Hernandez injected a mild sedative and installed an intravenous line.

***

His ravenous hunger returned despite the sedative. He knew he would be waiting much longer than he wanted before savoring any meals. Then, he told himself, he was going to have a steak, medium rare, with all the trimmings. Although no one was around, he held the back of his gown closed modestly with one hand as he moved himself from his bed onto a gurney brought in early that morning. A few minutes later an orderly wheeled him into the waiting area next to the operating room.

It was 5:54 a.m.

Dr. David Shepherd walked up beside Paul's gurney.

"What are you doing here?" Paul asked, shocked and pleasantly surprised.

Paul was caught off-guard, despite the calming effects of the sedative in his system, to see the world-famous cardiothoracic surgeon standing beside him. Dr. Shepherd had led the team that performed life-saving surgery when he was shot, removing the fragments of the other two shattered bullets from his right chest and lung.

"Dr. Moore consulted with me in Chicago about your operation," Shepherd replied, as Lillian Moore walked up to them. "Decided to come back and help finish the job. Couldn't let her have all the fun, now could I?"

The two surgeons exchanged smiles. Both were dressed in pale green operating room scrubs.

"Not sure I have room in here for both pairs of your hands along with all of your toys," Paul joked, pointing to his chest.

"Hey, that's okay," Dr. Moore replied with a grin. "If it gets too crowded we'll find something to throw away – a spleen, liver, stomach … whatever."

Dr. Moore's manner turned serious.

"Paul, needless to say, I'm thrilled that Dr. Shepherd has agreed to join us. He's the best there is. You know that from personal experience. Although this bullet entered from your back, Paul, Dr. Shepherd and I both agree we need to go in from the front."

Dr. Moore continued, "This operation will be much like open heart surgery. We do an incision, cut through your breastbone, and open your chest. This will give us access to the site where the bullet appears to be lodged."

Two hours into the operation, Dr. Moore was ready to extract the bullet. To their surprise, the bullet had somehow lodged between Paul's aorta and pulmonary artery. The two surgeons wondered if Paul would ever fully understand just how lucky he had been. A fraction of an inch either way could have been fatal. They exchanged looks over their masks and surgical lenses. Then, Dr. Moore nodded. Time to proceed.

Neither was expecting what came next.

Dr. Moore gripped the bullet with a long set of thoracic forceps and began to lift it out. It was stuck. She had to tug on it firmly. Without warning, blood spurted upward in an arc out of Paul's chest cavity. The bullet had punctured his aorta after all. The damage hadn't shown up on the x-rays.

They had to move fast or lose him. Quickly, the surgical team transitioned Paul onto a heart-lung machine. Dr. Moore had insisted one be on standby in the operating theatre, just in case. A good thing. The bullet had been acting as a plug, closing a rupture to his aorta caused by the bullet itself. It was being held in place precariously by pressure from the pulmonary artery and some muscles around the heart. Natural healing provided a fragile seal of scar tissue also helping to hold the bullet in place.

"David, we need to repair that section of the aorta with mesh. Agreed?" Dr. Moore said, pressing her thumb down on the hole to reduce the blood loss. She'd already ordered blood transfusions to be started. "We'll stop his heart as soon as we get him fully transitioned to the heart-lung support."

"Agreed," Dr. Shepherd replied. "A good thing you anticipated this, Lillian. Thanks to you, we came to the party prepared. Look, you get that bullet out and then let me do the mesh. I've done hundreds of aortas. It'll give me something to justify for all that time I'm gonna bill for," he added with smiling eyes and a grin no one saw behind his surgical mask.

"We've started administering the first units of blood," Dr. Moore said. "We ordered 10 units. Hope that's enough. Good thing he's Type O positive. If we need more, we've lots of donors on standby."

It took another three hours – transitioning to the heart-lung machine, removing the bullet, repairing Paul's aorta, restarting Paul's heart, transitioning him back off the heart-lung machine and stabilizing him. They were in the operating theatre a total of five hours. Finally, the two weary cardiothoracic specialists turned the operation over to junior surgeons to complete closing Paul's chest cavity and preparing him for the recovery unit.

Anne jumped up and ran toward Dr. Moore and Dr. Shepherd as they walked into the waiting room.

"How is he? You've been in there a long time! Is Paul okay?" Anne asked, clearly overcome with fear. "When can I see him?"

"Yes, Anne," Dr. Moore said wearily. "First things first. Paul's going to be just fine. We anticipated the operation might be a bit challenging, and it was.

"Paul's in Recovery now," she added. "We'll be moving him into ICU in about half an hour. You can see him then, but just briefly. I guess you know the drill."

Anne collapsed with relief and fatigue into the chair she'd been in and out of while Paul was in surgery. Her hands shook as she dabbed at the corners of her eyes.

Dr. Moore smiled down at Anne. Dr. Shepherd sat in the chair beside her.

"Anne," Dr. Shepherd began. "Your husband is one incredibly lucky man."

She looked at him apprehensively.

"We couldn't see it on the x-rays or scans, but when we got in we found the bullet had punctured his aorta. Ironically, that bullet was acting like a plug ... like plugging a hole in a high-pressure pipe. The bullet was being held in place by the strength of his pulmonary artery and the muscles around his heart, and by some scar tissue that formed after the shooting. It was all very precarious.

"A hard fall or some other jolt could have dislodged the bullet," the surgeon told her. "I don't want to add to your discomfort, Anne, but Paul could have bled to death internally before anyone realized anything was wrong."

Anne recoiled inwardly in near terror as she recalled how she and Paul had been bucked off their horses during their encounter with the black bear and cubs.

239

"Dr. Moore and I are very relieved that you and Paul decided on this operation," Dr. Shepherd added. "You and Paul made the right decision. It probably saved his life."

Chapter Sixty-Five

Maidstone, England

Reggie woke in the police holding cell, also known as the drunk tank.

The fetid air was a repulsive cocktail of eye-searing odors – vomit co-mingled with acrid body odor, urine, and excrement.

Inspector Andy McKillop of the Kent Police called out, "Reginald Winston!"

He had to shout over the groans and curses of more than a dozen other drunks crowded into the large cell.

"Yeah, yeah," Reggie replied. His head was aching from another full-blown hangover.

"Get yourself over here, Winston," Insp. McKillop ordered, opening the cell door.

It troubled McKillop, seeing Reggie once again under his care. Here was a young man from a prominent and respected area family destroying his life with one alcoholic bender after another. It made no sense. McKillop recalled that in recent years, the number of Reggie's overnight appearances in his police cells had increased. Meanwhile Reggie's physical appearance had continued to deteriorate.

"Reggie, how many times must I tell you," McKillop said. "I'm sick and tired of your visits here. You're wasting scarce resources that we need to protect respectable people from genuine bad guys, not drunks like you. Go get yourself showered and cleaned up."

"Over there," the police inspector said in disgust, pointing to the locker rooms.

McKillop knew he was bending regulations once again by doing Reggie a favor like this, but he'd known Reggie's great uncle many years ago. While a young man, he'd worked on Percy's estate and had experienced the respect that the Earl and his wife showed for employees. The Earl had even written a letter of recommendation endorsing his application to join the Kent Police.

"I'll give you 10 minutes," he added. "Then I'll be in with a bucket of cold water."

Reggie knew better than to talk back. He felt like it though.

"Yeah, sure, Inspector," he muttered.

After being let into the staff locker room, and with the door closed behind him, Reggie muttered to himself, *Fucking copper. Why the fuck doesn't he just mind his own fuckin' business?*

Chapter Sixty-Six

Colorado Springs

Nurse Janine Hernandez had been given permission to work a double shift, determined to personally monitor Paul's post-operative care. In her opinion, it was the least she could do for him.

Paul was in ICU until midnight. Janine was there.

Anne visited him and then returned to the private waiting room, graciously declining suggestions that she go home for the night. In the waiting room, Anne fell asleep on top of a bed there. She'd sent their children home with Susan Willis.

Shortly after midnight, Dr. Moore considered Paul's progress good enough to move him to a private room in a secure section of the hospital like before. Janine got Paul settled and decided to remain in the room so she could keep an eye on him.

At 3:12 a.m., the door to Paul's room opened.

Janine was returning from the bathroom. She'd just changed one of Paul's intravenous bags and disposed of the empty. A man dressed in pale green hospital scrubs entered Paul's room. A surgical mask covered his face.

At first, Janine thought Dr. Shepherd was checking on Paul's progress. But this man was shorter and heavier. Something else was odd. It wasn't necessary to wear a mask now.

Without looking around, the man walked quickly toward Paul's bed. Something shiny flashed in his right hand.

"Oh, my god!" Janine screamed.

243

James Osborne

The man was holding a knife with a long, thin blade.

"Stop! Stop!" Janine shouted.

"What do you think you're doing?" she screamed as the man sliced an intravenous tube leading to Paul's right arm.

Janine rushed forward, forcibly jamming herself between the man and Paul. The man staggered back a step. She grabbed the call button with her right hand and pushed hard.

Her patient remained in a deep, drugged sleep. Janine lifted her hands to push the man farther away.

He was holding the knife in his right hand, the blade pointing away from him. In a lightning-fast move, he raised his hand across his chest toward his left shoulder, and then swung his arm down and to the right, across, in a hard, sideways slashing motion.

Searing pain shot across the right side of Janine's neck. Blood gushed out of a large cut, soaking into her clothing, and splashing onto the floor. The knife had severed her carotid artery and cut her windpipe.

Before she could react, Janine was knocked back against Paul's bed. A huge weight had slammed into her chest. She looked down, surprised. The handle of the shiny knife was sticking out of her chest between her sternum and her left breast. She didn't know it, but the point of the blade had penetrated deep into her heart.

Janine fell to the floor. Lying on her left side, she saw her attacker whirl around and run out the door. Her eyesight was growing hazy. Janine tried to push herself up from the floor. Her strength was gone.

A police officer ran through the door. His eyes grew big when he saw her on the floor in a spreading pool of blood. He rolled her onto her back and put his hand over her neck wound. The blood kept pumping out between his fingers. An intern Janine didn't know took over from the officer and tried without success to stem the gushing blood.

Janine vaguely made out more pairs of legs, one clad in a police uniform and others clad in hospital scrubs. The officer's feet stopped

244

briefly, then disappeared out the door and down the corridor. She heard confused shouting. Sights and sounds were growing more and more difficult to make out clearly. In the distance she thought she heard two shots, then a third and a fourth, as everything went black.

And then the life of Janine Hernandez, BSc, RN ... wife, mother, sister, daughter, nurse, and friend ... ebbed away in a rapidly spreading pool of her own blood.

Officer Juan Lopez had stopped briefly in the room, seen his colleague attending a severely injured nurse and then had sprinted after a man clad in blood-splattered hospital scrubs, running away down the hospital corridor.

"Stop!" Lopez ordered at the top of his lungs. "Police! Stop right there!"

Lopez cursed himself for leaving his post at Paul Winston's hospital room door to get a coffee. Again, he ordered the retreating figure to stop. The man ignored him and disappeared around a corner. Lopez was close behind.

The man slammed through a pair of steel fire doors and leaped down the concrete steps. A split second later, Lopez burst through the doors. The fleeing man was on the landing below. He raised his hand, pointed a handgun, and fired.

Officer Lopez ducked instinctively as he heard a bullet slam into the fire door above his head. He leveled his service pistol and returned fire at the fleeing suspect. He missed. With a supreme force of will he focused hard, aimed carefully, and pulled the trigger three more times in rapid succession.

All three shots from Lopez' .357 Magnum hit the man. They threw him back heavily against the wall. Then the man's knees crumpled. He fell sideways headfirst down the next flight of stairs.

Lopez held his weapon at the ready. Two other police officers ran up behind him. Both were part of the detail assigned to guard Mr. and Mrs. Winston and their three children.

One officer ran down the stairs to the fallen man. The other stayed with Lopez. Both kept their weapon ready in case the man lying on his back at the bottom of the stairs made a move. The first officer carefully approached the fallen man and kicked the handgun away from his hand. The man's eyes were partly open but sightless.

The officer put his fingers on the man's neck to check for a pulse. He looked up at his colleagues. He shook his head 'no.' The shooter was dead.

The police officers checked, but the body carried no identification. Even the pockets in the street clothes under the scrubs were empty.

It was a shock later to the Colorado Springs Police Department when fingerprints confirmed his identity. The name that came back from the police identification unit was Stephen Joseph Hooper. CSPD knew him as the registered franchise owner of Master Tailor Men's Wear store in Colorado Springs and husband of suspended lawyer Roberta Winston.

CSPD homicide investigators were mystified by Stephen's presence in the hospital and his apparent intent to kill Paul Winston.

Chapter Sixty-Seven

Paul was awake but still weak when Anne and their children visited.
He had been moved to another room. He'd overheard whispered rumors about why. There had been some disturbing events during the early hours of his recovery, but no one was willing to share any details. The responsibility became Anne's to tell Paul what had occurred.

Paul fought to control his emotions as Anne described how Janine had died defending him – the man, the benefactor, the patient who was so very special to her and her family.

"Oh, my god, Anne," he managed after composing himself. "What an incredible, incredible woman! Sometimes we just don't realize all the special people we are blessed to have around us.

"Can someone check on how her husband's doing?" Paul asked. "And is Ramon going to be all right? This will be awfully hard on him. He must be going through his exams right about now."

Paul turned to his three children.

"You guys have been through quite a bit lately," he said, a look of pride spreading across his face. "Sorry to put you through all of this. I just want you to know I'm proud of you, of how each of you've handled yourselves and supported your mother."

"Yeah, sure, Daddy," Catherine piped up. "You know you're behind on a couple of my riding lessons? I need you to get better soon. Okay? Enough of this goal bricking!"

"It's goldbricking, Princess," Paul smiled as he corrected his young daughter. "Gold," he repeated. Her mother and brothers chuckled, easing their tension.

Later that day, Lt. Lorente and another homicide detective visited Paul in hospital to take a statement. Paul racked his brain, trying to understand why his brother-in-law would try to murder him. Lorente knew about Roberta's lawsuit and her self-inflicted problems. Paul was certain they had nothing to do with Stephen's attempt on his life. He told Lorente about Stephen's improper approach to Anne and the encounter between himself and Stephen in Roberta's office.

"Other than that, Dan," he said, "I've had little to do with him."

"By the way, Paul," Lorente said, "as we speak, our guys are doing a forensic analysis of the bullet they took from you. It's in excellent condition. We'll email HD photos of the rifling imprints to New Scotland Yard as soon as they're done, and courier follow-up prints right away. We'll send copies to young Gervais at the FBI in Denver as well. I texted a heads-up to both of them."

"I appreciate the update, Dan," Paul replied. "I assume that means Gervais is back on the job. I hear Schuler tried to fire him."

"Yes, he's back at work. Given the chance, I'd have hired that young guy in a heartbeat," Dan replied. "No pun intended," he added with a chuckle. "Well, all right, Paul, pun intended."

They both laughed. Paul needed that, after learning how Janine Hernandez had died protecting him. He pulled a soft heart-shaped pillow a bit tighter against his incision. He was told to hold the pillow firmly to his chest and cough regularly to clear his lungs. The pain was intense. Laughter was even more uncomfortable, but more welcome.

"Yes, Gervais is going like a house on fire," Lorente repeated quickly, trying to hide the guilt he felt for causing his friend Paul's discomfort.

"Schuler's apparently on his way to Washington to answer some tough questions," Lorente said. "And it couldn't happen to a more deserving son-of-a-bitch," he added with a grin, unrepentant for his outburst of colorful language.

Chapter Sixty-Eight

"We're going on a wonderful adventure," Roberta told her two young children as she packed their luggage into her Lexus SUV.

"We're going to visit Disneyland first," she told the youngsters. They responded with squeals of delight.

"Then we're going to Sea World in San Diego, and maybe even to the San Diego Zoo! Would you like that?"

"Oh, yeah, Mommy," the two excited children replied in unison.

There was nothing to keep her at home. Her license to practice law had been suspended. Facing disbarment and criminal bribery charges, she'd been told to take a leave of absence from her law firm.

Given all this, Roberta decided that doing the right thing might benefit her later, so she reported her travel plans to CSPD and the disciplinary counsel.

Roberta had recently filed for divorce from Stephen, who didn't oppose her bid for full custody of their two children. He could hang out with 'his whores,' as she described them. She didn't need him anyway. Roberta had more than $2.2 million in a bank in the Cayman Islands. She'd set it up but kept it secret from Stephen after learning of his infidelities.

An unmarked police car drove up while Roberta was getting the children settled in their car seats. It pulled in crossways at the end of the double driveway, blocking her car.

Lt. Lorente got out of the passenger side. A uniformed female police officer Roberta didn't recognize got out of the driver's side.

"Looks like you're going somewhere?" Lorente asked.

"Well, yes, Dan," Roberta said. "I've informed the disciplinary counsel and CSPD. Stephen and I are getting a divorce and I need to get away for a bit. I'm taking the kids on a road trip to Disneyland and maybe San Diego, and then well, wherever. I'm not sure."

"Would you mind stepping inside for a minute, Roberta?" Lorente said coolly. "I have something to discuss with you. Officer Rita Hudson here will stay with the children."

Roberta glanced at Lorente then at Officer Hudson. She felt unnerved by the tone of the police executive's voice. She knew he was still in charge of homicide although recently promoted to deputy chief. His visit troubled her. She led him inside to the living room.

"You'd better have a seat," Lorente began coldly.

After an uncharacteristically nervous Roberta was settled on the couch, Lorente forged ahead without preliminaries. He knew all about her recent history and had little sympathy for her.

"I have some bad news for you, Roberta," he began. "Your husband Stephen has been shot. He's dead."

"What!" Roberta said, jumping to her feet. "Oh, my god! What happened?"

Lorente explained the events, as police understood them, at Memorial Hospital in the early morning hours.

Roberta's eyes were wide in amazement and dismay. She racked her brain trying to figure out why Stephen would try to kill her brother. Surely it couldn't be out of spite over their divorce.

Roberta sat down and began to cry quietly. She had not been in love with Stephen for a very long time, but they had been high school sweethearts and he was the father of her children.

Lorente questioned Roberta whether she knew of any reason why Stephen would want to murder Paul. She told him she was mystified by what her late husband had done. Roberta didn't ask once about her brother's wellbeing, which Lorente found unusual and disturbing, although predictable under the circumstances.

Chapter Sixty-Nine

Paul wanted to be home from the hospital for Anne's birthday. It was not to be. Dr. Moore told him he hadn't recovered enough from the surgery in only three days. Anne stayed with him each day.

At Paul's insistence, instead of using the private room the hospital had provided, she slept the second night at their home in Colorado Springs. The second home had become practical, since their business, social and personal commitments had increased to the point that they were being kept late in town more and more.

Elsie Solomon now was employed full-time, looking after both homes. Her schedule had been adjusted so she worked two days at the ranch and three days in town. Elsie liked the schedule a lot and knew the home well after working for the Brownlees there. Besides, the three days working in town and weekends helped Elsie plan for the growing number of dates she was enjoying immensely with Dan Lorente.

Paul and Anne were delighted with the home in town. They'd purchased it from Richard and Kathleen Brownlee, the retired ranchers who years ago had been valued neighbors and customers for Two-Dot Ranch purebred cattle. The aging and ailing couple had moved in with their daughter and her husband, John Everett. The only minor drawback was Paul and Anne's concern over the size of the attached one-car garage nestled beside it.

The phone rang at the house just as Anne was leaving for the hospital, but she was going to ignore it. It was her birthday, and she wanted to get to the hospital early to surprise Paul. Anne knew he was disappointed by having to remain there on her birthday.

She answered the phone, only to find, to her surprise, that it was Paul. After exchanging their usual affectionate endearments and receiving birthday wishes, Anne heard Paul say over the phone, "Anne, look out the kitchen window ... the one by the driveway." He was unusually insistent.

"What for, Paul?" Anne asked.

"Never mind, my love. Just look out the window if you will, please," he said. "Then come back and tell me what you see."

Anne was curious by nature. It drew her to the window. What she saw startled her. She hurried back to the phone.

"Paul!" she said with alarm. "Someone's parked a big car out there. It's blocking our driveway! What should I do? I was just leaving to come see you. I can't get our car out of the driveway with that thing parked there. Should I call the police?"

"Anne," Paul replied calmly. "I'd like you to do me a favor. Will you go outside and open the garage door? Then will you back our car out and see if that car in the driveway will fit into our garage. The keys are in it."

"What?" Anne asked. "I can't do that, Paul! Not with someone else's car!"

"Never mind that, my love," Paul answered patiently. "Just do it for me. Okay? It'll be fine. I'll hold on."

Anne was thinking, *Well, whatever*. She agreed to go out, move their car to the side of the wide cement driveway, and then try fitting the strange big car into their one-car garage.

A few minutes later, Anne returned to the phone.

"Yes, Paul," she said, "I drove that car into the garage. It fits just fine. And I drove it right back out again. It's parked at the curb. Whoever owns it can come and get it there.

"And do you know what? It's a brand-new BMW convertible!" Anne said. "What should I do with the thing?"

253

The BMW was just like the sporty car Anne had been thinking she might treat herself to someday. She was looking forward to the added independence that her own car would bring her, especially now that she was handling more and more of their business affairs. She and Paul had just been too busy with work to go car shopping.

"Oh, and Paul," Anne demanded, "Are you going to tell me what this is all about? Have you any idea whose car it is?"

"Well, yes, Anne," Paul replied. "I do know whose car it is. Happy Birthday, my love! The car is yours!"

Chapter Seventy

Now they had confirmation.

Ballistics tests on the bullet lodged beside Paul's heart had been performed immediately by the Colorado Springs Joint Crime Lab, and photos of the bullet's rifling showed excellent detail. The HD photos were emailed to Superintendent Archibald at New Scotland Yard in London and sent as a courtesy to a reinstated Gervais at the FBI's Denver office.

Superintendent Archibald called Lorente the next day.

He told Dan that using the better-quality photos, forensic experts at New Scotland Yard were able to confirm that the bullet removed from beside Paul's heart had come from the Webley Mark IV registered to Willard Winston. They also used the new photos to confirm that the fragments from the other two bullets taken from Paul's chest had come from the Webley. Rifling marks on the fragments matched marks on the complete bullet.

"Deputy Chief," Archibald said. "I believe you will agree that based on the evidence we have so far, our prime suspect has to be Reginald Winston."

"Yes, Superintendent, I would most certainly agree," Dan said. "What are your next steps?"

"Well, I have to tell you, fingerprints taken from the Webley and from the shell casings are a problem," Archibald said. "They're not clear enough for our people to conclude definitively who they belong to.

"You see, prints taken from the weapon appear to be those of both Reginald Winston and of his father, Willard Winston ... and that poses

255

a problem for us, I'm sorry to say. We've concluded that the prints are not distinct enough to be admissible as evidence in court.

"I'm sorry to say, we feel it would be inappropriate to proceed with charges, at least at this time," he told a disappointed Lorente.

Archibald said The Yard had received no evidence placing Reggie in Colorado Springs, much less at the crime scene. Lorente understood decisions about charges against Reggie were in the hands of New Scotland Yard, but that did little to ease his impatience.

"Superintendent," Lorente said, "Would it make any difference if I told you we've just taken sworn statements from eyewitnesses connecting Reggie with Stephen Hooper and placing him in Colorado Springs at the time of the shooting of Paul Winston?"

"Oh, my, that sounds most interesting," Archibald said.

Dan told Archibald that a number of Stephen's girlfriends had been interviewed after his death. One of them, Margie Schechter, a former employee, gave police a statement describing an encounter between Reggie and Stephen. She'd told them it was more like a verbal altercation. The encounter had occurred one evening in Stephen's office at the back of Master Tailor Men's Wear. Margie didn't mention why she was in Stephen's office at the time, but her detailed description of Reggie was clear, placing him in Colorado Springs at the time of the shootings.

She confirmed her account of seeing Reggie when she showed detectives several British silver coins he'd given her as souvenirs. She'd put them away in an envelope. CSPD had lifted from them usable samples of both Margie's and Reggie's fingerprints.

"Ah, hah, my good man," Archibald said with a touch of reserve. "Perhaps that might very well be just what we need, I should think. Can you send that evidence along to me, please?"

Archibald said he would forward the evidence to the proper authorities. The comment confused Dan. He thought The Yard was the proper authority. Then Archibald told Dan something he did not want to hear.

"Chief Lorente," he said, "I will be blunt with you. The evidence we have so far is, in my opinion, not sufficient to overcome a reluctance in my country to prosecute members of the peerage or those closely related.

To complicate matters further, Archibald said he had a confession to make.

"I must tell you that while The Yard is responsible for the security of the British Royal Family, that jurisdiction does not extend to the peerage. I got involved in this case initially quite by accident and out of sheer boredom. I will admit that I kept myself involved simply to help that bright young guy, Agent Gervais, and because it felt good to get back into the action for a while.

"The fact is, Deputy Chief," Archibald said, chuckling, "Young Gervais should really have been dealing with Kent Police. I've been liaising with a contact there, Superintendent Andy McKillop, an old friend who's been kind enough to let me take the lead at this end, for now."

The call ended amicably enough but left the Colorado Springs deputy chief deeply frustrated.

Chapter Seventy-One

Two-Dot Ranch

Paul had been home from his operation only a few months when George announced one evening he'd decided to get away for a while. He told them he was planning to go on a cruise.

The three adults and three children were finishing supper at Paul and Anne's house at Two-Dot Ranch. George had been an occasional guest for supper after Elizabeth was murdered. By inviting George for supper, Anne knew she could get at least one good meal into him from time to time. He didn't always show up. It was clear he was still not coping well without Elizabeth. George had aged dramatically. He'd continued to lose weight, his face was sallow and deeply lined, he often went unkempt for weeks, seeming too preoccupied to look after himself properly.

Paul and Anne assumed the recent attempt on Paul's life by Stephen Hooper as well as Stephen's death had upset George far more than they expected it would. George's reaction reinforced their view that their friend was still emotionally fragile over Elizabeth's murder, and the possibility of losing Paul in addition to losing Elizabeth had made that worse. They welcomed George's announcement that he planned to get away for a while.

"Where are you planning to go?" Paul asked.

"I think I'll go on a cruise through the Panama Canal," George replied. "I've never been there. I've not been anywhere much outside of Colorado. Not sure where I'll go after that. Maybe I'll take one of those trans-Atlantic flights. Never done that either. Or maybe Australia. I'm not sure. Need to think on it a bit."

"That's exciting!" Anne said happily. "We're really pleased for you, George. Maybe that's just what you need right now."

"We're going miss you, Uncle George," Catherine chimed in. Her brothers nodded.

Catherine, Douglas, and Michael had grown close to George and Elizabeth after their move from England. The children were devastated by Elizabeth's senseless and still unsolved murder. Like most children, they were recovering and able to look to the future, but they did share their parents' deep concern over how poorly George seemed to be coping with the terrible death of the loving woman they'd called Aunt Elizabeth.

"When do you plan to leave?" Paul asked. "Is there anything we can do to help you get ready?"

"Oh, that's all right, Paul," George answered. "Thanks anyway, but I was thinking of going over to Denver next week. I can make the arrangements then."

They would have been happy to help him, even get him the attractive company discounts that Prescott Enterprises and Two-Dot Ranch were able to get. But they didn't want to interfere. Besides, making those arrangements would give George something to look forward to and keep him busy until he left. They were encouraged by George's plans. Perhaps it meant that finally George might be coming out of his deep depression over Elizabeth's murder and was finally ready to start moving on with his life.

Five weeks later, Paul and Anne drove George to the Denver International Airport for a flight to Panama City, Panama.

Chapter Seventy-Two

Five years later
Colorado Springs

"George has been missing for more than five years now," Paul began. "What do you think, Bill? Do we wrap it up, or is there still a chance he might be found?"

Paul and Anne had invited their friend Bill Radford to spend a few days with them at their home in Colorado Springs. Bill was now president of Global Security International. They were discussing the mysterious disappearance of George Underhill. He'd gone missing without a trace while on a cruise through the Panama Canal. The trip followed a year of grieving over the still-unsolved murder of his wife Elizabeth.

A few weeks after George had left, much to Paul's surprise, he'd received a phone call from George saying he'd changed plans. Instead of visiting Britain or Australia after his cruise through the Panama Canal, he'd decided to visit Indonesia instead. Paul had thought the change and destination unusual. George had never expressed an interest in Southeast Asia. What he had found even more unusual was George had asked him to notify his son and daughter of the change in plans instead of calling his grown children on his own.

No one had heard from him again.

After two months had passed without hearing from George, Paul had hired Global Security to track him down, fearing that George might have suffered an emotional breakdown from the grief over losing his wife.

They were also worried that their emotionally vulnerable friend, an inexperienced international traveler, might have become a victim of foul play.

"Paul, our people have chased down every lead we could find," Bill said, "and we appreciate your patience. But to be honest, we've simply run out of fresh ideas. This man has disappeared so completely it's like he never even existed. I hate to admit it, but I think it's time to throw in the towel.

"As you know, Paul, our hottest lead came when we traced over $5 million of George's assets to the Cayman Islands," Bill continued. "That was a few months after you asked us to help find him. We called in some hefty favors down there just to get that much information.

"The money was transferred somewhere else not long after that account was opened. We couldn't find out where the money went, or where he went, or even if he was there for sure at the time.

"Speaking of money," Bill said, "I feel obliged to point out that you've personally spent more than $1.6 million with Global so far trying to find George. Don't you think you've done all you can?"

"I guess you're right," Paul said reluctantly. "I hate to admit it, but I suppose that has to be the end of it. Kathleen and Chester, George's son, and daughter, have asked me to help them get the paperwork in motion to have him legally declared dead.

"They're pretty upset about having to that," Paul added with a sigh. "It's a huge step, having a parent declared dead. I'm sure it feels to them like they're ordering their father's death. It must be a terrible emotional dilemma."

"It's sad," Anne said. "Understandably, they're confused and hurting over all of this. They never heard from their father after he left on his trip. He probably didn't know he had grandchildren.

"George never seemed to get over losing Elizabeth," she added. "Or the attack on Paul."

James Osborne

"We sure do miss that big guy," Paul said, struggling with his emotions.

Anne reached for his hand.

"Damn, I'd give almost anything to know what's become of him," he sighed.

Chapter Seventy-Three

George was now legally dead.

John Everett, personal and business attorney for Paul and Anne, had completed all the requirements to have George Anthony Underhill declared legally dead. His estate was divided evenly between his two children. After taxes, fees, and costs, each received $1,276,823.31.

Paul and Anne organized a memorial service for George on behalf of his and Elizabeth's two children. At first, Kathleen, Chester and their spouses were apprehensive about attending. They relented after a call from Anne helped them realize the memorial service was as much to bring a measure of closure for Paul, Anne, and their children as for the two of them.

None of the local churches or funeral chapels had facilities large enough to accommodate the crowd of people expected for George's memorial service. Paul and Anne booked the Pike's Peak Center. It was more than two-thirds filled with business friends and associates, second and third generation ranching families who had known George and Elizabeth as well as Paul and Anne, and even some who'd known Paul's parents. The Colorado Springs news media described it as the largest civilian memorial service anyone could remember.

Paul and Anne delivered the eulogy together. It was obvious to the assembled crowd that both had idolized George and Elizabeth. They were well known and widely respected. Elizabeth had become like a favorite aunt to Paul and a dear friend to Anne, and George had been an integral part of Paul's life since childhood.

James Osborne

With the memorial service over, that chapter in the history of Two-Dot Ranch had now been laid to rest.

Chapter Seventy-Four

London

A tall man landed at Heathrow Airport in London, England. He'd arrived on a Qantas flight from Melbourne, Australia.

The man wore a beard dyed dark brown, as was his abundant head of hair. The dye job was amateurish, leaving obvious that his hair and beard were naturally a light color, perhaps grey or even white.

The man got directions to his destination at the car rental booth, or 'car hires' as they're called in Britain. He made his way to where his car was parked and drove away.

He didn't see the two men following him.

They'd picked him out from among deplaning passengers. The bad dye jobs made it easier. They waited until he left to pick up his car before approaching the rental agent. The two detectives, one from New Scotland Yard and the other from Kent Police, were shown a copy of the car hire agreement.

The agent said the man had asked for directions. The clerk dug from a wastebasket some rough notes she'd scribbled down before re-copying them more neatly for her client. The notes were for the directions to Maidstone in Kent County. There was no specific address.

The man's last name, Sutherland, wasn't familiar, and nothing showed up on the computer when the two phoned their offices with details from the man's Australian passport. Regardless, when his photo was scanned by Customs, it fit the description of someone on Interpol's wanted list. The FBI in America had added the photo, name, and description. The clumsy attempt by the man to alter his appearance encouraged the police officers to continue their pursuit, to find out where he was going and what he was up to.

Within minutes, the hired car was being followed on the M25 Motorway by police surveillance teams. It was tracked to the M26 and then on the M20 to Maidstone. There the tails followed it to where the driver had parked the car, but by the time they'd parked theirs and returned to the hired car, the man was nowhere to be seen.

"Terribly sorry, Charles," Supt. Andy McKillop of Kent Police said into the phone. "Our guys seem to have lost him. Any suggestions?"

McKillop was calling Archibald as a courtesy on the superintendent's cell phone. Earlier, Archibald had told his friend Andy McKillop that he'd been alerted by U. S. authorities about the possible arrival in England of someone fitting the description of the man they were attempting to follow. While the man was thought to be deceased, they had reason to believe that this might be a ruse, that he was very much alive and possibly seeking revenge. U.S. authorities told Archibald that their suspect may be heading for Maidstone and was wanted in America for murder, conspiracy to commit murder, attempted murder and several other charges involving a long-standing investigation.

Archibald was determined to help find out if this was the same man and if so, what the man was up to in England. If they could confirm an identity match, Kent Police would arrest him on warrants from the U.S.

"I think we can be very sure he wasn't looking for a hotel when he asked for directions at the car hire booth," Archibald replied. "My guess is he's looking for someone, Andy. From what the Americans had to say, I don't think we can view this as a possible social call, should he turn out to be who we suspect.

"You're not far from Earnscliffe Manor. Based on evidence from here and America, my guess is that Earnscliffe could be the connection. Look, Andy, I'm at home in Gillingham. Maidstone's just a few miles from here, so I'm coming over. Can you hold where you are while I do some checking? I'll call you right back.

Six minutes later, McKillop's cell phone rang. It was Archibald.

"Andy, I think you should get over to this address right away. I'll meet you there," Archibald said. The urgency in his voice was obvious. "It's the address for Reginald, a.k.a., Reggie, Winston. There's a very good chance he may be in considerable danger."

"I know him well," McKillop said. "Too well."

Fifteen minutes later Archibald, McKillop and two Kent Police investigators met around the corner from the address.

James Osborne

Chapter Seventy-Five

Maidstone, England

"What the hell are you doin' here?" Reggie was startled and frightened. He backed away from the tall man standing in the doorway.

"I've come to settle up, you dumb little shit," came the reply. "It's long overdue."

"Look, man," Reggie said, making no attempt to hide his fear as he walked backward into his cheap two-room flat.

"I'm really sorry for what happened ... I really am. Honest! I didn't mean it to turn out that way!" Reggie whined.

"It wasn't my fault, you know. Christ, talk to Stephen, man. That rifle he got me was a piece of shit. He forced me to do it that night. Any other time, I wouldn't have missed, honest."

The man pulled a large handgun from behind his back, pointing it at Reggie. The trembling little Englishman back-pedaled almost at a run into the sitting room/kitchen until he bumped up against a chair at his table. His mouth was drooling, and his eyes were full of fear.

Reggie wished he hadn't returned his father's old revolver that he'd taken to America to shoot Paul Winston. It would have come in handy right about now.

"Stop sniveling, you disgusting excuse for a man," the tall man said. "You can't even take responsibility for your own fuckups. I oughtta to put an end to you right here; put you out of your goddamned misery.

"Don't you know Hooper is dead, you asshole? Turn around!" the big man barked at him. "Face the other way. I hate the sight of you."

"Wha ... what? He's dead? How come? What're ya gonna do?"

Reggie was startled. He'd not heard about Stephen.

Well, so much for the other $15,000 dollars that shithead still owes me, Reggie thought.

"How'd it happen?" he stammered.

"Enough with the questions, you asshole," the man commanded

"I'm gonna tie your hands. Then I'm gonna take you on a little trip," he continued. The big man made a strange-sounding chuckle deep in his chest.

"Where? Where are you taking me?" Reggie managed from his trembling mouth.

"Never mind! You don't need to know just yet. I said turn around!"

Reggie did as he was told. Now he was so terrified that he was on the verge of tears. He could feel himself wetting his trousers.

God, I sure could use a stiff drink, he thought.

His hands were pulled behind him roughly. They were tied together with something that felt like cable ties. They cut into his wrists, hurting him.

The man remained standing behind him. Reggie couldn't see the tall man reach in and pull a slim cylinder out of his jacket pocket. It was a silencer. He screwed it onto the muzzle of the gun.

"Pull that chair out and sit down for a minute," he told Reggie. "Face backwards! Don't turn around!"

Reggie did as he was told.

He found it difficult sitting on the hard wooden chair with his hands tied behind him. His wrists hurt from the ties and his shoulders hurt from the strain of his arms being pulled back.

Reggie hoped the pain in his shoulders would ease once he could stand back up, to go wherever he was going to be taken. He realized the anticipated relief was an ironic thought, but he would still be tied up, the outcome uncertain.

It was his last thought.

The man pointed the muzzle of the silenced handgun behind Reggie's right ear and pulled the trigger. A red-gray mist exploded from the socket where Reggie's left eye had been an instant before.

Reggie's head slumped forward onto the table.

A pool of blood and brain spread on the table and spilled over the edge. It dribbled down beside his foot, forming a puddle on the cheap rug on the worn wooden floor. The big man calmly unscrewed the silencer and tucked the gun into the belt behind his back. He pulled the back of his jacket down over the gun. The silencer was returned to the left pocket of his jacket.

The keys to the rental car were in the right jacket pocket.

Chapter Seventy-Six

An aging George Underhill turned and walked calmly out of Reggie Winston's flat. He looked carefully up and down the hallway, then closed the door quietly behind him.

As he went down the two flights of stairs to the street, George peeled off the surgical gloves he was wearing. He carefully wrapped the silencer in the gloves, being mindful not to touch it with his bare hands. Then the silencer and gloves were placed in a self-closing plastic bag which he stuffed into his left pocket. He'd toss everything into a trash bin when he got to the airport.

George's carefully thought-out plan was to drive the rented car back to Heathrow for his flight to the Cayman Islands. The name on his ticket and on his fake Australian passport said, 'George Anthony Sutherland.'

He walked out onto the sidewalk heading for his car parked at the end of street. At first he didn't see the tall, distinguished man in a tweed wedge cap and raincoat standing out of sight to his right, 10 feet back from the doorway. The man's large hands were folded casually together across an ample mid-section.

Nor did George see McKillop and the pair of armed Kent Police investigators to his left, a few feet back from the left side of the doorway.

"George Underhill?"

George wheeled around, surprised to hear his real name. He'd not used it for years.

"I'm Superintendent Charles Archibald of New Scotland Yard. We'd like a word with you. Please come with us."

ne

George began easing his right hand around toward his back, where he'd tucked his gun.

Archibald unclasped his hands. In his big right was a .357 Magnum, pointed at George's midsection.

George changed the direction of his hands, slowly raising them upward. On the orders of Supt. McKillop, one of the three others with guns also pointed at him, George laced his fingers at the back of his neck. His face bore a look of resignation, yet with a hint of relief.

While Archibald and the Kent Police officers stood guard, McKillop frisked him carefully, removing the pistol and the plastic bag, and then handcuffing his hands behind him. McKillop carefully placed the plastic bag into an evidence bag, secured the gun, smelled the muzzle and then offered it to Archibald, who smelled it. They exchanged nods.

Using a note with the address found in George's pocket, McKillop send one of the investigators up the stairs to the apartment George had left moments earlier. He found Reggie Winston's body.

The silencer and the plastic bag, plus a chair back in Reggie's apartment, yielded several excellent examples of George Underhill's hand and fingerprints.

272

Chapter Seventy-Seven

Colorado Springs

"What in the world could have possessed him?"

Paul and Anne were in Dan Lorente's office.

A distraught Paul asked the question over and over again – of himself and of no one in particular. He was devastated, trying to make sense of something that made no sense at all. He kept shaking his head in disappointment, despair, and anger.

They'd just finished a phone conversation with Superintendent Archibald of New Scotland Yard and Superintendent Andy McKillop of Kent Police in England. The London police executives had agreed to brief Paul and Anne on George's arrest and the British police investigation. Lorente filled them in on the CSPD and FBI roles in the investigation.

"Archibald and McKillop told me earlier that after some hours of interrogation, George finally broke down and became quite cooperative, admitting his prime motive was financial," Lorente said. "George had a shaky plan at best that went terribly awry. And there's more. George admitted to interrogators that he was jealous of you, Paul. He felt that after he'd helped to build your ranch, you'd pushed him aside."

"Good god!" Paul exploded. "I put him in charge of Two-Dot, and my parents left him a 10 percent interest in the ranch. When he decided to retire, and it was his decision, we bought him out at his request. We paid him more than $4 million for his share."

"I'm afraid George's duplicity didn't end there," Lorente continued. "He must have had quite a hate on, Paul. It seems George was also involved in Roberta's lawsuit against you. Evidently she promised him a percentage of what they won if he would side with her and, basically, spy on you. She's admitted to our investigators that he did. The big prize for him would have been control of the Two-Dot Ranch. He thought that if Roberta were successful, their combined holdings would give them control. That depended on inheriting from your estate a portion of the ranch after your death. I expect you know what that's about."

Dan went on, "As we understand it, Roberta's plan was also to take over your interests in Continental Del Rio Oil and Gas. She expected that she and Emily would inherit a large number of shares in Continental from you. Roberta was going to buy out Emily's interest, then pay top dollar for enough of the other shares to get control of the company.

"Roberta hatched her plot after she found out Philip Tremblay had reduced his controlling stake in Continental to 41 per cent, less than a controlling interest. That's because he transferred a big chunk of his personal holdings into the Continental employees' share purchase program to assure its future.

"George had a role in the Continental plot as well. We have reason to believe he was behind that explosion at the oil well on the South Platte that killed those two men and caused that big oil spill. All the evidence points to him as the one who stole ten sticks of dynamite from Two-Dot Ranch. There was an intact blasting cap found at the scene that was traced back to a box of blasting caps at Two-Dot.

"He refused to comment about this during the interrogation, but we also believe he hired Marvin Solomon to handle the explosion. We think the plan was to cripple Continental financially, so that Roberta could buy in cheaply. A takeover would have been much easier after you and Anne were murdered.

"If you think that's complicated, trust me, it gets even stranger," Lorente went on.

"George said that Roberta knew he and Stephen had worked together on both of the attempts to murder you, Paul, and the attempt on your life, Anne. It was Stephen who hired Reggie as the gunman, at Roberta's suggestion.

"Evidently Reggie had jumped at the chance to get his revenge on you for inheriting your uncle's estate. He believed his father's accusations that you had cheated his father out of the late Lord Percival's estate and that his father should have been the rightful heir.

"The irony is that Stephen didn't know Roberta was in this plot up to her neck. She was planning to cut him out of everything she could. So much for marital bliss. Bizarre! So that's about it, as we know it," Dan concluded.

"Roberta … George ... Stephen … Reggie," Paul sighed heavily. "I can hardly believe it. What an unholy alliance!"

"Just think – their entire bloody scheme depended upon the reliability of a convicted felon and drunk," he added. "Serves them right. It would be laughable if it wasn't so damned tragic."

"I'm afraid there's something else I need to tell you, Paul," Dan said.

"We have reason to believe it was George who caused the plane crash in which your parent died. We're certain that he tampered with the fuel line and the right brake wiring that caused the explosion on landing.

"My god!" Paul said, looking over at Anne. "Surely not!" Her heart hurt at seeing the pain in his eyes. "My parents give him everything, gave him his life's work! How could he do this to them?"

"After George was arrested in England," Dan said, "El Paso County investigators visited his home on your ranch. They found tools in his garage wrapped in dirty rags that were consistent with tools that could have been used to damage the fuel line, particularly a small hand metal saw. But the clincher is that analysis of the rags revealed traces of aviation fuel. I recall you mentioned one time that George never wanted anything to do with flying, because he's afraid of heights. So, the tools and the rag are too much of a coincidence, and besides, he refuses to answer questions about the crash."

"For all those years, I trusted the man!" Paul said. "We trusted him implicitly. You're right, George never showed any interest in Dad's plane or in flying. Dad even offered to pay for his flying lessons. George wasn't interested. You're also correct that Dad was scrupulous about looking after every detail himself.

"There's one last thing," Dan said.

"You should know that Roberta was arrested two days ago at Los Angeles International. She had tickets for her and her two kids to the Cayman Islands. Evidently Roberta has a bank account there and was planning to 'lose' herself and her children in the Caymans.

"LAPD returned her to Colorado Springs last night under police escort," he continued. "As you can imagine, she's now facing a long list of charges, including accessory to murder, conspiracy to commit murder, accessory to commit theft, attempted miscarriage of justice, and bribery of a judge. She was also charged this morning with attempting to flee to avoid prosecution for each of the charges she's facing.

"She's being processed in this building right now," he added.

"Oh, her two children were seized by the Department of Child Welfare and turned over to the custody of Stephen's parents in Boulder."

"Christ almighty," he sighed. "My own damned sister! What in the world got into her?"

He looked over at Anne and slowly shook his head again in sadness and disbelief. Anne gently took his left hand in both of hers.

"Well, everything's backfired on George and on Roberta too. And those two bloody well deserve it," Paul said.

His biggest struggle was to make sense out of the betrayal by George. He was a man that Paul had admired and looked up to all of his life.

"They blew it, didn't they?" Paul said rhetorically. "They all blew it!

"Just so that you know, Dan, before leaving for England years ago, I made a new will. In the event of my death, George would have inherited another 10 percent of Two-Dot Ranch. That would have given him 20 percent. My sisters' shares would have been 35 percent each. George and Roberta would have had control.

"I never thought to tell George that after Anne and I were married, I made a new will," Paul continued. "That 10 percent was deleted. I just assumed he'd expect it would have to change. Anne and our children are my primary beneficiaries now. And I've made provisions in my will for Emily, a few charities, and Roberta. I guess I'll be changing my will again.

"Well, it's too bad for him, and it's too bad for her," Paul said with a lingering sigh. He stood, squared his shoulders, set his jaw and then said, "I guess in the end, each of our lives comes down to the sum of all the decisions we make along the way, good or bad. They made theirs."

As Paul and Anne stood to leave, Dan asked,

"Do you want to see your sister, Paul? I can arrange it if you want."

"No," Paul said.

Epilogue

London, England

George Anthony Underhill was ordered for trial in London's Old Bailey Court on charges regarding the cold-blooded murder of Reginald Willard Albert Percival Winston.

He was found guilty and sentenced to life in prison without the possibility of parole.

Reggie's parents, Willard, and Alice Winston attended every day of the trial. Alice wept frequently. Willard sat through the trial in stoic silence. The only sound Willard uttered throughout the trail was a barely perceptible 'Yes!' under his breath when the verdict was given, and again when the sentence was read.

None of George's children, other relatives or former friends attended.

Prosecution witnesses during the trial included Dan Lorente

He testified that Stephen Hooper and Mr. Underhill were co-conspirators in the attempts on the lives of Paul and Anne Winston, the Earl, and Countess of Prescott. The hit man was Reginald, a.k.a. Reggie, Winston, hired by Stephen Hooper and the defendant.

The American police executive also told the London court that Stephen Hooper was shot and killed by Colorado Springs police after a second failed attempt on the life of Lord Prescott, a.k.a. Paul Winston. During that attempt, Hooper had murdered Nurse Janine Hernandez.

Lorente testified he received a call from Superintendent Archibald advising him that ballistics tests confirmed the British made Webley

The Maidstone Conspiracy

Mark IV service revolver submitted in evidence at the trial was used in the first attempt on Mr. Winston's life. However, despite verbal evidence linking Reggie to Colorado Springs at the time of the shootings, The Yard felt it needed stronger evidence before laying charges against him, a man connected with the British peerage.

Partial fingerprints on the gun linked the late Reggie Winston to the shootings and thus to George Underhill. The information helped confirm other evidence pointing to Underhill and Paul's sister Roberta as the prime suspects behind the conspiracy to take over key parts of Prescott Enterprises by murdering the two owners.

Police believed that George and Roberta had been operating on the mistaken assumption that George was still in Paul's will and that they would inherit enough assets to exercise control over those parts of Paul and Anne's estate both craved.

Superintendent Andy McKillop of Kent Police told the court Reggie Winston had called their station in Maidstone a few days before being shot by Underhill and confessed to the shootings. He had been on one of his drinking binges and had not been taken seriously. Reggie claimed Stephen Hooper had hired him at the request of Mr. Underhill. Unfortunately, the call had been received late one night by a young recruit who'd dismissed the drunken voice on the phone as the meaningless ranting of an alcoholic.

It took several weeks for transcripts of the recorded conversation to resurface, too late to prevent Reggie's murder, but they helped to confirm information received from the FBI. Reggie had also been videotaped earlier while in the Maidstone police drunk tank, ranting about a shooting. It was submitted at Underhill's trial as corroborating evidence.

*

Three weeks after George was incarcerated in Her Majesty's Prison Wakefield, Britain's Home Office received a formal letter from the

James Osborne

United States Ambassador to the United Kingdom requesting his extradition.

The Secretary of State for the United States, on behalf of the Attorney General of the State of Colorado, requested George's extradition to the United States on several warrants for his arrest. The extradition request listed the charges as: first degree murder in the deaths of Ted and Catherine Winston on April 3, 1990, in the crash of a light plane; conspiracy to commit murder in the inadvertent death of his wife, Elizabeth May Underhill and the attempted murders of Paul Richard Winston (The 12th Earl of Prescott), his wife Anne Victoria Winston (the Countess of Prescott) and Sergeant William Stewart Thornton of the Colorado Springs Police Department.

The request was referred to a British court. It ruled Mr. Underhill was to be turned over to U.S. authorities for return to the United States for trial. But the court, in a touch of uncharacteristic dark humor, further ordered that their ruling could take effect immediately upon the completion by Mr. Underhill of his life sentence without parole currently being served in the British maximum-security prison at Wakefield.

Colorado radio and TV stations and newspapers covered George's trial and sentencing in England live. Major news media all around the western U.S. carried highlights.

Throughout his trial and subsequent imprisonment, George maintained a stoic silence. To some observers, he gave the impression that he was indifferent to what he had done and to his fate at the hands of the law.

In fact, he was a broken man.

Until he died six years after beginning his life sentence, George berated himself every single day for hiring the man who had accidentally murdered his wife, Elizabeth. He'd loved her dearly and missed her terribly. He never forgave himself. Nor did anyone else.

For years, a bank in Zurich has been awaiting a reply to its annual correspondence to a client with an address in the Cayman Islands. The client's account has been inactive for eight years. It currently is valued with interest at more than US$17.7 million. The name on the account is George Anthony Sutherland.

James Osborne

Acknowledgements

I am immensely grateful to Trevor Apperley and Tim Young who undertook extensive reviews and critiques of The Maidstone Conspiracy as it developed. The value of your contributions is beyond measure.

Sincere thanks also to some very special people who generously provided their advice and suggestions as this novel progressed: Marilyn Cottrell, the late Keith Critchley, Michael Flood, the late May Gollinger, Kent O'Conner, Lorelei Piotto, Dr. Brian Proskiw, Betty Ann Stimson, and Gail White. Gratitude is due also to A. J. Kohler, the talented editor who mercifully insisted on saving me from myself, time after time, and to Travis Miles, a gifted cover designer, for his considerable skill and patience.

Above all, I am immensely grateful to my wonderful wife Sharolie Osborne for her abiding tolerance. This novel could not have been written without her willingness to sacrifice countless hours that we could otherwise have enjoyed together.

As always, any errors and omissions are mine alone.

-- James Osborne

About the Author

James Osborne is a former investigative journalist, college teacher, vice-president of a Fortune 500 company, entrepreneur, and army officer. His work has received numerous awards and other acclaim, including an Amazon #1 bestseller with his novel, The Ultimate Threat. *In addition to his novels, Osborne's short stories have been published in dozens of anthologies, magazines, and professional and literary journals.*

Social Media Links

Blog/Website: http://www.JamesOsborneNovels.com
Amazon: www.amazon.com/author/jamesosborne
Goodreads: https://www.goodreads.com/JamesOsborne
Facebook: https: www.facebook.com/jim.osborne.140
Twitter: http://www.twitter.com/okjo1
LinkedIn: https://www.linkedin.com/in/jimosborne5/

James Osborne

Other Books by James Osborne

Having enjoyed **The Maidstone Conspiracy**, I hope you'll also want to check out the next novel in the Maidstone Suspense Series, SECRET SHEPHERD, as well as the other books below.

SECRET SHEPHERD

A single act of kindness plunges young philanthropists Paul and Anne Winston into jeopardy. After rescuing a gifted youth from an international drug cartel, the gang retaliates with huge bounties for their murder, tracking them relentlessly around the world as the couple persists with their mission of bringing desperately needed help to deserving others.

https://www.amazon.com/Secret-Shepherd-Maidstone-Book-Two-ebook/dp/B09L78RJGK/ref=tmm_kin_swatch_0?_encoding=UTF8&qid=&sr=

THE ULTIMATE THREAT

This novel tells it like it is. It's a chilling look at the senseless brutality of ISIS, while also offering a compassionate exposé of the horrendous suffering their savagery has imposed upon millions of innocents.

The Ultimate Threat steps beyond fiction, reaching firmly into the realm of the possible, even the probable, in a disturbing forecast of how ISIS is planning to aggressively expand its terror around the world … especially to America!

https://www.amazon.ca/Ultimate-Threat-Enemy-Has-Arrived/dp/B085DSR4G1/ref=sr_1_1?crid=GXQQEU033JT9&dchild=1&keywords=The+Ultimate+Threat+--+The+Enemy+Has+Arrived&qid=1635971557&s=books&sprefix=the+ultimate+threat+--+the+enemy+has+arrived%2Cstripbooks%2C123&sr=1-1

ENCOUNTERS:
Tales of Living, Loving & Laughter

This delightful cornucopia of 36 captivating stories guarantees to entertain you, and to lift your spirits! Many are rib-tickling funny ... a few are chilling adventures ... some are heartwarming ... all are entertaining!

Author James Osborne has woven these engaging tales into an amazing collection ... many inspired by his experiences as a journalist, teacher, publicist, army officer, corporate executive, and business owner. Read a few and you'll want to read them all!

https://www.amazon.ca/dp/B09LSPGK27/ref=sr_1_1?keywords=ENCOUNTERS%3A+Tales+of+Living%2C+Loving+%26+Laughter&qid=1636871436&s=books&sr=1-1

Printed in Great Britain
by Amazon